Charles Bogue Luffmann

A vagabond in Spain

ISBN/EAN: 9783337229597

Printed in Europe, USA, Canada, Australia, Japan

Cover: Foto ©Andreas Hilbeck / pixelio.de

More available books at **www.hansebooks.com**

Charles Bogue Luffmann

A vagabond in Spain

A VAGABOND IN SPAIN.

BY

C. BOGUE LUFFMANN.

LONDON:
JOHN MURRAY, ALBEMARLE STREET.
1895.

DEDICATION.

THE days of rich patrons have gone by; the wanderer and tale-teller are without a friend! But as I owe the pleasures of my journey to the poor of Spain, it is to them I turn;—to those who gave me of their simple fare and protection in pigsties, fowl-houses, and barns; of their cold and warm floors in prisons, hospitals, and palaces; of the cool shade of their dear Mother Church, castle ramparts, and posada chimney-corners;—to all who have given me their meanest crust, their "maravedi," their full-hearted pity, their blessing, smile, or praise.*

With all the many simple and varied friends who helped me on my way must be joined the name of one who has been my constant companion and support; one who throughout each day has been a defence against

* *Mite.*

malicious hands, and each night has lain beside me ;— the friend on whom I have leaned and been helped forward over all the long and stony road, who has humoured all my wanderings, and in the hardest times kept his dear old head ever close to mine.

To my hosts in Spain, and to the one companion who is still strong and willing to accompany me to the end— to " Durandal," my walking-stick, I dedicate this story of the journey we have made.

PREFACE.

THIS book claims to be nothing more than the experiences and impressions of a tramp in Spain.

My journey has not been a mere caprice. It was undertaken with the object of getting a practical knowledge of the condition of agriculture in Spain, and of learning to understand the life and social conditions of the common people.

Although warned by the English, French, and Spanish authorities that I should certainly receive my quietus at the hands of some of the murderous brigands believed to exist in wild Spain, I was able to make the journey of one thousand five hundred miles, alone and unarmed, without a single interruption or insult. After a trot through the Gironde and the great pine forests of the Landes, I passed through the Basque provinces and crossed the Pyrenees into Spain. On my way from Biarritz to

Malaga, I crossed ten great barriers—the Pyrenees, the Arriba Mountains, Montes de Navarra, Sierra de Moncayo, Sierra Minestra, Montes de Toledo, Sierra Morena, Sierra Nevada, Sierra Alhama, and Sierra Tajedra. The last three being covered with deep snow afforded anything but a comfortable experience to the lonely pilgrim.

As much time as I could spare from my practical researches (which will find no place in these vagabond pages) was devoted to visiting the famous cities and monuments of old historic Spain. La Mancha, fragrant with the memory of the immortal Don, had special attractions for me, and an account of the famous Cave of Montesinos (Albacete), where Don Quixote encountered Merlin, will be found in my journal.

During the journey of one hundred and forty-five days and nights, I lived entirely in the society of Spaniards (chiefly of the humbler classes), conforming myself strictly to local conditions and customs, and keeping eyes and ears well open. I hope the kindly reader will be satisfied with the result.

A word to disarm criticism. I frankly own this to be an egotistical journal. The personal pronoun " I " plays first fiddle throughout my tale.

This is readily explained by the fact that " I " was

my own guide, philosopher, and friend, my own "mentor," my own companion, sometimes my own consoler, and always my own judge.

Another word in defence of my position as a tramp.

Across my MS. a friend's hand has written : " The tramp's is an ignoble life ; he does nothing, he earns nothing," together with the profound, deep-reasoned inquiry, " What right has one person to live on the work of others ? "

This last question is so broad that it embraces most of the great social problems of our day. Had I time, I might endeavour to show that the majority of the comfortable classes live in no other way.

If I had travelled through Spain as a first-class tourist, I should have seen and heard no more than is known to all the world. As a tramp I have broken up new ground. I have looked on life through a tramp's eyes, suffered his sorrows, and rejoiced in his pleasures.

I did not act the character. I lived the life in real earnest. The vagrant's rest-house was my only hotel ; the succour doled out by the alcalde my only means of sustenance. Had I lined my pocket with gold before setting forth on my journey I could never have found courage to fulfil the hard

task I had set before me.   Every now and then,
when I reached a large city, I came up—for the time
being—to a higher level.   But the money I drew
there was spent within the precincts of the city, and,—
out on the road once more,—I lived the life of an
ordinary wayfarer.

How else could I have penetrated into humble
homes and learned to know the life of the toiling
masses ?

The road across Spain is long to him who takes
it on foot ; but it repays the toil.   It reveals wonders
in nature and in art, which will with difficulty be
rivalled elsewhere.   It shows the Spaniard under
many and varied aspects, for every native of Spain
is not either a courtier or a cut-throat.

All that this tramp saw, and a little of what he
felt, is at the reader's disposal.   If this journal,
written on the spot it deals with, can enable others to
see and feel with the writer, they will not regret
their journey in his company.

C. B. L.

CONTENTS.

CHAPTER IV.

ARRAGON.

CHAPTER V.

ARRAGON (*continued*).

CHAPTER VI.

ARRAGON (*continued*).

CHAPTER VII.

OLD AND NEW CASTILE.

CHAPTER VIII.

OLD MADRID.

CHAPTER IX.

OLD AND NEW CASTILE.

CHAPTER X.

OLD AND NEW CASTILE (*continued*).

CHAPTER XI.

OLD AND NEW CASTILE (*continued*).

CHAPTER XII.

OLD AND NEW CASTILE (*continued*).
DON QUIXOTE'S COUNTRY.

CHAPTER XIII.

ANDALUCIA.

CHAPTER XIV.

ANDALUCIA (*continued*).

A VAGABOND IN SPAIN.

CHAPTER I.

VASCONGADAS.

MY START.—PROPHETS OF WOE.—FROM BIARRITZ TO ST. JEAN
DE LUZ.—BEHOBIA.—I AM IN SPAIN.—A NIGHT IN RENTERIA.
—SAN SEBASTIAN.—THE VALLEY OF ORIO.—THE INN OF
ANDOAIN.—TOLOSA.—SYMPTOMS OF FEVER.—THE TURNPIKE
KEEPER.—FAREWELL TO VASCONGADAS.

WHEN I threw a few things together and said,
"*I am going to walk through Spain,*" I had
not one thought or care as to how I should live,
or what I should have to go without. If a round
twenty years of footing it up and down the world
have taught me anything, it is—that only he who
needs little will ever get enough!

Future ages may be interested to learn that when
I set forth, July 6th, 1893, with the intention of

walking from Biarritz to Malaga, my costume consisted of a knickerbocker suit of brown linen, a veiled
hat, and extra broad welted boots, and that I carried
on my back a knapsack of twenty pounds' weight.
It held two complete changes of flannel under-
clothing—two white flannel shirts with collars, two
pairs of long stockings, two pairs of flannel knickerbockers and a coat of the same ; a bandage thirty
feet long (in case of a weak knee), two handkerchiefs,
two neckties, a towel, a soft brown felt " Sombrero,"
a cloth cap, shoes, and a rug which had sheltered
me through all sorts of weather during ten eventful
years.

A small linen bag held my spare clothes and
formed my pillow at night. This was rolled inside
my rug, and secured by a tight piece of webbing
with a flying loop at each end, drawing the bundle
tighter and tighter as I jogged along.

I also carried a satchel, shaped like a game-bag,
with a centre partition. One side was dedicated to
food, the other held my books, passport, map, " Spanish
text-book," writing materials, a small card-board box
for geological, entomological, and botanical specimens, a silver match-box, and a flint and steel tied
fast by a kind hand to a book whose pages bristle
with needles and pins. Last, but not least, came
shaving materials. By way of defensive weapons, I

carried—a pocket-knife. It once possessed three blades; but one expired on the battle-field of Magenta, and another went overboard in "Merrie England," so that I was left to defend myself in "navaja"*-loving Spain with a blade barely two inches long, and without a point.

My most important possession is my "Recommendation"—a document informing the world of Spain that I am Somebody (which is indeed true!), that I have been here . . . and there . . . and am going somewhere else, and wishing me "Good luck" to the end.

Think of that for a Tramp! A stout walking-stick of Australian tulip-wood, and a pocket-case containing a photograph completed my equipment.

It will be seen that I carried with me neither beef lozenges nor condensed essences. I intended to live on the food of Spain. If hard and unpalatable I should but share the common misfortune of seventeen millions of my fellow-mortals.

As I set out from Biarritz my appearance was sufficiently striking to attract a crowd of idlers, who straightway proceeded to inquire into the nature of my journey.

Little as I understood their foreign lingo, I soon

* Knife.

became aware that they were describing for my encouragement and edification all the known methods of brigandage and murder. The violence of their gesticulations was meant to impress my mind with the fact that every other Spaniard I should meet on the road would be a villain and a cut-throat !

How consoling this was to a poor devil without house or home, or one sweet face to call his own in all this strange land, can better be imagined than described. Fortunately, I have heard a good many people talk in my time, and I could have told them a few facts about former tramps of mine in other lands which would have made them open their eyes. So, undismayed by these blood-curdling prophecies, I shouldered my bundle and set forth by the southern road for Spain, the land of my dreams.

It was something like a drag from Biarritz to St. Jean de Luz—ten miles of wild moorland country, with occasional glimpses of the sea and of the Pyrenees, looking hot and dry through the dusty air. After some days of dissipation at Biarritz I did not feel in the right mood to enjoy my load of twenty pounds and a sun pouring one hundred and twenty degrees of heat on the white, glaring road. St. Jean de Luz was pretty and cool and inviting, but I did not linger there. Spain was beckoning me on !

The mountains rose before me as I advanced. I

love mountains, but these looked uncomfortably high for one so burdened to scale. The high road was quite "high" enough for me just then, for I was growing tired, and there was neither water nor habitation to be seen. After travelling over heath-covered ground for many miles I sighted a valley, the valley of the Bidassoa.

The road began to descend rapidly, and I found myself going out of France at a headlong gait. Behobie was soon reached, and I was as soon out of it again. I wished to rest there, and pass in review the incidents of my previous wanderings in France, so that I might sum them up, and then go into a new country with a clean sheet. But it was not to be. The one gendarme in Behobie told me there was good accommodation "across the bridge." I went across the bridge and I was——in Spain.

Behobie had become Behobia now, and custom-house and sanitary officials seized me as their lawful prey.

I was questioned and examined till officialdom was tired of the game, and then, without being invited to do so, I took a chair and sat down. I am "only a Tramp!" No matter, I am not to be done out of well-deserved rest.

The wretched custom-house officer discovered that I had brought into Spain—a pound of chocolate too much! He informed me that it was the "property of the State," and that, if I wanted it, I must buy it over again.

But I never bought it at all. It was a present made me by my good friend the Consul of Biarritz. After a vigorous expression of opinion on my part I was given back my precious chocolate and presented with a sanitary passport.

I found there was no accommodation for me at Behobia, but before leaving the dirty little frontier town I went back to the bridge to look at the famous position occupied by the Anglo-Spanish allies in 1813. Before me rose the green knoll of St. Marcial, where the English protected the passage.

Every slope, saddle, and peak of the surrounding country is decked with earthworks, look-out towers, and stone barricades. The water-way is broad and unprotected. The position must have been a terrible one to occupy when the surrounding heights were swarming with French soldiers.

The victims of military glory sleep in that lonely spot, encompassed by wild, bare hills, lying where they fell.

As I stood musing on the bridge I did not hear a sound. All was silence and sadness.

I journeyed on, keeping the Bidassoa on my right, to Irun, where I found a dreamy, dirty, noiseless set of people crowding its half-dozen streets, and every window darkened by dishevelled heads.

Not liking the look of the place I pegged off, along the narrow dusty road which led to San Sebastian. Spain did not impress me at all. I didn't like the country. I felt too close to Ireland! The Spaniard, like Pat, is inseparable from his pig.

The ground floor of every house is the barn where cows, pigs, poultry, and other animals herd together. The odour is simply intolerable. After the filth of Irun it was pleasant to strike a real country road. Hills rose on either side, and apple orchards ran up the slopes. The fruit was small, green, and bitter, fit for making cider. Here I encountered two villainously dirty carabineers (military police). They were undersized, ugly little wretches, and their clothes were patched in a hundred places.

To these sorry personages I had to unbend and expose my all ; first my passport, which they couldn't read, and then my "swag"; but here I fear that curiosity, not duty, was the constraining motive. I felt inclined to resist these brutes, but knowing such a course would be unwise, I bottled up my indignation and yielded to their commands. Then I went on my way.

There were many pretty, shady places where I might have slept, but as the road was easy, I plodded

on till dusk, when I struck a small town. A cara-
bineer standing at the entrance gave me a ticket,
which I had to show to a little man at the town hall,
who was the image of Mr. Toole. He was extremely
affable, and offered to conduct me himself to a place
of rest. He did so—more's the pity! Of all the
disgusting odours that ever arose from a square of
this earth none could beat those emitted by that
horrible house in Renteria. I am not proud, and I
travel to learn; I will also own to an acquaintance
with some of the plague-spots of our century. I
have indeed spent days in Port Said, and I have
passed a night in Belin. But now, those old
experiences have an atmosphere of virtue in comparison with my night at Renteria. Mr. J. L. Toole
led me to a large archway in a wall. Then he waved
his hand as one might do to a dog, pointed to a
dark staircase, and shouted something to those above.
A shrill female voice replied. I went up. A large
galley-like room presented itself on the first floor.
A woman, engaged in nursing a baby and peeling
onions at one and the same time, beckoned me in.
Oh the horrors of that moment! I flatter myself
that I am a strong man, that I can put up with a
good deal, that I can rise or fall to all degrees of the
social barometer: I confess that I *could* not feel at
home in that unspeakable room.

About a dozen tramps, maimed and halt beings, were sitting round a long table examining the contents of their bags. Others were engaged in cooking onions and soaked bread in flat stone saucers over the charcoal fires which glowed red in the "incinerarios." A few brass and bronze plates of enormous size stood on a shelf above the open fireplace. Great wooden beams showed on the roof, and the walls were bare and covered with filth. I sat silent and shuddering, till the woman asked me if I should like to go to bed. She led me to a room across the landing, and I thanked Heaven that I was near the staircase. This room looked cleaner than the kitchen. It held two beds. The woman stuck an inch of taper about the substance of macaroni on to a nail in the wall, and I was instructed to blow it out as soon as I was ready for bed. I did so, and—made a discovery. I know something about parasites, for I have dabbled in agriculture and horticulture. I am an old hunter, having killed nearly everything except a Chinaman and a white elephant. But these experiences were of little service now. I could not cope with the bugs and fleas of Renteria. I had always believed them to be sworn enemies till I came here, when I found that they lived on the best of terms—and on ME!

All this happened thirty-six hours ago, but my

blood is still rushing and my flesh creeping on account of the hideous experiences of that night. An old man came to bed soon after me. He re-lighted the taper several times to hunt for—parasites. And he always crossed himself piously before extinguishing it.

I only slept about an hour. Bells were tintinabulating all night long. It *was* long! All the lights were out in the other rooms, and snoring was general. Some woke and cursed their lively bed-fellows. Others lighted their tapers and smoked cigarettes. I was glad of this, for the fumes dissipated the disgusting odours from the pigsty below.

I waited nervously for the first ray of light that I might up and away. It came at last—accompanied by ominous sounds. The boss of the establishment and his wife were evidently having a row. In the midst of this conjugal duet I rolled up my knapsack and departed. Never did the outer air smell more sweet. There was a public fountain by the roadside. Here, in defiance of a printed notice to the effect that "Any one using soap or washing in this flood will be fined five pesetas,"* I bathed and lathered and made myself feel wholesome and sweet. I was glad to shake the dust of this vile place off my feet, and had no desire to look back.

* Peseta = about one franc.

San Sebastian is one of the prettiest little places in the Old World. This was my verdict after looking at it from every coign of vantage. The streets are beautifully ordered. The open spaces are decorated with flowering and foliage plants. The houses are lofty, and everything looks clean. The bay is a perfect gem. A little belt of golden sand, not more than a hundred feet deep, runs round three-fourths of a circle of clear, emerald water. A cone-shaped island forms a natural breakwater to the outer ocean.

The patron saint of the town is treated quite humanely here, compared with all the stabbing he gets in other places. With only one arrow through his midrib, and another planted on his right knee, he stands, Mercury fashion, on tiptoe over the main doorway of the church dedicated to his memory.

I set out about midday, when all the little green bay was alive with women and children floating and splashing in the clear water.

The road was ill-made and dusty. Cider houses were frequent, and as a sou buys a large glass I slaked my thirst frequently without sinking much capital. My English shoes felt heavy and hot in this scorching climate, and I determined to try walking in " espargatos " (cloth slippers with soles of plaited flax). At a small store by the roadside I offered to exchange a good pair of trousers for two pairs of "espargatos." After a good deal of bargaining I agreed to take *one* pair of slippers, a plate of haricot beans, and a glass of wine, and to give up my bags.

The country suddenly became very wild, and all the people I met seemed equally so. I passed a lot of rough, gipsy-like fellows, whose appearance did not please me.

My first rural village was Hermam, which may be briefly described as all pigs and filth. As I did not wish for a repetition of my ghastly experience at Renteria I did not linger here. Just beyond the village I struck the Orio, and the scenery at once became wonderfully beautiful.

The mountains are of limestone, and the waters have chafed and fretted the cliffs into a thousand fantastic shapes. All these nooks and crannies are clothed with a rich mantle of luxuriant vegetation.

The river rushes over huge boulders, and the old weirs which have been thrown across the stream lock up the waters into long peaceful reaches. Watch-towers and look-outs are perched on almost every peak. I was enchanted with this lovely valley, as I saw it bathed in the ruddy glow of sunset lights, and I hoped that the Orio might be my travelling companion for many pleasant hours.

It *did* accompany me all the way to Andoain, where

I regret to record the youngsters received me with shouts, and pelted me with canisters filled with dust.

Appealing to one of the inhabitants for a night's lodging, I was referred to the alcalde, who sent me under the care of a small boy to a " posada " in rather a rough situation (Andoain is only a big village).

The landlord and his wife read the ticket and then read me, and I think they liked the ticket best. I offered the man fifty centimes, and told him that I was very tired. But he did not seem in the least affected by my sufferings. He kept me sitting on my bundle outside in the street while he sent the boy back to the alcalde.

Suddenly he changed his tune, invited me in, spread a cloth on the table and gave me eggs, fried bacon, bread, and wine.

Then a buxom girl brought in black coffee, red and white brandy, and a green cigar. Under the influences of that coffee royal and that green Indiaman, I shut my eyes awhile, and alone in that Spanish inn I was a happy fellow, talking with and in turn listening to those I love best in other lands.

I was shown to a dear little bedroom, everything clean and white, and the pillow-case embroidered by hand. Nevertheless, I arose in the morning with an aching head and a pair of legs that didn't wish to carry me. I thought the unpleasant sensation would pass away with an hour's walk ; but it didn't. The country was still very lovely. The hills were getting higher than ever : they were dangerously high—they would fall and I should be killed, crushed under the full weight of a giant mountain. This was the result of fever. My head was going round and round, and everything was topsy-turvy. When I stooped to drink from the springs by the wayside I dived my head quite under the water, while imagining myself a foot away from it. I was in a bad way. I knew it. I felt it. Had I been poisoned at Andoain? My hosts had given me in the morning a glass of warm sweet milk, a " bola," * and a roll, had refused to take the fifty centimes, and had wished me " God speed " on my journey. Was there any subtle motive for all this generosity ? Ah no ! That little woman's eyes had too much of the " mother " in them for her to treat me with cold-blooded cruelty. I knew it, and yet— what had overtaken me ? I was ill. God help me in this lone land.

I struggled on to Tolosa. The road swarmed with people going to market there. It is an old-fashioned little place, doing no trade with the rest of the world. All its merchandise consisted of a few reams of coarse shop-paper. It is situated on a bend of the Orio, and surrounded by an amphitheatre of grandly pre-

* A mixture of sugar and white of egg baked.

cipitous mountains with bold, rocky summits. Here, after refreshing myself with a glass of good cool wine from a skin, I visited the church, which impressed me on account of being the first clean one I had seen in Spain.

As I moved away from the town, I overtook a man and woman driving a lot of pigs. It came on to rain heavily. The pigs enjoyed it. I did not. Night was drawing in. The river had now become small and unimportant, the mountains higher and more rugged. Dark clouds were resting on the black ravines. No human habitation was in sight. I was wet, cold, and ill. It was a dreary look-out.

At last we reached Lizarza, a tiny hamlet perched under a great cliff. There was no alcalde, no secretario to be found ; and while I was searching for a tramps' rest, my friends with the pigs moved off, and I was left alone. An old man whom I " button-holed " led me to a cellar in an empty house. Here I spent the night racked with pain, and in a burning fever,—a prey to nervous terrors.

The old man let me out at an early hour, and I made off. I rambled many weary miles up a long valley, ever ascending by slow degrees. The lower slopes of the hills were clothed with walnut and sweet chesnut trees. Tiny patches of maize, grain, and root crops nestled one above the other on the sides of the gully.   The houses were little better than barns, built of enormous stones, and roofed with coarse pantiles.   Holes serve for windows, and a linen blind does service for a door during the day. All the pigs, poultry, horses, goats, donkeys, mules, and cows live on the ground floor.

In the course of the morning I arrived at a turnpike kept by a great fat man, very proud of his person and his office.

I showed him my recommendation from the Consul at San Sebastian, and then I offered to wish him "Good-day."   He pressed me to take some wine, and set bread and cheese before me.   I was touched by his friendliness, till the secret cause came out— "*Would I write him up in my book?*"   "God bless him—yes."   I will write up any man who helps me on my way.   He was charmed with my reply.   He would not say "á dios," but insisted on accompanying me on my way.   He did so for about five hundred yards, when we came to a culvert across the road conducting the water from a little torrent rushing down the mountain side.   There was a coping to this culvert, and we sat down.   The big, fat man stuck his thumbs into the armholes of his waistcoat and surveyed me with a bland air.   Then he lifted a hand from its perch, and showed me—the kingdom of Navarra.

" This," said he, "where I am sitting, is Vascon-gadas, but *you* are in Navarra. That little stream is the original boundary in these mountains."

Ill as I was, a thrill of joy went through me as I realised the importance of my position. The little I had read rushed back into my mind. I thought of the old, old days when Navarra did not exist, and when and how it became a kingdom. It is a beautiful, glowing story. It always touched me in the past, it will touch me still more in the future. It is so like Romance, and yet so true that it has the charm both of the Ideal and the Real. Here are the plain facts. Two weary wayfarers—priests, or monks, or penitent sinners—set out on a pilgrimage to a shrine in the West Pyrenees. They encountered a hill so precipitous and dangerous that they could not find strength to climb it. Accordingly, they built a little nest, and set to work to make an easy road to the top of the hill. They lived on native produce and on gifts bestowed by grateful wayfarers. Their fame spread, and these road-makers became objects of worship. The mountaineers went up the high hill to pay homage to the two self-sacrificing old men. They looked out on the surrounding country, on the towering hills, and then on themselves. They realised their power; they were six hundred strong, and Hidalgos. They confessed their sins, took counsel with one another, and there and then on that lonely hill, to which they had come to offer their thanks to the aged pilgrims, they founded the kingdom of Navarra.

I thanked my good host the turnpike-keeper, bade farewell to Vascongadas, and went slowly on my journey, which now lay across Navarra.

CHAPTER II.

NAVARRA.

THE country I now passed through was beautiful, but a sick man is a mean thing, finding interest in little but himself. I got a little bread, but I could not eat it. They do not make black bread in the north of Spain, but their brown and white bread is villainously hard and heavy stuff.

Towards evening I reached Le Cumberri, a long, straggling village in a mountain gorge. I was too tired and ill to trouble any alcalde, so I took up my quarters in a cheap shanty. My companions were a rough set—hawkers, tramps, and one dreadful cripple, whose legs were turned behind him and who went about in a " Billy-in-the-bowl fashion " on his haunches.

As he was the innkeeper's son he busied himself

with the dozen little pots and jars stewing over a fire in the centre of the kitchen. The fireplace was a circular platform, about a foot above the floor, ornamented with enamelled tiles. In the centre burned a charcoal fire.

The kitchen utensils in this part of the world are very simple. The saucepan is unknown. Everything is cooked in tiny jars of clay or iron. The bowls, spoons, and ladles are usually of brass, very old and curiously designed. The clay pitchers and jars resemble those shown in the Roman rooms of the British Museum. I saw a child playing with a little drinking pitcher which had two handles and three lips. A piece of ribbon fell loosely round the neck, and heavy lace decorated the lower edge. If it had come from Etruria all the art critics would go mad about such a thing; but made by a living Spaniard, it is of no value.

The cost of my accommodation was not great: fifty centimes paid for bed and board. Another night had passed. I still felt ill, but my spirit did not leave me; I struggled on in the direction of Pamplona. The stream had now become a noisy cataract, rushing down in clouds of snowy foam, and falling into dark depths hidden by boughs of overhanging trees and long grasses. The mountain road skirted the edge of the torrent. The ascent was rapid and formed a double zigzag. I toiled wearily along, and was rewarded by reaching a point whence I could look up to hundreds of peaks, capped with mist, down into deep black gorges, and away over bright spots touched by the sun on the lower hills. The air grew thinner and colder as I approached the Arriba Pass. The water rushed from a thousand springs, and the cow bells tinkled on the slopes below. The winds howled round lonely rocks, and through rents and rifts on the heights above. The sun showed a silver disc through the misty clouds, and the valley below looked like a dark death hollow. It was a weird, impressive scene.

About 1 p.m. I reached the pass, and now for the first time I was able to look eastward. A stretch of wild mountainous country met my gaze. A few tiny patches of cultivation showed that the country was not absolutely unpopulated. My journey was now all down-hill. In the evening I reached Betelu, and made at once for the alcalde.

The "Civil Guard" are generally civil to me, but here, when I asked the guard to grant me a night's lodging, he replied, "No entiendo,"—which I easily translated into "didn't intend to!" I had tried that game myself in France, and now these Spanish rascals were turning the tables on me. I badgered that fellow for nearly half an hour—reviling him in

all the vernaculars with which I am familiar. But it
was no use, I had met my match. He sent me off
to a casa blanca (white house), where a little hot-
headed woman drove me away. I went on to a
"posada" kept by a mother and three daughters. It
was very clean for a Basque house. The elder woman
looked suspiciously at me, and asked what brought
me to this out-of-the-way spot. Her daughters
entered into the romantic side of my pilgrimage, and
were enthusiastic in their remarks. They saw that I
was ill. They had but little to give; but such as
they had was mine. They made some excellent soup,
and cooked me a veal cutlet. I ate this with a glass
of good wine, and went to bed in a clean room.
In the morning I gave the woman thirty-five cents
(the price demanded) and asked her name—for such
kindness deserved encouragement and recognition in
a practical way. This she refused, and I was forced
to go away ignorant of the very names of those
who had done me such good service. One of the
daughters was the most beautiful woman I saw in the
Basque country. She was tall and well made, her
hair dark, her skin clear and fresh. She had fine
features, and a noble, generous, sensible expression
of countenance. The Basque women impressed me
favourably. They looked good. There was no
artfulness or hypocrisy about them; nor were there

any meaningless smiles. They seem to age very quickly. Women of thirty are set and hard-featured. The instinct of maternity does not appear to be strong. There are no large families. Amorous swains do not appear in public; at all events, I have looked for them in vain. The men show little interest in domestic affairs. Wives and children are mere accessories, and there is no "climbing of knees the envied kiss to share."

I soon got away from the gloomy mountains where I had suffered so much, and came out on open country, where wheatfields and vines were growing freely.

I passed what I shall always regard as the "champion team" of the world on this bit of road. It was composed of two black bulls, three grey mules, a rusty-coated Jack donkey, and two brown horses, pulling a dray loaded with wine barrels.

I have been a bullock "puncher," and I know that a strange variety of animals is often strung together to make what is called a "team"; but I never saw such a queer lot as this in all Australia. The sight was so comic that I laughed aloud.

I met dozens of donkey-boys with "thimble rigging" shows, and blind men with fiddles led by big Basque dogs. There were girls, too, looking as if they could dance a bolero, and tambourine maidens, thick and clumsy limbed. It was clear that a feast or a fair was in preparation.

I journeyed along for many weary miles, passing through hot, dry gorges before I reached a tributary of the Arga. The water was deep and clear. A range of hills rises in front, and a magnificent rent affords the river a clear way between massive limestone precipices, five or six hundred feet in height. This is a grand bit of scenery, well worth a weary pilgrimage.

A dozen or two of eagles were towering round the height. The water was rushing wildly through the gorge below, and far away in the centre of a vast wheatfield rose the towers of Pamplona.

The Gorge of Irurzun is more than nine miles from Pamplona, and the village looked big enough to hold me for the night. But the alcalde's wife was a thick-headed woman, who told me that I should get accommodation farther on, just a *little* farther on the road. She gave me a handful of dried prunes, and, munching these, I went on my way. I met a fat priest who smiled benignly on me. I asked him if he spoke English, and the old rascal replied that he "didn't intend to!" I was furious, and asked him how he could possibly desire to remain ignorant of a language that gave so much delight to half the millions of the earth. "No entiendo," he said again.

Then he pulled a two-centime bit out of his greasy pocket and held it out to me. I took this as a signal to decamp!

The sun had gone down, and the lamps of Pamplona were twinkling in the distance. The roadside was aflame with lights, which might have been the cigarettes of crouching brigands; but a closer investigation proved that they were given out by peaceful glow-worms. The phosphorus rubs off, so that they are followed by " trails of glory " as they move along the grass.

Late in the evening, I reached a little cluster of houses. One was a wine shop. A big, fair man (a rare sight) with a sprout of hair growing from his chin, told me that this house was " *bad*—very bad," and, fearing lest some infectious illness should lurk within its walls, I prepared to depart. The fair man assured me that a nice rest-house existed a little farther on ; but it turned out to be a villainous crib with four or five crippled vagabonds lying on its sand floor.

No, not for all creation will I sleep in this den while there is a bit of clean earth outside. But the plain of Pamplona did not boast of a single tree, hedge, fence, or shed. Nearly all the corn was cut, and the bare, stubbly fields did not look inviting. In spite of my weariness, I felt that I would rather go on to Pamplona and seek a decent bed than lie down exposed to the chilly night air.

The lights of the city increased and died away in turn as I journeyed up and down the rugged plain. As the night grew blacker the houses seemed farther off than ever. Hour after hour I trudged wearily along, and just as the church clocks were striking ten I entered the northern gate and stood within the capital of Navarra.

I tramped round, asking directions to posadas and hotels for two weary hours. A soldier handed me over to the guidance of a couple of drunkards going to a house which he felt sure would just suit me. (Complimentary, wasn't it?) One fellow soon became too top-heavy to go on. So I tramped round with the other singing snatches of old lays at the top of his voice. It was just midnight, and I felt not a bit too respectable.

At last we reached the desired haven. I disliked the look of the street, but with bleeding feet, and ready to drop from sheer weakness, I could not afford to be particular. We made a row, and the door opened. Dancing was going on. An old man with a kindly face was thrumming a guitar, and three or four girls were tripping up and down the kitchen. The other people were rough and ready but "square-headed" folk, and I felt I could trust them. I asked for milk, but they had none.   An old woman brought a spoonful of poor soup, and asked me to try it.   It was better than nothing, so the soup was warmed for me.   Then I retired to rest and slept soundly on the bare floor under the tiles of a five-storey house.   The next morning I procured some remedies from a local chemist, and, feeling better, I went round the town, which is one of the dullest "capitals" on the face of the earth.   It stands to the north-west of a broad, undulating plain of wheatfields and vineyards, and is surrounded by a high stone wall.   The Arga bounds the western side.   But for this river I could have run round the place in twenty minutes.   It just covers a quarter of a square mile.

The Plazas Constitution and Valencia are good sites, and a little trouble might make them beautiful, but this has not been taken.   A big theatre, a few dull cafés, a "tora" circle, and the Cathedral of St. Ignatius, a richly gilt but unattractive edifice, exhaust the sights of Pamplona.

What interested me most were my table companions.   The house turned out to be a very respectable one, frequented by dealers in live stock, grain, oil, and wine, men who talked and acted roughly, but who possessed a fund of practical information on a variety of subjects.   They were all dressed in blue blouses, "espargots," and "berets," which they kept on

during meals; and every man was clean shaven.
They were most kind to me, and did all in their
power to make my stay pleasant.

The meals were roughly but cleanly served, the
viands abundant, the cooking excellent. Here I ate
my first piece of chamois, and I thought it a delicious
meat.

As I still felt too ill to write, I wandered about the
dull old streets, peeping behind canvas and reed
blinds to see the contents of the stores; for there
is not a shop with a shop-front in all Pamplona.
The goods are kept in boxes, barrels, and enormous
jars, on the ground floor. A block forms the counter.
Here people sit, stand, and knit stockings as the
goods are dealt out. It is a slow, tedious method.

I strolled one day into the little Church of St.
Nicolas, a mere porch with a tiny dome ornamented
with rich tracery in amber and gold. The light was
such as penitent sinners love. It was a soft blue,
born of the stream of sunshine flowing through the
cupola. I sat down, and there, in front of me, was
written, " Here is peace." Ah, God ! is it so? Had
I come so far to find it at last? Was I to find the
crisis of my life here, in the place where the great
Ignatius Loyola had met it ? A sweet sense of repose
and satisfaction stole over me. My languid state was
conducive to meditation. I would give the world to

be able to recall at will the feeling that came over me that day in St. Nicolas of Pamplona, but I fear I never shall.

Two pretty, sweet-voiced girls came in with their mother, and fell to admiring the dome, and the blue glass vault above, and the inscriptions; and, not knowing me to be a heathen and an alien, said it was "Muy bonita!" (very beautiful).

"Si, si," I said; and this was all the Spanish I could muster.

My two days and nights in Pamplona cost me nine pesetas fifty centimes; yet I marched out of the gate of San Nicolas little wiser for my sojourn there.

CHAPTER III.

NAVARRA (*Continued.*)

IT was a beautiful evening when I left Pamplona. The sky line seemed farther off than I had ever seen it before, nor had I ever beheld a vaster extent of cloudland or a more lovely collection of forms and colours. Thousands of plots of corn and grape-vines, east, west, north, and south, made the scene a rich one.

Pamplona was soon lost behind the evening clouds which came down from the hills.

I walked nearly seventeen miles that evening, and slept in a fowl-house near Garicoain. The next morning it rained hard. I took shelter in the church, where I found nothing to look at save half-a-dozen effigies with swords stuck through their bodies.

By this time I was far away from the plain of

Pamplona — traversing wild, broken country, that carried nothing but patches of lavender, broom, gorse, rosemary, and wild brier. Just above Tafalla I struck the Cidacos. It is but a drivelling creek, a tributary of the Arragon ; but the people have turned its waters to good account, and distribute it over the gardens by means of elevated channels. Grapes flourish in this little hollow, and olive trees, which serve as break-winds to the vineyards in rough weather.

Tafalla turned out to be an ugly, insignificant town, its only attraction being a citadel perched on a clay hummock, which was held by two Basque dogs and a fat woman. I drove out the Basque dogs at the point of my stick, and claimed an indemnity from the fat woman—to wit, one green pear—agreeing to evacuate the place in ten minutes. I sat down on the old outer wall and looked down on the mass of tiles and rotting walls and filth below. It was as sad and silent and dead as Pompeii. The church of Santa Maria was bigger than the other buildings, but not one whit more inspiring. Having eaten my pear I went off towards Olite. This is a very old and fortified city, standing on a shingle spit in the centre of a broad, dry valley which soon widens out to the dimensions of a plain. The old buildings are very paltry, and the stone walls are guiltless of cement. There is not—there never was—a square yard in all this fortress which three English navvies and a crowbar could not displace in ten minutes.

A brother-at-arms, a strong, well-made Frenchman, tried to strike up an acquaintance with me.

He wore a grey fur cap, and a blue blouse reaching to his heels. He carried a recommendation from some important personage, but what his weakness was (I think light labour) I failed to discover. He pressed me to journey with him, as he was "tired of travelling alone." I was not; so I shook him off and departed.

After a long fag across an open, dirty plain, I reached Caparroso, on the banks of the Arragon, which, like most of the Spanish rivers, has a great name, a broad bed, and very little water.

Caparroso is at once striking and peculiar, in its rude primitiveness and effective position. It occupies the sides of two long ravines lying between three bold ridges of close, gritty clay. With the exception of the boulders on the bed of the Arragon, there is not a stone or rock within sight, and not a vestige of vegetation. Where the ravines converge near the river there are a few houses of stone and sun-dried bricks, but up both gullies hundreds of dwellings are cut out of the solid hills. The scene is most striking. There stand the houses—veritable temples of Kylos—hewn out of masses of native clay. The world-known temple is entitled to no more respect than these isolated cabins by the "hills of silence" —the local name for the ridges. Although the architect and engineer have not been consulted, the plan of construction is excellent. Enormous mounds and spurs of earth have been honeycombed within and decorated without, so as to afford shelter to the body and satisfaction to the eye.

Difficulties have been recognised only to be overcome. In many cases the hills have cracked and sent the houses over towards the gullies below. The floors have been squared down to a horizontal plane again, and the walls, roofs, and chimneys left leaning at frightful angles over the chasm. There are no military earthworks half so curious as these civil dwellings, and no monolith reared to perpetuate the memory of a nothing or a nobody could impress one more than these necessary domestic hives.

A frightful monotony reigns over all. Everything wears the same shade of buff-grey. The windows are but tiny holes, and the doorways are screened by canvas blinds faded to the same dull hue.

The people are almost as silent as their natural surroundings. There is no voice in nature here, and man seems half afraid to break the stillness.

They live on the produce of a few miles of river flat some distance below the town, and journey up and down with mules and donkeys laden with water, corn, and garden stuff. You will never find a Northern Spaniard's house situated on good ground. He wants the soil for other purposes ; so he perches his cabin where nothing will grow, even though it be miles from wood and water.

The dwellers at the head of the ravines had to carry their water fully three miles. They take their bit of clothing to the river, and lave and bang it over stones till it is a little cleaner than before. A really clean article I have not seen in all the " pueblos " I have visited. Judged as a whole, the Northern Spaniards are a very dirty people ; but I, a victim to their negligence, can afford to say—and with much emphasis— look at the conditions they are born to! Hard native surroundings *will* tell, and poverty produce indifference to cleanliness, as long as the world runs on.

They did not treat me badly at Caparrosa. The alcalde gave me a ticket entitling me to bed and board at the hospital. This was not a clay dwelling ; it was built of sun-dried bricks, and stood on a flat by the river. It was a wretched place, but I managed to put in a fair night.

I could find no shop or bakery in the morning, so I started for Valtierra, trusting to pick up some breakfast on my way ; but, alas! there were no houses on the road.

I had to cross the most terrible bit of country I have yet encountered. The wold of Caparrosa is twenty-four miles broad and holds only one house. At this house there was no bread. I could only get a glass of wine. The heat was intense, the wold a blighted desert. Its composition is interesting, but a tramp is a man who *feels*, and you must give him something to eat if you would show him anything worth looking at. The wold is composed almost entirely of alabaster, much of it beautifully laminated and clear as rock crystal. I was able to read with ease through some pieces half-an-inch thick. Some rifts are mottled like marble, pink, blue, and white. Other patches are clear as Parian and hard as flint.

The spot is full of interest to the geologist, but I was "only a tramp," and little short of getting to the end of the wold would satisfy me.

When at last I reached the valley of the Ebro I "struck oil" at once. At a little stone cabin I got some bread and wine, and took what I felt to be a well-earned rest. Here there was a picturesque old shepherd wearing a beaver hat shaped like a Chinese sunshade, with two huge knobs like powder puffs dangling one from the crown and one from the side of the hat; a coarse blue cotton shirt, with a dirty white front let in, and large splashes of flowers embroidered round the neck and buttonholes; a black plush coat shorter than an Eton jacket, and worn brown and ragged ; tan leather breeches, the seat and pockets strengthened by patches of leather fancifully scalloped round the edges and sewn in cross-stich ; leather sandals on his feet, and a strip of brown saddle cloth bound two or three times round his lean calves, and tied with a bundle of leather laces, the ends of which dangled as tassels about his ankles. He was a very good-looking old man, and I found his company, to say nothing of the bread and wine, a great relief after the miserable wold.

Valtierra was now in sight, and early in the evening I presented myself at the Town Hall.

The secretary was a young man with a very white face and a very red shirt. As neither knew the other's tongue there was something like a dead lock, till the secretary bethought him of a fellow-citizen who knew English ; and I was soon introduced to Señor Julian Zapatéro, who explained that I was a " deserving case," and I was forthwith granted accommodation at the hospital. I was grateful to Señor Zapatero for his assistance, but still more for his conversation. He showed himself entirely free from prejudice. The accuracy and force of his reasoning was clear. Navarra and its people began to wear a noble aspect. Zapatero spoke English

well, having spent three years in London. He is--
wonderful for a Spaniard—a cosmopolitan. He
judges people and places as he finds them. Tradition does not influence his estimates.

We were soon at home with each other. We
chatted about "things in general." Then we got
back to Spain. What did I think of it?

I told him that I was surprised to find the
Northern Spaniard so unlike the character usually
ascribed to him.

"Yes," said Zapatero, "we are not the cold-
blooded savages England has heard so much about,
are we?"

"How is it that the Spaniards have got such a
bad name?"

"That is a big question! I consider that nothing
has done more to set the world against Spain than
the writings of the elder Dumas. He wrote at a
time when the world well-nigh lived on sensational-
ism; and with his facile pen he made his romances
read like every-day facts. Dumas has made Spain
the stink-pot of the world. The world is slow
to unlearn old beliefs. The mother's fable becomes
the child's fact, and sticks to him through life. The
'reading public' are the stupid public, people who
are too lazy or senseless to prove things for themselves. The world finds it easier to swallow Dumas'

Spain than to adopt *your* plan of action. You will learn to know something of Spain as it is, but I fear the knowledge will sadden you."

"But," I interposed, "will you not yourselves refute this universal calumny by sheer force of character and internal growth?"

"No, we cannot grow. What is the use of great men in Spain? They cannot make her great. Men do not make countries, countries make men! Washington, Kossuth, Garibaldi were great, simply because they were called on *at the right time.* There are always men for occasions.

"No," added Zapatero,—and there was a ring of pathos in his voice,—"we are a quiet people and we must remain so. We have nothing to gain by being 'educated,' as the world uses the word. Education is not the certain key to a better life. It often leads us to neglect the little we naturally possess, and to suffer accordingly. What becomes of the Spaniard who professes to be educated? He neglects the needs of stomach and brain to clothe his lean shanks in some town with eighty per cent. of underbred people like himself.

"Our 'internal growth,' as you call it, is in proportion to our national resources. And what are they? You have journeyed nearly the entire length of Navarra, and could you or your people do more with the country than we have done ? Ours is a struggle for existence. We can never hope to advance. Here for ages we have carried on the most intense system of cultivation, and we have exercised rigid economy. We have had few endemical disasters. Yet, with all this, we have no surplus. We are just where we were centuries ago. It is a sad fact ! " *

Señor Zapatero sent to my hotel (*i.e.*, the hospital) a note of introduction to a friend of his in Tudela. This was accompanied by a few kind words and good wishes addressed to myself.

There is nothing like a heart for giving a man heart. If you can find a human soul it will kill all the devil out of you in less time than all the salves and emulsions in the world.

I cast in my lot with three old men and a woman at the Hospital, and I really enjoyed being down on their low level. The fare was poor, yet the feast was sweet. The old men might have sat as models for portraits of heroes. Their rich brown faces showed above long muscular necks, looking like toughened bronze.

When I set out from Valtierra the Ebro appeared about three miles off. After walking for six hours and passing through a couple of untidy villages, it seemed farther off than ever, and I was apparently

* These remarks apply particularly to the province of Navarra.

marking time right in front of Valtierra. It was
Sunday ; but I was not able to keep it holy. I had
to walk the whole day, anathematising the confounded idiots who caused this road to wind like a
watch-spring and never made one solitary yard in
a straight line. It looked as if the river once wound
round under the hills and the road followed it, but
the river has gone over to the opposite side of the
valley, and the old road still serves, so I had to
journey seven or eight miles for the sake of
advancing two or three. But at last—at last—I
reached the green river, and profited by it to wash
my clothes. I rested while they were drying.

Tudela rose before me—a mass of red-tiled towers
and spires, chimney-pots, and tumble-down houses.

A line of poplars showed the river's course as far
as eye could reach. It spoke of new life. After
barren hills, sandy ridges, shingle spits, and ugly
hummocks of clay, I was glad to look on the strip of
green which followed the great river.

The country was changing rapidly. I missed
many things to which I had become accustomed.

I had suddenly lost the " Rebeccas " with their
wooden buckets banded with bright steel, the only
thing the Basque and Navarra folk take a pride in
keeping clean. I met no more tiny, black, one-eared
donkeys laden with country produce, and a woman or

two perched on top of the heavy load. I was no longer tormented by the big Basque dogs, trained to hunt the unfortunate tramp through every village street. My ears were no longer filled with the jangling music of cattle, dog, donkey, and mule bells (they put a bell on everything in the north except a pig. The Spaniard knows that any pig is industrious enough to leave traces of his handicraft behind him.) And I was leaving piggy behind me too! He is all very well when written up as " Dublin cured " or " Prime York," but he is a less respectable creature when met as a grunting bed-fellow. It is no misfortune to be a " black sheep " in Navarra. The majority are black, and the old shepherd who " drives his flock to pick the scanty blade," generally gives effect to the oddness of things by having two or three big crop-eared, white dogs. They crop all animals here instead of branding them. It is a cruel and ugly custom. These people have no sense of beauty. They are not to be blamed. Away from the Pyrenees there are no refining influences in the north of Spain. The scenery and the surroundings are always harsh and brutal, and the people's spirit is governed by them.

I entered the old town of Tudela by way of an early Roman bridge spanning the Ebro, which has seventeen arches all of different designs. There is not room for two carts—scarcely for two well-laden donkeys—to pass abreast. The bridge is neither a crescent, a curve, a regular set of angles, nor a straight line; it is something unique.

Tudela is in two parts—"old" and "new." The "old" is very old, and the "new" far from modern. The old buildings are sombre, and resemble high fortresses with their walls of Roman brick and black-tiled roofs. Curious contrasts are seen at every turn: coats of arms and crests over doors leading to pigs' hovels, and the former abodes of nobles turned into the grimy haunts of vagabonds and beggars. New Tudela has few attractions. It boasts a "New Plaza," which is two hundred years old and looks its age.

I was here reminded of a famous fellow-tramp, "Old Benjamin the Friar," who was born in this town. He journeyed round the world (which was small in his time) from 1159 to 1173, and wrote an account of all he saw and experienced, which, if he kept eyes and ears well open, must have been a considerable amount.

I found Zapatero's friend at the "Café Impérial," enjoying himself in true Sunday fashion. He entertained me, and then pointed out the sights of Tudela. They are not many. The cathedral is an immense old building, one of the earliest Gothic buildings in Spain. It has some beautiful archways, and fine marbles, but the effect is ruined by many repulsive figures in relief on the dome, reminding my Philistine eye of the decoration of a menagerie. This church has played a great part in the ecclesiastical history of Spain, but to a casual tramp its greatest gift was a few minutes' rest and escape from the hot sun.

Coming out of this old-world building, I confronted the French tramp I had left at Olite. I had some difficulty in dodging the rascal, with whom I would not be seen for worlds. My new acquaintance is a leading man in Tudela, and no good Spaniard loves a Frenchman, especially a French tramp! But I did not linger long in this dead-alive place. In the evening I found myself out on a flat, open road, lying off a mile or two from the Ebro. I journeyed along for many weary miles, till I reached the village of Riba-forada, where I slept in a little hut made of river grass standing in a back-yard. It was clean, but hard—the natural earth—and at daybreak a woman drove me from my lowly bed. Having shouldered my bag, I started for the Imperial Canal, which flows parallel with the Ebro, hoping to find shade and coolness amidst an abundant vegetation. But it was not so pleasant as I had hoped to find it. The locality is a second Venice, and, like Mrs. Partington, I was visiting it when the place was in flood! The canal flows at an average distance of twelve miles from the river, and the intermediate lands are cut up into little blocks, over which the waters are distributed by natural gravitation.

This artificial river is sixty-six feet wide and twelve deep, and has a current of five miles an hour. It is a magnificent flood, displaying in unmistakable language the disposition and enterprise of these Northern Spaniards. After two or three hours of toilsome wandering across the boggy flats created by the floods, I went back to the main road, where all was bare and blighted as ever. The only welcome feature in the landscape was a near glimpse of Arragon.

My experience of Navarra was at an end. Two ragged-faced old stones mount guard on either side of the road, close to the "pueblo" of Mallen. They stand as the boundaries of the two ancient kingdoms. I sat down beside one of them, and thought of the sage of Valtierra, and of the truth of his words. I felt like a man in the witness-box compelled to give ugly evidence. Navarra wants re-modelling! It is not designed to meet human needs. If we could pull down these barren hills, which are piled to no purpose, and turn on the wasting waters of the world, Navarra might breathe and grow like the rest of Europe. But man is not master of all matter, and all the scientific discoveries in the world cannot make Navarra a great country. It needs a

Moses to strike the rock and send a fertilising flood down every barren range and arid plain.

Some people declare that aluminium is the coming factor in utilitarian and decorative work. Navarra has enough clay to produce aluminium for centuries, but it lacks the working forces—wood and water. I have heard white-handed men glory in the fact that Navarra has political autonomy. What of that? Will local government change the face of nature, and the miserable condition the people are born to? Political reform does no more than knock a few rascals down that another set of scamps may step up.

Bad laws may injure, but they cannot kill and wholly impoverish a country. Where there is native wealth a people will always rise superior to the decrees of men. Show me the rich countries of the world, and I will show you the rich people.

For their laborious effort and great perseverance in the face of tremendous difficulties the inhabitants of Navarra deserve all praise.

Praise is a factor in economy. We should cultivate the habit of praising all that is worthy, as by so doing we create impulses which increase the native wealth of the world.

CHAPTER IV.

ARRAGON.

MALLEN, the village on the frontier of Arragon, was too busy with its own affairs to pay much heed to me, a tramp. It was harvest time, and threshing was going on on the circular-paved floors round the village. The mode is of the simplest description. The tools—forks, shovels, sieves, screens, harness, and accoutrements—are all of wood, bent to various shapes by steam, and the straw plaited or twisted with twigs.

The threshing machine is a broad sledge resembling the bed of a cart—one end turned up representing the footboard. The grain is spread three or four feet deep on the ground, and a couple of mules, yoked to the sledge, are driven round and round—generally by the help of a dozen youngsters, all nursing babies, and highly delighted to get a ride for nothing.

The bottom of the sledge is roughened with rows of flints, chipped and sharpened till they look like sharks' teeth. These stones cut up the straw into coarse chaff. When the wheat has been trodden from the ears, men with wooden forks toss the mass against the wind, and so divide the chaff from the grain.

The latter is then screened through sieves made of straw or leather. The wind, acting on the chaff, piles it in various places according to its size. By this simple means a complete division of material is effected with speed and economy. Wherever you journey at harvest time there is the same process, and you meet scores of mules and donkeys moving along the roads half hidden under their immense burden of chaff, which they are conveying in huge nets rigged over a wooden frame to the barns.

The valley of the Ebro looked lovely as it opened out before me. It is one vast garden, and as I stood on a high bank overlooking eighty or a hundred square miles of country, bearing fruit, vegetables, and cereals,—with occasional rows of trees, and straight streaks of water showing between,—I was filled with the delight of living. When a tramp's eyes can feast, there must be something really good before him.

There were plenty of people at work on the irrigated lands, and I received from them a generous supply of fruit. With these and a piece of bread I had bought at Mallen, I sat down to enjoy my feast, when suddenly my French tramp came upon me.

He wanted to be friendly (I fear it was cupboard love), but I didn't. I shook my head and pointed over the green valley, and at last, seeing the game useless, he took himself off.

I followed the bank of the Imperial Canal, through rough cuttings of terribly hard stone, which showed how big the task had been and how energetic the workers, for this great work was carried out before the introduction of steam. Late in the evening I reached Gallur. Gallur has cursed the whole world, and made a special appeal to ME (a tramp!) to make its complaint known.

By desire of the mayor I beg to inform you that Gallur is not to be found on any map *—which shows how ignorant and careless are geographers! Gallur was born A.D. 1788. Its inhabitants are the descendants of those hardy spirits who dug and delved the Imperial Canal ; and yet, in spite of this, their heirs, and the town they have built up, are to live unknown!

This is not my speech. It is the Mayor of Gallur who asks these indignant questions. He would have his flock of five thousand souls made known to all

* I have since discovered that Gallur is clearly marked in the map to accompany Murray's Handbook.—C. B. L.

peoples. I agreed with him. I said I would do what I could for him, and, even though he chose to give me no more than a shakedown in a stable between mules and donkeys infested with lively fleas, I'll speak of the inhabitants of Gallur as a most industrious people—busy from dawn till dark with their waterways, garden plots, and garnered grain.

I caught sight of the French tramp again here—only for a moment, for I rushed off to avoid his company. It proved to be my last view of him, as many days have passed since I saw him in the starlit street of unknown and complaining Gallur.

I began to enjoy a little shade now, for poplars line the banks of the canal. Every few miles I came to a lock whence the waters are dispersed over the valley. Towards evening I broke away from the canal to cross the green plain to Alcala. It was from this place that Don Quixote's enchanted barque set out on its short but classic journey. Alcala is a very out-of-the-way place. I could find nothing there to remind me of the age and civilisation of which I try to persuade myself I form an honourable part. My experience is the reverse of that of Rip van Winkle, for I find that hundreds of years have brought no change to this lowly spot. The houses round the little plaza and the manners and customs of the people are much as they were when Moor and

Arragonese lived side by side. The inhabitants are silent and sly. The bells have slipped from the old church tower, so there is no longer any weekly rousing by Sabbath peals. The river flows hard by, so I took a casual look for such a spot as the enchanted barque might have chosen to sail from ; but I looked in vain for any landing-stage, nor could I see any mills or barriers in the river.

I journeyed on to Pedrola, arriving at the station just as the train came in from Zaragoza.

A crowd of country folk were waiting to receive some grandees, who were returning to their country-seat. A pair of fine mouse-coloured mules, coarsely harnessed and attached to a third-rate cab, formed the aristocratic chariot.

Four badly-dressed women, without face, form, or intellectual beauty, stepped in. They were members of a ducal family. Their house is a grand palace—at least it is grand for Spain—standing in the centre of the village, and surrounded by decayed and frightfully dirty dwellings. A long deep archway—almost a tunnel—leads from the narrow street into the courtyard.

It occurred to me that this would be a favourable moment to seek admittance to the palace of the Duke of Villa Hermoza. A page in a showy tunic led me to the entrance stairs, which were of black and white tiles with a medallion in the centre of each. I noticed all I could because it occurred to me, "If I am received I shall have to talk about the doings of the family. This house has entertained stray characters and knights without armour in its time. Did not Don Quixote and Sancho Panza receive good lodging here, and was not 'Rosinante' stabled somewhere in sight of me? Ah! I thought, they will like allusions to this! There is nothing like the ancient traditions of a family for touching its vital spot, be it pocket or larder." (But here let me say that the devil of it in Spain is that there is no larder! The people cook no more than can be eaten at a meal, and when the meal is over, God help the dog who is expected to fatten on the bones.)

Let me make a clean breast of it. I didn't gain an audience with the Duke or with the family of the Duke of Villa Hermoza. A neat maid-servant informed me that cards were not received that day; she asked me to take a piece of bread instead, and expressed the hope that I would find my way out!

This I did quite easily, for the palace was in no sense bewildering. It neither charmed nor dispirited me; on the other hand, I felt glad that I was a tramp privileged to roam under the free canopy of heaven, and not bound to such filth and unsight-liness as surround the palace of Pedrola.

I wanted rest badly, but there was no alcalde or house for vagrants in this village, and as I learned there was a decent " pueblo " some three miles away, I set off to it. The road was over a dry but cultivated piece of plain land, all vines and wheat stubble. The plain crossed, I arrived at Ferruginelles, a dirty little village perched up on a ridge not far from the canal. The houses are built of sun-dried bricks, a strip of whitewash round the doorways being the only decoration of these miserable hovels.

All the washing is done at the stream which flows at the foot of the hill. The women journey up and down before and after meals, first to prepare the vegetables, and afterwards to wash the utensils. These Northern women are great gossips. I have watched them for hours, and have seen the hands hang idle while the tongues worked at railroad speed.

The young alcalde directed me to a house where I could get a night's lodging. I was received by a quiet, grave-looking woman, dressed in dingy black, a kerchief round her shoulders and another on her hair.

The house had two stories. A mule and some pigs held the ground floor, the woman and her husband lived in the room and cupboard above.

When the little oil lamp was lighted and I took

a look at my new home, I was in no way cheered. The room was very small, and the walls black and shiny as a chimney. The fireplace was a raised platform of mud and stones in the centre of the floor. A broad wooden tube drew up some of the smoke to a hole in the wall, the rest found its way through the door and light holes. A few stone platters and bowls, a chocolate pot, and big cooking vessels in clay, made up the decorations and furniture of the chamber.

A little fire glowed on the pile of stones, and the contents of a stone jar bubbled on its margin. A three-legged frying-pan held something covered over with a plate, and a stone jar filled with water hung in the cool draught of one of the light holes. We sat waiting for the husband, who came in holding his hand to his face, and almost crying with toothache. I had some strong mint in my bag, which I gave him, and he got some relief.

The woman pulled out the small stool—which is the only dining-table known to the Spanish peasantry—placed the stone jar and the frying-pan upon it, and pressed me to eat. The frying-pan contained the centre spines of beet leaves. I was hungry and ate it gladly, although it had little flavour to recommend it.

After this, she turned out the contents of the

stone jar : potatoes, onions, and—something else, which proved to be snails. They had been well prepared, and I ate them with much gusto. The meal over, my hostess gathered the wooden spoons, bowls, and cooking utensils into a hand trough, and said it was time to go to bed. " He has to be up at three," she explained, " and he is tired."

The labour conditions in the valley of the Ebro are truly frightful. This man, who was only fifty, but who looked like a worn-out old man, works in the summer all the hours of daylight, and ten hours in the winter. For this he receives five pesetas a week (little more than three shillings), and not one single extra in any shape or form. Sunday is a rest day— he works eight hours ! Think of this, my brother Britons, and ask yourselves if the Spaniard is to be most blamed or pitied ?

My heart ached for these poor human slaves born to such hard conditions ; to me the terrible pang of their existence lies in the fact that it knows no change. A condemned prisoner hopes for a coming day, but these poor mortals have no hope for the morrow. The future only fills them with dread, for it will find them less capable of earning their living. A cloud of sadness seems to hang over the land. Even the children do not play as others do. There is no life—no *abandon* in their games. They mimic the hard labour of their parents, in which they all too soon have to bear a part. And this is European civilisation!

No one can complain of the Spaniards' lack of friendliness if once they take to you. I lay down and slept with the man and his wife on the floor of the room. I was awake a long time thinking of my poor bed-fellows' life and the comparative blessedness of mine, even though I am but a tramping vagabond. It was a short night. I left the house too early to get my passport (which is usually held by the alcalde when one gets assistance), so I had to sit on a doorstep and wait three long hours for his arrival. This afforded another opportunity to watch the matutinal customs of the villagers.

Each swept the space in front of his house, and so all the "calle" was clear,—not because anyone values cleanliness in the least, but in order to collect the rubbish for manure.

Servant-girls from the big houses fagged up and down to the stream for more than two hours, carrying heavy pitchers on their heads or on their broad hips. No wonder that they are old hags at thirty. When I tell people my age, they put their tongues out and try to let me see they don't believe all they hear. I am a youth of twenty in the eyes of Spain.

When I had got back my passport, I took the

road towards Zaragoza. I came across a figtree, and, as I had not breakfasted, I speedily gathered and ate a dozen or two of excellent figs. Then the owner came along, and though he spoke not a word he said in the plainest possible way, "Come down." So I came down and stood before him, and awaited orders. But there were none. On recognising that I was a foreigner, his voice seemed to leave him. I saw his position and I held my own. I looked him in the eye, indicated that I had eaten enough, and departed.

The Spaniards can't fight as we understand the word. If you like to enter into a war of words you will be beaten, but fisticuffs are not to their taste, and silence is a terror to them! They think it implies much evil. When I want to triumph over a Spaniard I shall say nothing at all!

Some of the men of this province dress very fancifully. The ordinary costume is blue cotton trousers, a short blouse with braid round the neck and sleeves, and a handkerchief tied in a ring round the head, leaving the crown exposed to the full force of the sun. "Espargots" are on every foot ; but those who keep up the old local dress wear knickerbockers of velvet or cord, which are open from the hips and loosely buttoned or caught together by loops of braid to the knee. Underneath are white drawers with

embroidered edges, which the wearers love to display
—especially when fresh from the "lavandera." Below
are black stockings and espargots. A short coat
cut like an Eton jacket comes down to the "faja"
encircling the waist. The faja does not exist in
Vascongadas ; to the south of Navarra it appears as
a heavy waistband, and it grows more extravagantly
large as one journeys east and south. I have
measured one thirty-six feet in length, and it may
not be the largest I have seen.

The faja is the Spaniard's pocket. In it he carries
all his treasures. I have seen men in the markets
going round with a complete sample of the season's
produce—grains, fruits, and vegetables—all rolled up
in the folds of their fajas. It also holds his smoking
requisites and usually a 20-inch "navaja" (blade).
The "Spanish blade" is a bogey. It is a big pocket-
knife, nothing more. Rest assured the Spaniard
dreads the knife more than we do ! I have lived with
my fellow-countrymen on more than one continent,
and I am ready to maintain that the Spaniard fears
strife and is far slower to enter into it than the
average Englishman. True, the blade is his weapon
of defence as much to-day as ever it was, but he is
not led to take action without cause, and the best of
all proofs of his harmlessness is the extreme order-
liness of every Spanish crowd. There is a peculiar

hardness in the character of many Spaniards, but take them all round I believe they are as humane as any other men. I cannot believe England faultless and the rest of the world so much dirt. The Spaniard is as much my brother as any man alive, and so far as I see manliness in him I will proclaim it. Don't tell me I am dreaming. I of all men am testing his worth. I am asking him for crumbs and he invites me to share his feast!

But Spain is an enormous country, and its people are not to be summed up in a single sentence. Each province, nay, each hill, each valley has its own peculiar stamp: one must always be local if one would be true to its people. Climate is allpowerful in the development of national customs. If England shared the geographical situation of Spain, mules would draw her burdens instead of horses, bull-fights might take the place of horse-racing, and the pleasures of the fireside would be lost in the enjoyment of open-air life.

The mules of Arragon are the finest in the world. They are bred to suit the climate, and the splendid work they do proves that they are not bred in vain. They are of immense size and splendidly proportioned.

The valley of the Ebro grew wider and greener and more luxuriant as I journeyed onward. Fruits were in abundance. Vast areas are planted with grapes, pears, and plums. Clumps of olive trees of enormous size (some trunks are five feet in diameter) vary the landscape, and rock and water melons are too common to be noticed.

I passed through Alagon, a busy though antiquated town. Thousands of tons of wheat were stacked round it, and at every turn quantities of fruit met the eye.

But I was still a tramp, and few of these things were for me. I took a peep at a queer old church with a leaning tower, and got the benefit of a little cool shade in a convent which was once a mosque. The old dome is still in very good repair, decked out in pantiles of very varied colours. A little way beyond Alagon I crossed the Jalon, a blood-red babbling stream, hurrying along a rocky bed to mingle with the Ebro and change its green flood into a creamy hue.

I slept that night in a miserable posada at Las Caselas, and rising early the next morning I soon came in sight of the tall towers of Zaragoza. I could only discern one chimney, but it was evident that I was nearing a great city.

The air was as clear and pure over the distant town as that I was breathing on the country road. "Smoke spells money," is the commercial man's cry, but how much misery and discomfort does it bring with it! I had grown very footsore and way-weary; but thoughts of a speedy rest (a tramp's supreme joy) cheered me till I reached the Puerta de Pamplona, and a new world revealed itself to me.

CHAPTER V.

ARRAGON (*continued*).

I ENTERED Zaragoza at midday, with the thermometer standing, or rather jumping, at 140° in the sun. The place looked like a tropical city with its yards of drapery sighing and flapping over all the house fronts, and its glaring atmosphere.

My first impression was of a vast barrack, for I saw nothing but soldiers and soldiers' quarters. With the exception of a fruit barrow and its owner, there was no sign of business or a civilian. It was evident that the inhabitants did not care for the sun. After a time I got away from the soldiers' quarters, and wandered through a maze of narrow streets which led on towards the great towers of La Leo and the Holy Pillar. I pulled up at the Engracia, the finest street

or boulevard I had as yet seen in Spain. The promenade is fully two hundred feet wide. The margins
are planted with trees and flowers. Fountains, kiosks,
bath and sedan chairs are placed at intervals, and
trams run on either side. The surrounding houses
are high and well built. The best shops and cafés are
under a fine colonnade about three hundred yards in
length.

I took but a momentary glance at this fine
street, and then turned towards a more modest
quarter in search of an hotel.

A young fellow seeing me looking about offered to
show me to a posada. He was a genial young man.
There was nothing of the " don't intend to " about him.
He bowed to and understood all my wants. He introduced me to the fat landlord as though I were a poor
child who had lost its way. He pointed to my feet
to indicate that I was weary, and asked to be shown
to a room at once. It was a decent little place with
two beds. I sat down on one, my guide and mentor
on the other. Then I had a wash and shave, dusted
my clothes, got out my best things and put on all my
feathers. My companion complimented me on my
improved appearance. Then he handled my belong-
ings, combed and brushed his hair with my articles,
wiped his face on my towel, and set himself down
again and looked smug !

I wanted to go out; but I wanted to go *alone*. I asked my mentor if he would like a glass of wine.

" No."

" Well, then, here's twenty cents."

All his kindly smiles vanished. He looked at me as though I were a toad. " Give me a peseta and I will go," he said.

No doubt! I found it necessary to show my little temper, and after we had squandered a few words over each other, he took himself off.

I had no reason to complain of my Zaragoza home. It stood in the plaza of La Leo. Cleanliness and good breeding were all around, although I was very second class. I had a live marquis for a near neighbour, and the bishop's palace was just over the way. The square was very picturesque, shaded by trees and bright with flower beds, and rockeries covered with showy creepers. In the centre stood " Our Good Lady," pouring water from a real pitcher. Being a woman of importance she stands far off from the crowd, who gather round her all day long.

In the midst of a large circular pool she holds her pitcher of clay, and pours an everlasting stream into the long metal pipes which women and girls carry to the fountain to conduct the water from the pitcher's mouth to their own stone jars. By this system the water can never be polluted by mischievous or dirty people.

It was too hot for sight-seeing to afford any pleasure, but I had no time to lose. I visited the Café " Ambos Mundos," said to be the largest in the world (which really means the world of Zaragoza). The saloon, which is splendidly fitted up and lighted by electricity, is two hundred and fifty by two hundred feet. It is a marvellous place, and, what is still more marvellous, it pays. Although a cup of coffee usually costs fivepence in the cheapest house, here, in this gorgeous saloon, you can get one beautifully served for twopence halfpenny. A little farther on, the Engracia opened out on a circle of prettily decorated houses surrounded by gardens filled with the choicest flowers. The scene resembles the view from the Arc de Triomphe looking towards the Champs Elysées, but instead of the Arc rises the colossal statue in bronze of Pignatelli, Bishop of Zaragoza, author and giver of the Imperial Canal.

My Lord Bishop, I beg to tender you my humble but sincere respects. I beg you to regard me, although a heretic and an alien, as a profound admirer of your genius. I have had cause to thank you a hundred times for the cool draughts I have taken from the flood of your creation, for the sweet, luscious fruits which are the work of your great hand, for the green foliage that has shaded my path, and for the cool air that has fanned my brow. For these and for the great blessing you have bestowed upon my fellow-man receive my hearty thanks.

Pignatelli's face resembles that of George III., but I fancy that his brain must have been of another quality !

Zaragoza does not forget its benefactor. The centenary of his death was celebrated last month (June, 1893), and tons of wreaths and offerings lie round the base of the column. Theatres, pleasure grounds, cafés, and people of both sexes are named after the great man.

Just beyond the statue of Pignatelli is the outer boulevard—the playground of the children of Zaragoza, where mimic bull-fights, exhibitions, and Spanish games take place. As I was in search of a familiar feature, I made for Pignatelli's theatre, and asked to see it. The door-keeper told the actors that " a pilgrim was at the gates," and the principal comedian came out to see me. He could speak English, and being a genial soul he showed me over the fine theatre, and introduced me to his chums—to fascinating Señora Romera, the prima donna, and to the artist actor Enríque Lacasa, who could do better things in a better town than Zaragoza ; and then a large party proceeded to show me round the town. Ambrosio Rusti, my first friend, acted as interpreter. He led me through scores of streets, some fashionable and beautiful, others dreary and unclean, to the great cathedral of the Holy Family—a most impressive shrine. The building is nearly square, and its vast groined and fluted roof rests on twenty massive columns a hundred feet high, with bold basements of black, brown, and grey marble. It made one feel rich, and glad to be alive, only to see such splendid proportions. The marble floor shows mosaics of rosettes and wheels representing the traced roof. There is not a particle of stained glass in all the building, and it does not seem to need it. Pictures cover the walls. One large one, which might be called the "offering of the firstfruits," as it represents the presentation of children, and flowers, and other earthly glories, is a perfect gem. The grand altar has stalls like those in Henry VII.'s Chapel at Westminster, and the choir also resembles our Abbey, although Zaragoza strikes me as larger and richer in materials of art. The books in use are four feet by three, and weigh each one hundred and fifty pounds.

The deep Gothic doorways show traceries in stucco and carved marble which are a delight to the eye. The wood carving is also very fine, and the shining brass which is everywhere displayed fairly dazzles one. There is enough solid brass in this cathedral to make a flat candlestick for all the people in the world, and perhaps enough to spare to make its presence felt here. Some spiral columns of rich black marble are rare and very beautiful. Four of these support a canopy of hand-wrought and chased brass, which displays such an amount of fine workmanship that one feels it must have taken centuries of time and men to develope it. There is an altar (one of about twenty-four), of mottled alabaster, with an altar cloth bearing a fringe and a device of flowers and Crusaders' armour, all of solid gold. A few feet off and one feels that that cloth could be taken off and shaken ; but it is not to be done. It is a solid, immovable thing. Many visitors come to this shrine. Pilgrims hold it dear ; and though they suffer by the way, they think they have the best of the bargain when they kneel within its walls. As for me, I felt I was becoming Catholic to the core ! I had found no romantic castles as yet, but I should never tire of Spain so long as the Church doors stand open.

My friends had some reverence but little admiration for the old place. They took me off next to see the palace of a former Infanta of Arragon. It was not unlike a fifteenth-century English mansion, although the arabesques, and Greek and Moorish "plaques" around its entrance hall looked foreign to my eyes. The house stands in a back street, and is valued for its associations rather than for its beauty.

We went to the Lonja (Town Hall), a big, richly-decorated building. Here the Mayor, representing the infant King of Spain, sits and draws the black and white tickets which decide the fate of the conscript. There are scores of colossal effigies with highly-painted faces and wickerwork bodies ranged along one side of the hall. These are the property of the city, and are used to delight and terrify the children at feast-time. They are dressed in the costume of all ages, and men get inside the wicker bodies and run up and down the streets after the children, carrying gifts in one hand and weapons of castigation in the other, so that the pursued child never knows whether he is going to get a handful of sweetmeats or a whipping. The discovery of this time-honoured custom was pleasing, but I soon made one of more importance.

When the Moors held Zaragoza they beautified it in a wonderful way. Amongst other things they erected a high tower, and put in it a brass bell made in Fez. In dangerous times this bell was rung and the people gathered to receive their arms, and be marshalled for action. "At the foot of the tower" is a phrase which to this day means ready to fight. Seven centuries (1118) have slipped away since any Moorish foot pressed the dust of Zaragoza, but the tower (rebuilt in 1504) stood till a few years ago, when by common consent it was pulled down. Only the old brass bell laughed at the Master Time, and being a thing of beauty, the Spaniards decided to preserve it, and it is now resting and waiting for a new term of service in the Town Hall. It is about four feet high, and three across the mouth, chased at both ends with Moorish emblems of peace and war.

We visited the great church of " The Virgin of the Pillar," and saw the paintings and frescoes of Goya. The church is almost a little town—hundreds of feet long, and nearly as many wide and high. It has domes and vaulted roofs, and sky-piercing cupolas to the number of twenty-four, and within their vast and airy depths Goya has displayed the wonderful virtues of his brush.

What I admire about this great master is that he brings his subjects so close to the spectator. He can represent every type of man, woman, and child, and he has a marvellous way of contrasting effects of light and shade. You feel the hot rays of his sun and the damp chill of his dull days as you look at the little worlds he has made.

A black eagle with an outstretched wing looks

down from one frescoed dome. It is a wonderful bird ! It terrifies and maddens you, and you want to get out of its way. It is not just so much paint on hard stone : it is a living, greedy thing which is about to swoop down and fix its talons in your flesh. Goya's frescoes remind one of the " Judgment " in the Sistine Chapel, and yet there is a great difference. The " Judgment " is heavy and cold—Goya's terrestrial and celestial worlds are animate and warm. The skin of his children and cherubs is full of budding life, and what is more, they look and rest and play as real children do. Nor does he give to his base characters the grim smile and black upper lip of a Judas. His men and women are such as we see in every-day life. There is one allegorical figure, high up in a vault of light, with a wand in her outstretched hand. A blue cloud gathered round her shoulders falls off into other tints about the lower limbs. It is a lovely human figure, but that remnant of a garment deifies and glorifies it. There are some domes under which you fear to stand lest those great giant rocks and rushing rivers and thunder-clouds should break upon your head. In the great central dome Goya has depicted wonderful groups of human forms which you see through a cunningly wrought gossamer-like cloud of ethereal blue. You can imagine nothing more natural up

the great height. Goya is numbered with the great
dead, but the work of his hands is safe to last long
in old Spain.

I went again and again to visit this church. It
took me out of myself, and I seemed to be sharing
the life of the blest. There, I was far away from
long pilgrimages and dusty roads, from the need of
beggars' crusts and fear of yelping, growling curs
who drove me from out the streets and obtained
a smile from their masters for the service.

At the Church of the Pillar I could rest. It is
the holy of holies, and I lived. I did not want to
crane my neck into a black cavern to kiss a dirty
stone which has a hole deep enough to put a loaf
of bread in, worn by the pressure of believing lips.
Nor did I wish to feast my eyes on the three hundred
odd robes which adorn the image of the Virgin, or
to gloat over the million pounds' worth of gaudy
jewels which decorate her person. Rest is the
tramp's luxury, and I found it here. Outside, the
church looks poor enough. The children and the
elements have wormed holes deep enough to sit in
along one side fronting a well-decorated square.
The legend of the pillar is old and tame. " Our
Lady " is said to have appeared to St. James standing on a jasper pillar, and she commanded him to
build a church on the spot. He obeyed her, and

to-day it is one of the most popular shrines in Spain.

Foreigners who know anything about the English always expect them to be " warm " on the subject of beer. My friends of the sock and buskin took me to a café where we drank the cool draught so dear to Britishers. Then we rambled on through streets like those of Naples and " old England," where the light is shut out by overhanging roofs and " parquets," and the sheet or counterpane stretches as a sunshade from narrow balcony to balcony. We got into little noisy squares and irregular spaces where life seemed to be equally irregular ; we entered wine shops where " swells " were taking wine side by side with dirty, unkempt women, who brawled and wrangled about giving *two* or *three* " perras chica " (halfpennies) for a few beans or green vegetables. For wine shops, greengrocers, oil sellers, and fish vendors are generally enrolled as one business in the north of Spain.

This was a varied day. In the morning I had entered Zaragoza as a tramp ; in the evening I was launched in the world of society. Only those who have been tramps know how delightful it is *not* to be one.

In the evening I shared a box at the summer theatre. These summer theatres are very pretty and comfortable. The dress circle is on a level with the stage. The ladies do not wear ordinary evening dress, but something of the " tea gown " order, an abundance of white lace, and far too much powder.

Not a man in the house was in evening dress; consequently, I was not out of order. I am an oddly dressed stranger, nothing more. My " tramp " life has not so far impressed me as to make me look like one. The Spanish actors can act! So can the singers—which is a rarity. They work frightfully hard.

The strolling players' day is from ten in the morning till one o'clock (after midnight), when the curtain is finally rung down. The play begins at nine, and runs four hours. The first " call " is at ten, and with a break of a few minutes for refreshments, they run on with the thing in hand and " coming attractions " till five or six in the evening. In this climate such work is killing. No wonder that the Spanish actor is pale and thin.

Little attention is paid to appearance so long as a man can sing or act. I saw some truly wretched objects in the chorus, but their music was excellent. It was half-past two when I reached my posada in the Plaza del Leo. An old-fashioned night watchman with his bunch of keys, lantern, and pike let me in, and I was glad to sink upon my truckle bed.

I spent the following day wandering up and down the streets and looking into the shop windows, full of glorious representations of the Virgin of the Pillar. They are of all materials, some of fine bronze, some of silver and gold studded with real gems.

There is quite a commercial side to this myth ; it practically keeps Zaragoza alive ; but I am glad it exists. We should be without the frescoes of Goya were it not for the church and its legend.

At night I sat in the moonlight under the shadow of the statue of Pignatelli, and heard the bee-like hum of the throng of promenaders in the Engracia. Half Zaragoza—which means fifty thousand persons— must have been there. Beggars were numerous, and so were fine women, many almost giantesses, with rich luscious faces, spoilt, alas ! with powder. No hats or bonnets were to be seen, only a mantilla of black- or cream-coloured lace, and a fan or sunshade. Hats are worn at the theatres and cafés.

A belt of sweet flowers and shrubs made my position a pleasant one, and I lingered long. Men and women moving about the throng of strollers were vending cold water and lemon juice from clay pitchers and jars.

Cigarettes, lights, and a thousand odds and ends were hawked for sale. Music was in the air. A score of string bands were playing within and without the cafés. On one programme I saw selections from Chopin, Weber, Liszt, Verdi, and other famed names, and it seemed that the " common people " have a good wholesome love for the best pieces.

There is little colour in these northern crowds. Doubtless the church is the cause of so much sober black.

Home once more, I held a conversation with a pretty waiting maid, who enlightened me on a point which had perplexed me all along the road.

I have been asked over and over again a question which I could not understand. This girl's eyes speak, and I can understand her. She wants to know if I am walking round the world as a penitent ! No, no, pretty one, I am not such a clown. She tells me (with those eyes of hers) that penitents come here in sad plights. They come with snuff-brown cloaks and cowls, with wide green collars overlaid with shells, with huge holy-wood crosses and calabash (melon) water-bottles, with heavy rosaries dangling from a rope girdle, with a tinsel nimbus round their shaggy locks, and Moorish sandals on their bare and blistered feet. They sing Ave Marias and woful dirges by the wayside, they bless those who give and curse those who don't, and their sole companion is a wolf-like hound which protects them as they sleep.   I made it quite clear to the pretty little waitress that I was no penitent, and she went away satisfied.

Before bidding farewell to Zaragoza may I say a word on the all-important subject of eating and drinking?   At midday the inhabitants break their fast with a meal of six, eight, or ten courses, according to their means and physical carrying capacity.   Here is a sample of how I fared in Zaragoza.   Soup; salad, fairly floating in oil; vegetables with a highly seasoned sauce; "garvanzos"; butter beans and a suspicion of garlic eaten with sippets of toast instead of spoons; sliced tomatoes, cucumbers, and onion; boiled mutton and forcemeat; stewed beef; roast fowl; and grilled bacon.   After which dessert of all the fruits in season.   Then ten minutes' rest and a small glass of coffee.   It is an odd mixture, things hot and cold by turns; but it results in far less indigestion than the heavy, lumpy dishes of England.

CHAPTER VI.

ARRAGON (*continued*).

IT is a broad but truthful saying that " after the
Lord Mayor's show comes a dung cart."   I went
out of Zaragoza smoking a bad cigar and making a
great show, for a notice of my journey which had
appeared in the morning paper made me the topic
of the hour, and many came to the Theatre Pignatelli
to see me set off on my walk of two hundred miles.
Here I was a " lion " and a hero.   Six hours later I
arrived at La Muela (fourteen miles), with my tongue
hanging out, for I had done the last eight miles
without a drink, and the final four was a stiff uphill
climb.

But I struck gold at La Muela !   It was ten o'clock
on a Saturday night when I got into the little stone-
built and ugly village, which for a wonder was full

of good-looking and very tidy women. I may here mention that the habit of open-air hair-dressing affords ample opportunity for the study of female charms. No Spanish woman dresses her own hair; neighbours do this office for each other. About twice a week the plaits are uncoiled and combed, moistened with oil and *spittle* (I must write of things as I find them), and re-arranged in the presence of village gossips. I called on the alcalde, and my newspaper report of the morning hit him hard. He was entertaining some of his friends, and he entertained me right royally, and then sent me for the night to a posada. I had a good bed on the floor with two razor grinders, and the next morning got a couple of eggs whipped up with tomatoes, vinegar, and oil— the lot fried together. It was not bad. I am getting used to the olive in any form ; I can tackle him and his oil like a native.

While eating I watched my hostess cook her own morning meal. She poured a cup of olive oil into a frying-pan, filled it with sliced potatoes and about two inches of raw salt sausage. Then she stirred and turned and agitated the poor little sausage until he had lost his wind and went to pieces against the edges of the browning wafers. I call this economy. Enough potatoes for a dozen people, and a suspicion, a flavouring of sausage over it all.

On the following morning I gave the woman my best thanks, conferred my blessing on the entire community of La Muela, and shouldered my bundle. My journey to La Almunia under a scorching sun was not a pleasant one, and how glad I was to break the back of that one hundred and eighty miles, which looked so endless written in kilometres! I wish they wouldn't mark the distances to such far towns! It quite sickens a poor tramp when he remembers how long one kilo. (a thousand yards) is in such a hot, dry land as this. Thousands of acres of half-ripe grapes afforded me some sustenance, or it would have gone hard with me. My fame had preceded me. I was stopped by the gate-keepers of Almunia, and asked if I was not *the famous traveller*! I owned to being that unfortunate, and a crowd gathered at once. I was given bread and wine, and received the usual compliments, after which I went in search of the alcalde.

I found him sucking sweet juices through a straw in the principal café. He was a generous soul, and at once gave me an order for a bed within the arch of the Puerta de Calatayud.

I washed in the street under the public eye, and was followed to my crib in the arch by a crowd of noisy children, who are now beginning to follow me as they did the Pied Piper of Hamelin! I had to endure being stared at, and talked at, and laughed at, and fairly mobbed. Such are the penalties attached to fame!

I went to the principal church—a rich old place crammed with curious relics (among the latter was a large pig with a bell round its neck!). The stucco ceiling is lovely—white floral tracery on a pale green ground lined with gold. A funeral dirge was being chanted for some poor departed, lying under a pall bearing a skull and cross-bones in white satin. The choir was composed of only four singers, yet they filled the large building with beautiful sounds. The women mourners wore ordinary print dresses with little black cowls on their heads, and the men, in their everyday working clothes, carried three-caped cloaks over their shoulders. The four priests were gorgeous in black and gold, over white lace; the acolytes in cardinal and white, with their chalices and lamps adorned with emerald-green ribbons. La Almunia is a very old-fashioned place. The city is surrounded by a wall and ditch, both in perfect condition. The " Consumos " is exacted on all who take anything in or out of the town, and the general laws and customs are such as were framed nine hundred years ago. The Jalon flows near, and its waters are drawn off to irrigate the few miles of flat country lying round the town. I fancy that the majority of the inhabitants of La Almunia imagine the outlying hills to constitute the boundary of the world.

I was quite a curiosity, for very few had seen an Englishman. The children amused me by wanting to touch me, and yet they were afraid to do so. Spanish children are timid—though far from shy. The grown people have a great opinion of British pluck, and showed me how they admire our fighting with our fists. We are the only nation in the world who do so: is it not a significant fact?

I was told it was but a six hours' walk to Calatayud. I walked all day and made perhaps a third of the distance! One continuous climb over rugged hills, their summits bare, their sides clothed with grape vines, and in the gullies olive trees. There are a good many rivers on the map of Spain, but these courses are in reality dry, scorching hollows, carrying no more than the drainings of a thunderstorm or the thaw of winter snow.

I was not alone. I fell in with a fellow-tramp who would stick to me with the tenacity of a limpet. He too was journeying towards Madrid, and was rejoiced to find a companion. Under other conditions I might have welcomed him, for he was a strange character: a German-Swiss, a graduate of Bonn, and a master of five living and the Greek and

Latin languages. He owned to being a ne'er-do-well, with a weakness for making religious poetry which no one would buy, and for visiting shrines and monasteries; though with all this display of goodness he could swear excellently at everything in Spain. For a while I enjoyed him, but as I had work to do I wanted to be rid of him. I loitered by the way, and he ditto; I brushed along, and the pace suited him admirably. I decided to steal some grapes, and he admitted it to be his favourite crime. In short, he "*intends to*" all my ways. At last I told him plainly that I had work to do and must go my way alone; but all that day he hung leech-like at my heels till we arrived at the village of El Frazno, where I was able to bid him farewell. It was just growing dark, and every dirty house reminded me of Renteria. That town is always on my mind when night comes on and I am unprovided with a bed.

I was directed to the hospital, but after an experience which well-nigh rivalled my first night in Spain, I cleared out, and found very pleasant quarters at a posada. Here I got a chaff bed in a clean stable for three sous, and for three more I had a basin of oil broth and a glass of wine. The local doctor and some of his friends came in, and the balance of the early night went quickly over more wine and talk about many interesting things.

El Frazno is not marked on the map, but it ought to be, for it has more crooked streets, ugly houses, meaningless walls and angles, and quaint pavings, than any other place of its size in all Arragon. Furthermore, it has two churches, which are the most substantial enigmas I have yet encountered.

I have been round both these churches three times, and nowhere could I find an entrance to either of them. About forty women drove me off with broomsticks and donkey and mule collars, as I put my foot inside of what I at last felt sure must be the church door. But no! Both churches are on eminences, and all around them cottages and mud cabins are jammed together and packed into an indistinguishable mass. I have not seen the interiors of the churches of El Frazno—I have not yet found their doors!

The public fountain and bathing pool is in the plaza, and before six in the morning dozens of mothers and big sisters were there with their skirts gathered round their waists engaged in washing the entire juvenile population of the place. Hundreds of men of all ages and types loitered round or sat about the sides of the square. They were dressed in knickerbockers of brown leather, of black velvet and plush, of blue corduroy and coloured canvas; yellow kerchiefs tied like " Billingsgate rings " round

their heads ; dirty-fronted but fancifully frilled shirts ;
velvet waistcoats with the backs " flowered," or demi-
blouses of blue ; blue and white stockings over their
long legs, and " espargots " or leather sandals on their
feet. The general effect of this varied dress was
strikingly picturesque. This is a strange place, into
which no trace of " modern civilisation " has yet
found its way. At the posada I saw some fine old
brass and copper ware—circular, flat, and oval dishes
with loose brass handles ; curiously shaped and chased
drinking cups, a singularly formed brass lamp, and
a Moorish bronze pestle and mortar. There were
also some beautiful plates with perpendicular sides,
and a fine white china bowl with blue shamrocks
thrown over it.

There is no fuel in this region. The people make
their little fires entirely of olive and vine prunings,
and such bits of scrub and heather as they can gather
from the surrounding hills. In winter it is very cold,
and life must be hard indeed.

I set off in the company of a pleasant young
fellow who was journeying towards Calatayud. It
was July 25th, St. Iago's Day (which accounted for
all the scrubbing I had witnessed on the plaza of
El Frazno), and big feasts were going on in the great
towns, causing great talk of them in the little ones
and pueblos. We had a terrible journey over barren

hills, sweetened here and there with the scent of lavender and other herbs growing in the adjacent valleys.

The sun literally burnt our skin, and we were ready to faint from the intense heat. Towards evening we got our first drink and sighted Parracuellos. It was in its best clothes; still it did not look well. It is an odd mixture of mud-houses, narrow, alley-like streets, and fig-trees boxed up together on the spur of a giant hill. The Jalon flows at its foot, and orchards and gardens flourish along the valley. As Parracuellos extends no hospitality to wayfarers, who rarely find their way to this remote spot, my companion proposed that we should go to another village. We wound along the river banks through orchards of fruit, olives, and vines, and crossed scores of 'ducts and flumes carrying water to the various plateaux. It was a rich, sweet, homely scene.

We met many pretty and neat-figured girls, who, having nothing to " feast " on, were promenading in threes and fours within the cool shade of the orchards.

Sabinan was our place of refuge. Here my companion had a friend—the tailor of the village—and we were well received and pressed to stay the night. (I must own that I needed no pressing.)

The tailor was an old sportsman, and showed me

his guns, dogs, ferrets, and pigeons with pride. He had also some fine old red clay plates, cups and basins enamelled with white and elegantly flowered in Arabic and Spanish designs, and curious lamps in iron, brass, and clay. I feel sure that his wine skins and curious old bottles of glass, wood, clay, and stone would be looked on at Christie's sale-room by a crowd of envious eyes. Here they are old and useless, nothing more.

It is the custom in this part of Spain when you share a man's roof to pay for your fare and sometimes your host's as well! My friend of the day sent out for a sou's worth of potatoes, of tomatoes, and little strips of salt cod-fish. These, cooked in a large three-legged frying pan with some olive oil, an onion, and a handful of herbs, made a big supper for five of us. We ate from a big dish placed on a stool. Wooden spoons and one knife served for all, and a piece of bread was broken from in turn.

While we were supping my friend put up his hand and signed me to listen. I did so, hearing for the first and probably for the last time the sound of the " Nina's Campanilla." It is one of the most ancient customs in all Spain, and in the midst of all this cobwebby *bric-à-brac* and primitiveness I found it hard to persuade myself that I was an alien and living in the nineteenth century.

"La Nina's Campanilla" ("The Maiden's Bell").

Many centuries ago, when the world had little history but many witching legends and gruesome tales, a tiny "nino," tired of play and tale, sat nodding before the winter fire. His father and mother pressed him to seek his bed, but in vain. He feared the darkness of his solitary chamber, which his fancy peopled with goblins and legendary sprites. Deaf to his parents' voice, he sat dozing and nodding on the hearth till, overcome by sleep, he fell forward into the blazing fire. His wounds were terrible, and when he rose from his sick bed — his sight was gone. Never more would he see the sunshine or the flowers by sweet Jalon's brink. A sad and sightless boy, he fretted his early years away, and when his parents died he became a beggar-man, wandering through the vale and begging a pittance from door to door. The children learned to fear him as the dead, for, in his blindness, he fumbled round the doors and terrified the little heads he touched with his outstretched hands. Hence the blind beggar-man became a terror in Sabinan's Vale, and children grew to fear their quiet beds.

Then the mothers of the valley met together and sought a way to end this growing terror. The form was this : the prettiest girls were called into

the plaza, and the mothers bade them choose a
"Campanilla" maiden for a year. She had to vow
that she would never fail, when evening came, to
leave play or feast, vesper or toil, to ring her
"Campanilla" through the vale and tell in sound
of every house the tale of him who bred such fears
in Sabinan.

The song was brief, for the maiden had to hasten
and repeat it often ere the sun went down :—

> "Children now to bed must go,
> Or their lives be filled with woe."

And still to-day the maiden may be seen running
through the streets of Sabinan and ringing her little
silver bell. The scene is strange. Before her groups
and games and noisy shouts—behind her silence!
The little ones give but one shout, "The Nina
comes," and dart into their homes. No mortal, no
despot commands such calm as the mild maiden of
the bell.

What a long life is hers! Seasons come and go,
but Campanilla is unchanged. Fierce wars and feuds
have raged within the vale ; the storms of centuries
and manifold disasters have all been centred there ;
illness and death have overtaken forty* generations

* It is recorded in Parracuellos that in the twelfth century a
silver bell was purchased for the Nina (*por une aracion de la
noche*), but the custom is believed to be much older.

of the world ; but Campanilla is a child through all. Her voice will never cease till Sabinan itself is still.

This was a most delightful evening, and I took leave of my simple friends the following morning with real regret, for I knew I should behold their cheery faces and curious little nest no more.

This day was a hard one. I said good-bye to Sabinan and took another look at gloomy, fig-leaved old Parracuellos. I tramped along green gullies and bare hill-sides. I discovered and ransacked two or three nameless pueblos. I scaled and elbowed my way round mountain ledges which would have struck terror into the marrows of any Swiss guide. I crossed ten skeleton bridges swung high in air over the Jalon, and found my way through the semi-darkness of seven long tunnels. I begged and bought and stole bread and wine and cucumbers and fruit at lonely houses and from market-going girls. I survived the fury of a terrific thunderstorm, and found safety and rest within the great church of Calatayud. I looked up at its pure white plaster ceiling and dome, with its throng of saints and flowers, till, tired of my toils, I fell asleep in the main aisle, and was only disturbed by a very masculine and unchristian kick from the old verger. I called on the alcalde, who gave me permission to occupy the lower floor of the hospital, where I deposited my bundle and then marched round the old city. It is one of the dirtiest yet most interesting of Old World towns.

I was assured that the castle which tops the near hill is fifteen hundred years old, and that all Calatayud is antique and beautiful. Both statements are scarcely true, though I do not tell my informant so. It is bad taste to wound any man's pride in his home if he treats me well there. This man showed me wine skins in the making ; chairs and " espargots," webbing, brass, and iron ware are also made here. The "ninas" (girls) make lace fit for queens to wear, and the mothers and big sisters of these " ninas " were pretty enough to make me wish to linger. Ah me ! I am a tramp !

I lounged in the market-place of Calatayud, with its huge umbrella tents and half-naked women perched under them, vending comestibles of all kinds ; and, odd as it may seem for a tramp, I went shopping ; buying of cooked fish, and white wine, and " pan blando," and chocolate, and cucumber, and one pear, all for the sum total of fourpence halfpenny.

Having eaten and drunk all these good things I grew grumpy and moody, and fell to complaining at the dulness and sameness of a vagabond's life ! I am a mean, voracious creature. There is not a being in all Spain getting more variety than I am, and yet I am not satisfied. Doubtless I want rest—I am off to bed.

The foregoing paragraph was written at the close of that day, and when I wrote "I am off to bed," I thought that I should stay there for a few hours ; but I was not equal to it. There is no doubt about it, *I am a tramp*, and as such I am spurred to my task and my misery at all hours.

I was in Bugtown—Renteria the Second—and all the horrors of the former were around me. This den below stairs was alive with every classified kind of filth, so I made a move, though not without the expenditure of bad language. It was nearly midnight, but I decided to clear out.

I was assured it was dangerous to take to the road, as there are wolves in the hills round Calatayud. But I was prepared to be attacked by forty wolves rather than be eaten piecemeal by the brutes in the disgusting hole I had left behind.

The streets were in total darkness, and it was some time before I found my way out on to the main road for Madrid.

I tramped for over six miles, and then, too tired for further efforts, I turned into a hole by the roadside.

The mosquitoes were abundant, and as I had brought along a few of the parasites which had put me to flight, I had a wretched night of it. At daybreak I moved off to a water-hole and got a refreshing bath. Then I went on to the little pueblo of La Terrer, where I breakfasted on a pint of wine (price one halfpenny) and a crust of bread.

There is a singular geological picture at La Terrer. A number of almost perfectly formed pyramids— eleven in all—rise to a height of about two hundred feet. Five occupy one and five the other side of an equilateral triangle, and the odd one forms the crown. Standing at the base one sees what is probably one of the most perfect curiosities in the geological world. The composition is of hard yellow sandstone penetrated by thin layers of clay, and the caps are of alabaster. The scene is distinctly Egyptian.

From this spot I could look back on the accursed town which drove me forth a lone pilgrim at midnight. There it stood far up the valley, its plaza and principal streets on a plateau by the river, and the other part of it in the hollow and slopes of a rocky gorge.

Cliff dwellings, defensive walls, round towers, bastions, and mimic fortresses are there by the score, and, seen from a distance, the scene was a pretty one. But you are a vile old place all the same, and were incendiarism not a punishable crime, I could soon have seen you smoking and in dust!

After leaving Calatayud the country became less poor. The hills are more moderate in height, and carry sufficient soil to admit of grape vines on their summits. The land is still treeless (except in the valleys), and there is but one water source—the Jalon—and but one industry continually in sight; it is the vine, the vine, the vine—league after league. I travelled at a low level. The road crosses a railway, and the railway crosses the road, and the red river rushes under both a score of times in less than half as many kilos, so the journey was not altogether dull. Travellers by rail must get a very false impression of the country, as nearly all the lines traverse river-beds and watered valleys; hence they see nothing of the vast wastes which are everywhere away from the railroads.

At midday I reached Ateca. A small river here flows into the Jalon, and is locally known as the Bouverca. Ateca, like all these riverside towns, is dingy, tumble-down, and sleepy. It owns two decidedly beautiful towers, built of thin Roman bricks. One is octagonal, the other hexagonal, with curious bell domes of blue tiles. The brickwork is covered with fantastic designs, and the auditoriums have crescent-shaped holes under the eaves instead of windows. Both towers are far out of the perpendicular, which adds to the antiquated appearance of all around. I made for a chocolate agency, thinking I might get a good packet of that article at a cheap rate, but I was instantly met with two cents and asked if I were a penitent. For pure devilment I said, "Yes." "And why?" "Oh, I made merry at the death of my mother-in-law, and the priest got wind of it and ordered me a six months' tramp in the wild districts of Spain." Poor devils, they didn't understand a word of my explanation, but they looked aghast (evidently believing I had committed some fearful crime), and pointed to the door. I went off laughing, and they probably fell to telling their beads, and thanking Mary for delivering them from such bloody hands!

Pear trees abound in this valley, and I ate pears till I felt like one of the family. They are of all classes, and grafted on quince stocks, to produce hardihood, so all the fruit has a quincey flavour. It is rather nice in one pear, but all quince and no pear is calculated to pall on the palate, even though it be a tramp's.

I drifted on to Bouverca, a tiny hamlet of mud-huts, perched under a big rock beside the river. Its aspect suggested—parasites, so, though it was growing late, I elected to go on to Alhama.

The air was sweet with the balmy herbs which creep and hang about the cliffs by the roadside. All the little river flats were green with garden stuff and fruit trees, and Jack and Jenny donkeys, mules, and goats were munching and feeding from heaps of weeds which women and children were collecting from between the growing crops. I got a piece of bread and some tomatoes at a wayside house, and, refreshed by the food, plodded on till Alhama hove in sight. It looked exactly like the rest of the towns I had seen—an irregular pile of stone and mud, with a crazy old tower or two, toppling, half seas over, from its most out-of-the-way eminences. Its appearance was not a bit cleaner than that of the rest, and I could have wagered my only pair of boots against a toothpick that there was not a white-wash-, a paint-, a shoe-, or a tooth-brush in all the town. Looking through a gap in the hills I could see a kind of new Alhama, where houses are built of stone and mortar and have glass windows and clean doorways, and there is actually a little paint to be seen. I could not understand this ; but I was tired, and my thoughts were of the alcalde and the largeness of his heart. I had been told on the road that he was a " fine, fat man " ; but it was difficult to believe that. I could not imagine a well-fed turtle-eating mayor in this part of Spain. Rotundity is no part of the country's needs. These northern officials meet to work, not to grow fat at the expense of their poorer fellows. At least this is my candid opinion, no matter how bad or ill they may treat me. This alcalde was a rather stout man. He read my references and exclaimed with a big oath that mine was a remarkable freak! *He gave me a penny* and permission to sleep in the hospital.

At the hospital three women sent me under the care of a sulky, frightened girl to a filthy hole up in the cliffs, too disgusting for a Renterian pig to camp in. But the alcalde said the "hospital," and in the hospital I was determined to sleep. I told the three women so till we wrangled and rowed and swore at each other.

At last British determination overcame Spanish churlishness, and I was granted a bed. I went to sleep, supperless and hungry; but I did not complain, I had beaten those greedy women, and that was feast enough for me.

There was no chance to wash in the house, although it was a hospital, so next morning I went off to modern Alhama.

A stream was rushing down over a steep rock. The water was warm, nay, quite hot—a big thermal spring. I had a good bath and went on to the Gardens of Arabe.

I was told by some one before leaving England that I needed "a course of waters." I have been taking that course ever since I came into Spain! I believe I have drunk hogsheads of the Nivelle, the Orio, the Arga, the Arragon, the Ebro, and Jalon, and now I had arrived at the bath of Spain, the real old Roman, Moorish, Spanish baths of Alhama. They are extensive, rich in alkalies, but not beautiful. One Alfonso dipped here seven hundred years ago, but where are the virtuous atoms that touched his royal skin? Perhaps crystal fragments blocking Dr. Nansen's way to the North Pole.

As a matter of fact, I did not feel any the better for my bath in these remarkable waters. I felt cleaner, nothing more! I liked the great old-fashioned ragstone baths, with three steps inside, all cut out of a solid piece of stone. I liked the pools of crystal water and the beautiful kiosks built by the Moors. But I cannot echo the words of the local guide that Alhama is "that other Eden—demi-Paradise;" for the ancient lake is now a muddy swamp, and the "forest" is but a break of two acres of silver poplars and trembling aspens. You must be a Spaniard from the bare hills before you can realise that this is a "wood" and a lovely place.

I went on to Cetina, where I digested its castle and a few bits of bread which I had picked up on the road. I sat within the shade of the castle walls! Oh, yes! it sounds very well, and the place looked fine enough when I saw it five miles away. But a nearer view shows it to be only a meaningless, badly-built, ugly barn, with a crooked tower and minaret at each corner, and half-a-dozen square holes for windows on either side. It stands on a heap of drift mud beside the Jalon, which drivels past, a lazy, gory stream. These castles were great when man and his world were little. There is now just sufficient reality in their existence to enable tramps and vagabonds to get an hour's cool shade under their broad walls. True, they were admirable when imagination peopled them with the warriors and their lady-loves of earlier times, when it could be shown that here valour and beauty waged their wars or took refuge from the storms of a sinful world. But I must not waste my time over this heap of stones and sun-dried bricks. The folly of our forefathers is easy talk ; a little span of years, and the best efforts of the nineteenth century may appear of little worth.

My path now lay across an open plain or wold, without water or habitation. For six long hours I was exposed to the full force of a scorching sun, and when at last I reached a hut I was ready to faint and could scarcely find voice to ask for water. I had arrived at Ariza. It did not please me—all clay heaps and tile yards, in which paving-tiles of the finest quality are made. The secretario granted me accommodation in the hospital. I was shown to a decent room, where there was a nice little writing-table, a thing rare yet very dear to me.

I began writing up my journey at once ; but a big woman turned me out, saying. this room was for patients, and I was not ill, and so must sleep in a kind of chaff box.

My next care was to secure a good meal. At the butcher's I got some mutton for fourpence, and an onion for two centimos ; with these I made a stew. The woman charged me a penny for the fire, bread, and seasonings, and, with another penny for wine, and one to a fat baby, I made a good supper for seven-pence halfpenny. I ate my stew from the three-legged frying-pan in which it was cooked.

The room had nothing in it but a score of earthen pans and cooking jars. See how nature controls us ! These pipkins and tiny pots and pans are abso-lutely necessary in a land where there is not on any square mile enough wood to boil a gallon of water.

I enjoyed my evening. The family at the hospital were a rough lot, but I like to be much with the very poor. To my judgment they make the best pictures, and show the best side of life.

I thought by giving that penny away I should be allowed to use that nice little writing-table in the patients' room ! But no ! that woman was like a stone, and I believe she would have knifed me if I had not taken myself off just when I thought it best to do so.

It was quite early. I had walked nearly seven miles before eight o'clock. I came across a mob of navvies building a line of railway. They were break-fasting, and pressed me to share some bread and wine with them. Then the contractor appeared.

It was after eight o'clock, and the men were not at work. He began cursing and reviling them. He called on all the saints and devils known to Spain to maim and blind and perish them for their laziness and audacity.

Then he shook himself off his fine horse, and coughed and spat, and all was well. He handed cigarettes all round, and laughed and chaffed and hindered the men from their work. This may not be every, but it is at least one Spaniard's way of " bossing the job."

He asked me my business, and was pleased to compliment me on undertaking a walking tour under such hard conditions, through what he declared to be the roughest and hardest country in Southern Europe.

He gave me a handful of cigarettes, and we there-upon exchanged cards. We both laughed at the oddness of this, for a man does not, as a rule, hand his card to a tramp, or crave one from him. Soon after this interview I arrived at the southern gate of Arragon The boundary is an unseen line in the narrow valley of the Jalon. A triangular stone says : "This is Old Castile, and this is Arragon." I have walked two hundred and sixty miles in Arragon, enough to see it in its fulness, and it has not enchanted me.

Here is the best and the worst of it in a few words. It is snow-capped mountains, with defiant rocky slopes glaring glacier-like in the face of the summer sun. It is broad, undulating wolds, overshot with hummocks of alabaster, chalk, and sandstone, with plateaux between of shifting, arid sand. It is vast highland plains with a little poor soil and many stones. It is bleak and dreary moorlands of gritty sand, dark-stained with the juices of the casual vegetable growths which are scattered over them. It is old, dry river-beds of shingle, and rifts of silt and clay. It is the casual and uncertain streak of river with its narrow banks of green and gold, the vine and corn plots of the peasant slaves. It is the long, broad valley of the Ebro, the Garden of Pignatelli,—nearly four thousand square miles in extent. It is Zaragoza with its peculiar distractions and attractions. It is perhaps a thousand wretched pueblos, with twice as many antiquated temples, to the memory of San Sebastian and St. Iago, St. Ignatius, San Miguel, and San

Fermin, and I would add a few to San Pignatelli and San Goya. The addition would do no harm.

Arragon is hopelessly bare—not a tree of natural growth anywhere. It is well that her people like a simple life. I can imagine no one who has made a journey of five hundred miles being quite satisfied to settle there. Nature has placed hard and fast limits to its development : they will not soon be swept away. The extremes of heat and cold are known here. In summer the skies are lovely, the horizon farther off than in any land I know. The sunsets are gorgeous and soul-stirring, and the nights balmy, cool, and sweet, making it pleasant for labour or rest. In winter the cold is intense, and in these badly-built and fireless houses life must be hard indeed.

CHAPTER VII.

OLD AND NEW CASTILE.

A TOY CHURCH.—THE PALACE OF THE MARQUIS OF CASTILE.—
SAN MARIA DE HUERTA.—SOAP OF OLD CASTILE.—SPANISH
BABIES.—A USEFUL COMPANION.—ARCOS.—THE LAST OF
THE JALON.—THE CARPENTER OF ESTERAZ.—NEW CASTILE.—
ALGARA.—THE HENARES.—A BLIND BEGGAR.—GUADALAJARA.
—ALCALA, THE BIRTHPLACE OF CERVANTES.—MY UNDINE.—
ARRIVAL IN MADRID.

CHURCHES are the commonest of objects in
Spain, and yet not common. I have seen a
unique specimen on this frontier,—a little whitewashed building, fifteen feet long and eighteen wide,
with a tower thirty-five feet high. It looks a toy,
or a boy's model, but it is a real church, used by the
inhabitants of a village of five houses.

The floors of these cottages are paved with fine
river pebbles of all sizes, forming designs of dragons,
palm leaves, old armour, and swords. This work is
all very old and choice.

After leaving this place I soon presented myself at
the castle of the Marquis of Castile. I sent in my

card, and was interviewed by half-a-dozen servants in showy livery. The Marquis was at Zaragoza, and the house was not open to visitors. It is a tawdry but interesting place—everything for show, nothing for neatness, comfort, or convenience. Old breastplates, chain armour, saddle trees, helmets, and stirrups of steel and brass, hang on the walls outside the castle. The garden paths are lined with marble busts, and stags' heads and plaster and mosaic plaques decorate the balcony fronting the main parterre. The arms— two lions supporting an eagle and crown,—and the crest—a bearded head and flaying knife—surmount every door and window.

Within a stone's throw of the castle stands an old Bernardine monastery, said to have been the finest in Spain. It is now only a jumbled mass of stone and masonry, although two or three beautiful arches of stone and carved doors in wood still remain. The old church owns a doorway which would be treasured in any museum, as well as some effigies which might serve to frighten the crows.

This little valley of Santa Maria de Huerta was a wicked spot in bygone times. For here once stood the magnificent palace of Alonzo the Eighth, and here the amorous Rachel achieved her rise, her greatness, and her fall, as did her master the king. The Huerta is a good place now. Little tablets in all the houses say this is a "glorified spot," and the owners are religious and you are not permitted to swear!

I have no wish to swear in any man's house, but on this occasion it seemed as if I must break the decree, for I couldn't get anything to eat for love or money, and I was downright hungry.

There was but one shop, and it had nothing to sell! Wine and a bit of onion was all I could get. The shopkeeper was a big, ugly woman, wearing her hair like a figure 8, sticking up fully three inches from the crown of her head. She wore a short skirt, and white stockings, with an imitation garter and a dagger in open work, which did not add to the docility of her appearance.

I made the discovery of a " pueblo " where they don't sell wine! Contamina has twenty-six houses and no wineshops. It is probably alone in Spain.

I have not yet scented the soap of Old Castile ; in fact, I believe it is, like many a boasted thing, a fraud ; for I have not yet encountered an Old Castilian who uses any soap whatever! My own shaving stick has almost worn away from the effects of all the curious handling it gets from the natives.

Spanish babies have a rough time of it. Search from pole to pole and you will not find children subjected to harder treatment, more downright neglect, than the small inhabitants of out-of-the way Northern

Spain. No wonder the people are hardy! only those born with iron constitutions can survive the first year or two of life. I have observed these babies often, and pitied them as frequently. They may get a first washing, but I'm prepared to take my oath that they don't get a second till they are able to take it themselves. The peasant mother takes a real pride in the thick cake of black filth which coats the little skull, and rubs in a daily portion of oil or fat, so that it may not crack and peel off. They tell me it strengthens the hair! It is certainly strong enough to strengthen anything. The youngsters have splendid heads of hair, but I would rather be the "padre" of bald children than own such dirty ones as I see everywhere in North and Central Spain. There is one other hideous custom of which the poor babe is the victim. They coop up the children as greedy poultry farmers do their ducks and fowls, without room to turn or move. In every family is seen a kind of double stool, the seats one above the other, and a large hole through the centre. The child, swaddled like a mummy, is fairly jammed down the aperture, so that only its head and shoulders are visible. It cannot kick for pleasure or spite, as the under hole is very small, and there, hour after hour, perhaps half a day, whilst the mother is at work in the "campo," the child half stands and half swoons in the semi-darkness of the windowless cabin. It is a cruel, savage custom, and the authorities ought to prohibit the use of these veritable stocks. The poor little brats learn resignation early. They seldom cry, and peevish, fretful youngsters are unknown in the peasant homes. The babies are all dressed alike—when they are dressed at all. A close-fitting lace cap completely covers their dirty little heads, and a long yellow robe of coarse flannel, edged with black velvet and fancifully scalloped' seems to be their only garment. If they have shoes they are home-made of strips of red and yellow flannel, or list plaited into a kind of sandal.

Everybody was offended with me in Arcos because I expected to find a washing basin in the place. I was told that if I *must* wash I could go to the nearest water-hole. Arcos is not a generous place. It takes no pride in giving away. The night I spent in this town was a lively one—too lively. It was Saturday night, and all the young bloods of the place were tramping up and down the narrow cobble-stone "calles" bawling at the top of their voices, and extracting the most hideous sounds from mandolins and guitars. These are sweet instruments when understood and well played, but the country-bred Castilian makes a discord for all who hear him. And his voice! It is the most hideous for any purpose I have ever heard. If you should once hear a song from one of these Old Castilian natives you will never mention Spanish again as a part of the sweet things of earth.

Sunday morning did not unfortunately put an end to Saturday night's revels. These braying idiots continued to serenade me till nearly daybreak beneath my lattice balcony—no, no! beneath the *mule's manger*, where I was vainly trying to sleep.

Later, the place was quiet enough. The men went to work, and the girls counted their beads, and the women and old men fell to housework and farming out the pigsties and stables.

Arcos once owned a castle built of drain pipes filled with unburnt clay. Only a part remains standing. I will give it credit for being cleaner in appearance than most of its neighbours; but Arcos was not kind, and cannot expect many compliments from me.

I met a very sensible tramp here; a man who ought to go a long way and not fare badly either. He was accompanied by a tame nanny goat, with a fine full udder of milk, and so, go where he would, his wholesome wine-bottle was ever at hand.

It looked odd, but why not a goat instead of a useless dog? The dog is a dear, good fellow, feeling and sympathising with all our cares. There is no one like him when the way is long and the heart is low. You can't mistake the charity in his eyes : he is everything for you, and proud to be your companion in adversity—few men and women are like him in this. But you can't milk a dog, and you must feed him, while this " nanny " feeds both herself and her master.

I am selfish. I would like to have been the discoverer of the advantages of a goat companion ; but I will give the Spanish tramp his due : may he go far, and get fat on the rich nutriment which his little friend yields him.

From Arcos I got down to the present bed of the Jalon, and wound along its banks sheltered by the overhanging rocks from the hot rays of the sun. Garden plots showed green and cool, and pilferings of ripe fruit and vegetables kept me alive till I came to Samaen, a village of two or three hundred mud and red stone huts built on a horse-shoe bend in the river. A castle crowned a great rock above. It was a mere heap of ruins, but the sight was superb. The rock forms a colossal natural arch, rising high above the surrounding peaks. Viewed from the river the scene is magnificent.

I moved on to a gorge, where there are some fine caves and some grand rents and cañons between the hills. There are actually a few trees growing here : the Quercus Ilex. I could hardly realise this : a

wooded Spain is an anomaly! The Jalon was drawing to an end. It was now but a small cataract,
almost lost to view among the great boulders.

Juberru is a very high up place on the north-east
slope of the mountains of Baraena. From this elevated spot I could see over hundreds of miles of wild,
broken country, all bare and blighted with the hot
summer suns and winter snows. Juberru is but a
tiny village, living—Heaven knows how. As a rule
the people descend to the low country and gather
such sustenance as will enable them to exist; they
cannot be said to live. The place is built entirely
of stone. I have seen the last of the mud huts, and
I am not sorry.

No one could admire these towns and villages on
the Jalon. At the distance of half a mile they look
as if so many thousand tons of stone had slipped down
from the mountain and piled themselves in irregular,
shapeless heaps on the river slope, and then that the
flood stream had risen and deposited a thick coating
of mud and clay. That is what these villages look
like, and what in truth they are. Man has made use
of the fallen stones and the river mud, and without
an eye for beauty or anything else beyond the construction of a bare cabin in which to eat and sleep
he gradually evolves a "pueblo."

I have seen the first and last of the Jalon. I have

sat on its banks and watched it empty its sum total of red water into the green Ebro, and I have seen it at Sabinan, where it is clear and bright. I have traversed and tramped by it for more than a hundred miles, while it became a stream pushing its way eel-like under a few stones, till beneath a huge red cliff it shows itself a tiny, silent pool, a spring. It is not a big river, and its course does not exceed one hundred and fifty English miles. But, judged by what it achieves, by all it feeds and clothes and blesses, it is a grand stream. Long may it flow!

I made a professional visit to Medinaceli, which boasts a live duke, a palace, and other luxuries. But the duke was from home, and for me his

> "cupboard was bare,
> And so this poor dog had none."

The town occupies a very fine position on the side of a steep hill, and I have no doubt that if it had treated me well I should be able to say some kind things about it. Medinaceli blesses him that "gives" and spurns him that "takes," so, cursing the hardness of its heart, I went down the hill to the modern "pueblo," Salinas. Straight ahead lay an open, dusty road, and I was told, by way of consolation, that I should get no water till I reached Esteraz, seven and a half miles away!

I arrived here at dark, but could just make out that the place consisted of about two dozen decently-built and, marvellous to relate, whitewashed houses. A group of men and women were sitting under an old wall discussing local politics, and I appealed to them for information about the resources of Esteraz. A woman, with a long, thin, white face, wearing a black dress and head-covering, acted as spokeswoman. She appeared interested in me, as did her husband, a great, grave-looking man, with a wealth of black curls about his neck, dark flashing eyes, and a clean-shaven face, showing an abundance of early wrinkles, and as much good nature. This man could not read or write, but he possessed a well-balanced, intelligent soul, and nothing could be more touching than the expression of real sadness showing through the tears that rose to his eyes on account of the regret he felt that he was so ignorant of the outer world.

This interesting couple offered to give me bed and board for the night; so I followed them to their house, which was the cleanest I have seen in the country.

I was asked to the little board—truly a "little" board,—a stool bearing a large dish of bread and oil broth. The man, his wife, and grown-up daughter ate from the bowl; but they gave me my portion on a china platter, pure white, with a wreath of red poppies, which had a most natural appearance, as the petals were chafed and split by the wind.

My friend pressed me to accept this bit of china, but, much as I admired, I could not take it from this simple home. After supper we talked.

The man was greedy for knowledge. I never saw any one show such signs of living on learning. I was refreshed by my host's hospitality, and felt glad to be able to impart some welcome news. I gave him a description of some of the great cathedrals raised to perpetuate his Catholic faith. I gave him brief accounts of my wanderings in other lands. It was all wonderful to him.

There was no mistaking the look of wistful sadness that filled his fine, brave face. He longed to see the world. I pitied him from the bottom of my heart. I doubt if I ever felt as much like a brother as I did in the presence of this man. My simple words were a revelation to him, and I have since wondered whether I was over-wise in saying all that I did about that larger world which, sad to think, he will never know.

Later he showed me to a comfortable bed, and in the morning woke me at five, helped me with my odds and ends, and bade me farewell.

There was real emotion in his voice when he said "Buenos dias," and shook my hand. I shall meet many before I meet a better man than the village carpenter of Esteraz.

I walked twenty miles that morning before I broke my fast. Five miles from Esteraz I passed the boundary line between "Old" and "New" Castile. This was slightly interesting, but in no way fattening! Like every other Briton, I wanted my breakfast. And "want" became my master. The road lay through dry gorges, hot as an oven, and across flat-topped hills, with stones lying as close and evenly packed as if the place had been some giant's causeway.

I met a few mule teams, but they had no wine or water to sell or give away, and I was in great distress by the time I arrived at Sauca, a hamlet down in a hole surrounded by the everlastingly barren hills. I tried to get a crust at thirteen different houses, but without success. Then I went to a wine shop and got a glass of wine and bit of bread for a penny. The wine-seller was also the butcher of Sauca, and while I was eating my crust of bread a girl came to buy meat. She brought a square-sided stick, about a foot long, and handed it to the butcher. He marked the weight and price of the meat with his Spanish blade, and returned her the stick

I examined it closely. There were five different

kinds of marks. Those cut perpendicularly indicated the price, while those cut horizontally gave the weight.

Purchases were receipted by a brand burnt in the wood. This relic of bygone customs helped me to forget the uninteresting character of the place and people.

"Where God is not the soul dies." They had once a church at Sauca : it is now the quarters of the civil guard, and so the inhabitants get no instruction in the value and virtues of charity. There is one spot in Spain which I have not yet discovered—a cemetery. I now and then encounter curious tombs in out-of-the-way places, and have seen many piles of stones by the roadside, surmounted by a cross, showing where the victims of the highway have been murdered. Between Sauca and Torremocha there are several of these chilling landmarks.

At Torremocha I fared very well. An old man in an easy way of life took me in to his home. He also showed me a curious sight : a nest of young swallows resting on a horseshoe driven into a beam supporting the ceiling of the living-room. For thirty years two African swallows have made a home and reared a brood on that horseshoe. The date is well fixed in the old man's mind, for the birds first appeared just before his only son was born, when the house was quiet, and since that time they have never failed to come. I felt on better terms with my fellows after the old man's hospitality and stock of yarns about the French invasion and our own Wellington, who is mentioned as reverently as the Virgin Mother by the Spaniards of this region —though not so in many others !

Before leaving this place I discovered that there are some really patent fools existing in Spain. Men engaged in building a new church were carrying enormous stones up a forty-feet ladder, and then squaring them down to the weight of a few pounds, and throwing the chips overboard. At nightfall I crawled into Algora, after one of the longest journeys I have yet made, about thirty-five English miles. Though so tired, I had to put up with being hawked and poked about for two hours, before the secretario's wife could persuade any one to take me in for the night. At last I was accepted by an old couple of the type I like best,—real old-fashioned folk, living the lives their forgotten ancestors did well-nigh a thousand years ago.

My hostess was a dapper little woman, somewhere between eighteen and eighty, wearing a lock of white hair twisted like a big snail-shell on each temple, and little plaits on her wrinkled brow.

I had a good look at some old culinary articles

in brass, copper, and delf, and then went to a good bed.

Although midsummer, the night was very cold, for Algora lies several thousand feet above the sea. My hostess gave me an extra rug, made of plaited string. These rugs are common in Spain, though very singularly and tastefully worked.

The next day I passed over very bare and wretched country.

At Gragangos I was nearly starving, for hot weather and hard walking robs one frightfully. At a wretched posada I got a little bread and wine. I sat down in front of the public school, and watched the boys take their first meal, consisting of a wedge of brown bread and a tomato, or a raw potato. All the women of this village wore red or yellow petticoats. The customs, the dress, and the people are changing rapidly, and one is delighted to notice anything out of the common.

Tramping on in the face of hunger and dreadful thirst, I got into Trajique at night, having made twenty-five miles on the bit of bread I bought at Gragangos.

I was almost too tired to find out the alcalde, and had half decided to lie down on a heap of chaff against a wall, when hunger forced me to my feet. The secretario kindly invited me to his private house, and gave me a bed in the chaff house next door to his pig !

As my nose has long since become what a witty Australian terms an " insentient excrescence," I slept very well. In the morning I was regaled with coffee and bread, and had a pleasant chat with the local schoolmaster, the secretario, and his noble-looking wife.

With many good wishes from my host and hostess I bade farewell to Trajique, and an hour afterward entered the castle town of Torija. I rambled up and down its narrow " calles," and found nothing but dirt in them.

The ruins of a very substantial castle—the walls eight or ten feet thick—are placed on the edge of a precipice. The servants' quarters in the old court-yard still stand, and are used as private dwellings and stables, The heat in the " calles " was stifling, and I was glad to make off in the direction of a few trees shading the road to Guadalajara.

My travelling map turned out to be a vile fraud, for it showed a river as plain and blue as any other in Spain from Trajique to Guadalajara, and in reality there is not a square yard of water the whole journey of eighteen miles. There is a valley—but a dry one ! It is called Val de *Noches*. I prefer to call it Val de *Diaz*. It may be all right at night, but it is a hell upon earth by day. The hills on either side are of white clay, and the natural and refracted heat send the temperature up well-nigh to boiling point. I should consider six months' imprisonment in Old England a pleasure, compared with a week's forced residence in this death hollow.

May I never again revile a stream on account of its private notions! Rivers, like people, have a perfect right to choose their own course. An old lady once told me that she could never quite make out how rivers manage to find their way to the sea! Well, they generally do so, unless they pull up with a round turn under the lee shore of a Jungfrau or Rigi and form a Bienne or a Lucerne.

Once in sight of the Henares I didn't care how much it wound! After nearly a hundred consecutive miles of wretched, barren plain, anything in the way of change was welcome. Three days of internal and external drought had told on me sadly. I was parched within and also without, for the want of a bath and clean clothes. My feet were blistered and scalded, and I grew more crippled each succeeding hour. Before entering Guadalajara I was able to have a good bath at a public fountain.

Then I found the Town Hall, and the local powers consigned me to a very decent posada for the night, demanding my reappearance on the morrow. I slept alongside of an itinerant guitar player, his wife, and boy. In the morning he sat up in bed and strung and thrummed away at his guitar. It was sweet-toned, and the sounds quickened and strengthened me. Fellow-tramp that I was, I gave him five cents to play me the serenade from "Rigoletto," and yet another five for that sweet gavotte "Stephanie." Then I asked him the time of day, and he went to the window, but said there was no clock in sight. Later, whilst I was waiting in the plaza for the town clerk, my bedfellow came along. The woman was vending printed songs, and the little boy was leading the man, who, since he had looked out of the window for that clock, had become hopelessly blind! I really could not help admiring the admirable way in which he impersonated the blind man! Long practice in the black art had made him perfect. I did not expose the fraud. The man who wishes to do that can be constantly employed; but the remuneration is not high!

Guadalajara is a famous old place, containing many historic houses, gardens, and churches. But my time was very limited, as in accordance with a local law which I had unconsciously forced upon myself, I had to leave the town before midday. Alas! like poor Jo, I am always "moving on."

About a mile from the town I noticed a singular

engineering feat : the bed of the Henares was actually paved. Probably this was done to make a safe ford when means were not forthcoming for a bridge. The stones forming the bed are of enormous size, and the paving of great width, extending several hundred feet along the bed of the river. A stone bridge spans it now, and one can survey a scene which may have no parallel in the world.

I was not so fortunate as to be able to journey with the Henares for long. It ran away on its own selfish errand, hiding under rocks and cliffs, whilst I was left to pursue a straight, flat, dusty road. The dust did not last long, for a terrific storm broke, wetting and bespattering me from head to foot. I took shelter in a wine shop by the roadside, and scribbled a few notes till the rain left off.

A woman was engaged teaching a child to say prayers, and to count her beads. Every now and then she stopped and swore in a most revolting manner at a girl who was patching a donkey's pannier. Yet she could afford to look on me with quite a saintly expression as her lips muttered the litany. These people are not conscious hypocrites. They are too disgustingly ignorant to know what hypocrisy means.

I plodded on in the darkness. The road was now a river of water and mud, which was far from pleasant ; only one thing in my favour, it was cool.

At last I came to a house where a lot of harvesters were sleeping in the stable and out-buildings. The owner of the place gave me bread and eggs for fifteen cents, and I secured the entire floor space of a large shed for a like amount. It was a hard bed, but clean, and I would have slept comfortably enough if three mules had not come in and laid down close to me! These brutes snored and bellowed all night, and whenever I dozed off I was awakened with a start and the fear that they would tread or roll on me. This night in a mule shed was a humiliating sort of prelude to the classical surroundings of the day that followed.

Cervantes! Little did I think when first I laughed and cried over your immortal " Don " that I should ever stand before the house that gave you birth in your native town of Alcala de Henares. Yet this has really come to pass. Most people regret their vanished youth. I do not. Mine was *not* " a glorious springtime fraught with golden foreshadowings and fragrance of sweet flowers." All that I can recall with pleasure are my old book friends. I met them when I wanted them. They came to solace me when no one else would do so, and a kind of unwritten, unspoken compact has existed between us ever since. Time and closer intimacy give a firmer grip to our hands each time we meet.

And now in the year of grace 1893, in sight of the Calle Mayor, under the shadow of the great church El Magistral, in a narrow street with big tortuous river-stone paving, and houses not unlike the early home of our own Shakespeare, I stood before Cervantes' " casa."

No one was wise enough to be able to give me any homely particulars about the great old warrior. But three hundred years is a long stretch for memory, and the fight for life in modern Spain is keener than the desire to learn or to laugh.

I doubt if the Spaniards themselves made Cervantes great. I am ungenerous enough to think that the modern Spaniard is not thoughtful and earnest enough to discover true greatness in anybody.

Catherine of Arragon was born at Alcala, so was Ferdinand, Emperor of Germany, son of " Crazy Jane." The great Cardinal and Regent Ximenes, whose extraordinary versatility baffled all his contemporaries, passed the greater part of his long life here, and well-nigh every page of Spanish Church history records some heroic or impious deed done by the illustrious dead of Alcala. Still the name of Cervantes overshadows all. No one like him in all the past to make the present bright and bearable.

I visited the great church El Magistral, where Cervantes was christened. The walls are covered with exquisite Moorish, Spanish, and Italian tapestry, representing biblical, historical, and even hunting scenes. The rich colours—orange, cardinal, and celestial blue—have a quality and strength about them which modern art cannot show.

The church is full of lovely things,—sculptures in marble and alabaster, elegant wood carvings, jewelled robes, sacred relics, and amid all that is beautiful and costly, Virgins dressed in modern attire, which would be too common for a factory girl. I was charmed with the tapestry. I was lifted out of my tired self by the ravishing tones of the organ and choir.

But with all the historic associations of Alcala I had to turn my attention to more common needs. In the town of Cervantes I expended three sous on fried fish, bread, and wine, and I am sure if the old philosopher were to read my mention of his birth-place he would not deem it too poor, considering that I am but a tramp.

The rain of yesterday had no effect upon the roads. They were as dusty as ever, the sky as bright, the sun as cruel. I travelled over broken country, carrying a few vines and a little garden stuff, and in the early afternoon reached the Jarama. This is quite a real river, and the water is of beautiful quality. I decided to wash all my kit before entering the capital. A group of "lavanderas" were laving garments and banging them over stones and grooved boards by the river-side. They looked at my efforts with pity. One, a sweet girl, insisted on washing two shirts for me. She did not wash them clean, but in spite of my declaration that they were "no limpia," they were wrung out and hung on the bridge to dry.

I have had to walk six hundred miles to meet my first Undine. I am not sure that I would walk ten to meet another.

The women would have it that I was an artist, for all artists wear knickerbockers and have veils over their hats. Argument was useless, so I allowed them to enjoy their opinion. At sunset the "lavanderas" departed, and I was left alone on the bank waiting for the evening winds to dry my clothes; but the process was somewhat longer than my patience, so, rolling the wet garments within my bundle, I set off towards "Town." It was eleven miles distant, and I decided to do six that evening and enter the city in the morning. My six miles accomplished, I pulled up at a posada. The posadero was a churlish rascal, and wanted to blackmail me and extract far more from me than I was prepared to pay. But a couple of well-dressed fellows, who were sitting drinking wine, soon brought him to reason. They turned out to be artists, and we exchanged cards. Seeing the turn of affairs, the landlord changed his tune completely. He gave me a good bed, talked about Old England, and wished me "Buenos noches" in a really generous way. How much of the civilised and the savage exist in each of us!

Madrid was soon in sight. It opened out like an Australian town : no smoke, no chimneys anywhere, but a deeper blue haze than in the open showed above it.

At El Ventas, an outlying suburban resort, where the holiday-makers of Madrid meet to drink, smoke, and make small meals at big prices, I made a halt. All sorts of "shows" and "gaffs" were there ; but the great attraction seemed to be the river, a filthy hollow down which trickles a disgusting streak of polluted water. Well-dressed people promenade by the side of this scent-bottle, and think they are in the country. Ventas gave me the qualms, but Madrid proper turned out to be beautifully clean.

As I made my way down the Camino de Alcala, by the Plaza de Faros, the Retiro Gardens, and the Prado, the scene at every step became more and more grand. I had entered Madrid at the right gate. It was the most imposing entry I had ever made. The Puerta del Sol, the heart of Spain, is reached at last, and half my journey accomplished.

CHAPTER VIII.

OLD MADRID.

MY first care was to seek out a modest boarding-house in the Calle del Hostalza, kept by a widow named Clotilde, who hastened to assure me she had "*seen better days.*"

I notice that nearly every one looks back with regret on the past. As for me, I am satisfied with the present. I know more than I did yesterday, and to-morrow will increase my store of experience. This is the only kind of wealth I care to heap up.

The widow's terms were moderate, so I closed with her at once. Her only other boarder was a young girl of twenty, so that business was not brisk.

Here for a time I laid aside my character of a Tramp, and went forth to explore Old Madrid. Why it should be called "old" I know not, for it is one of the most modern-looking cities I have ever seen. It is Paris in miniature—the boulevards, the style of architecture, the street crowds, all reminding me of the French capital.

Under the protection of a beautiful grave-eyed boy named Julian, my landlady's son, who was most becomingly attired in a sailor suit of blue and white, and an immense *berêt*, I visited the sights of the town—the beautiful promenades, the Bueno Retiro Gardens, and the Church of San Francesco, which is being restored at the cost of thirty-three million reals. The seven great entrance doors display carved figures in relief representing Bible scenes, or incidents in Church history. This work is truly magnificent. It is Ghiberti over again, and the modern is equal to the old master. One is forced to remember the famed " Baptistery " doors, though these of San Francesco are distinctly original.

Madrid is so sensible as to open its museums, galleries, and gardens early on Sunday morning, so that those who wish it may enjoy an hour's communing with the old masters, or the breath of the roses in the Bueno Retiro, before breakfast. The Museum affords a rich treat to the art lover, no matter where or what he has seen. The display of Italian masterpieces is richer than that of any one gallery in Italy.

There are forty-three Titians; but I am growing sceptical. Every gallery in the world has a few of this old master, and I am inclined to think it must have been "Titian and Co. Limited." We know he lived ninety-nine years, and a busy man could cover a lot of canvas in all that time; still . . . one wonders and doubts . . . ! One of the most famous and precious pictures is a Madonna and Child by Raphael —the Spaniards call it "La Perla"; and there is a Christ by Correggio which even I can worship.

Albert Durer is seen to perfection here. Some of his faces are so full of living intelligence that it seems positively rude to stand gazing into them.

Murillo lights up many a corner, but Velasquez may be said to illuminate the whole gallery. Wherever one sees a crowd of gazers—there is Velasquez. Once seen, his "Barrachos" and "The Surrender of Breda" can never be forgotten. Goya is well represented in the Royal Gallery, where his genius has ennobled the portraits of many a trashy Bourbon. A fine bust shows this king of modern painters to be a large-headed, brave-looking, grave, resolute man.

Florentine tables taken at the battle of Lepanto, Moorish trophies, and magnificent bronzes,—figures of kings and queens,—fill the vast chamber. My Sunday morning in the museum provided me with a rich feast.   A kaleidoscopic picture of the world had passed before me, and the "fate of all things" may have saddened me for a moment; but the world is still real for those who know how to use it, and the great gallery of Madrid has helped to make it larger and richer for me.

The Royal Palace of Madrid is another of those things which are always spoken of as " the finest in the world;" but there is a little, almost unknown palace, where the guide-book's voice is all unheard, and where tourists rarely—very rarely—come.   It is the bijou Palace of Moncloa, standing just outside Madrid, in the direction of the Escurial.   Externally it is the plainest of buildings, but the interior is a dream of delight.   It is the merest cottage in size, its small suite of rooms limned out of gossamer, margined and streaked with sunbeams, rainbows, the plumage of bright birds, and floral wreaths so true and beautiful that they seem to scent the walls and pillars they cling around.   Fairies and cupids flit across the skies, or rest on billowy masses of cloud, under canopies blue as the heavens.   What does it all mean? Simply that this palace is lined with silk panels wrought by cunning hands, skilled in the art of flower-weaving. The fineness of the work is marvellous, and the blending and breaking up of colours so perfect that one becomes enchanted with all around.

Isabella's boudoir represents an aviary. The walls are in imitation lattice work : soft foliage and sweet tendrils climb round the pillars which support this mimic cage. Butterflies, moths, and wind-borne petals flutter on its golden wires, and overhead, perches, bars, and rings hold birds of every hue and type of beauty. Spring time freshness and summer glow are shown in the far-off clouds which kindly refuse to cast a shadow on the fair haven. This cottage palace stands a living testimony that Ferdinand VII. had an eye for beauty, and that he loved luxury—perhaps too well.

A grand bull-fight was announced for the Sunday afternoon ; and as I wished to see Spain in all her moods, I lost no time in securing a seat in the " Plaza de Toros."

The Madrid building holds twelve thousand, all visible from every part of the arena. It is built of solid grey granite in arabic design, and with hardly any colour in the interior decoration; but when full of people with twelve thousand coloured fans, and as many more hats, bonnets, dresses, and sunshades, the forty-eight thousand varied tints form a picture which cannot be equalled.

A few notes from a shrill bell proclaimed that the president had taken his seat, and then two knights, dressed in black velvet, cocked hats with red and white plumes, and mounted on splendid horses, cantered into the ring and saluted the president, who acknowledged them by throwing the key of the " Carol " (bull's-box) into the arena. Then the brass band struck up the regular air of " Pan y toros " (bread and bull-fights), and the vast fabric seemed to rock and sway with the foot-stamping and shrill vociferations and fan-fluttering of the great crowd. A moment later all was rapt silence, as the two knights galloped into the centre of the ring, doffed hats, saluted the president, and retired to lead in the glittering procession of toreadors.

First came the two knights, " their banners proudly waving," followed by " Espadas " (swordsmen) and " Bandilleros," their bright mantles flung gracefully across the shoulder. The Punctilias and Chulos came next, and after them the Picadors, mounted and carrying long pikes ; last of all the mule team—used to carry off the slain. Under the president's box all saluted, broke into single file, and retired to the narrow seat which runs round the ring. A moment later the knights and the mule team had left the ring, and amidst a roar of tongues all calling " Toro," the cage door flew open and the first bull rushed upon the scene.

The spectacle that ensued was fascinating in the extreme, but horribly cruel. The horses and bulls are foredoomed. No amount of courage and skill can save them from death ; hence the whole thing is always unfair. As a spectacle it is superb. It is impossible to conceive, without being an actual witness, how a dozen or fifteen men, a few horses, and a solitary bull can make up such a powerful picture. Yet such it is; and it is no wonder that in a land where religion teaches nothing better than self-love, and delights in the display of horrors, bull-fighting should have a wondrous charm for its people.

On this occasion six bulls killed fifteen horses, and nearly "finished" one human performer. A splendid-looking Bandillero, richly dressed in crimson and gold, was thrown three times into the air, and on each occasion twirled like a top, gored right through the trunk and the thigh, and the forehead crushed. Thousands of women were looking on this horrible spectacle apparently quite unconcerned. Many of the leaders of society were there, revelling in the "first-rate" nature of the performance.

The audience practically control the ring—marking their approval or disapproval by the wildest cries. The effect is bewildering when any of the actors is guilty of a breach of order or makes a bad move.

The audience throw bottles, fruit, confectionery, hats, bonnets, fans and parasols, and everything else they can lay their hands on, into the arena. At one time hundreds of cushions were flung down, in spite of the high prices their owners had paid for the pleasure of sitting on them. All this "flotsam and jetsam" was cleared off in a twinkling, and when a "fuerte" (bout) closed, showers of parcels and boxes fell on the arena—all containing presents for favourite performers. One young *débutant* opened some of his gifts on the spot, and I saw that they were nearly all of gold and silver. If these men live six or eight years before the public they secure great wealth. But it is a large "if."

A comic bull-fight terminated the entertainment; but although it was most amusing, it could not efface the impressions of the "real thing."

At the close of the performance I went down into the arena. Looking round the great circle with the clear starry roof above, I pictured what it must be to stand there before a vicious raging bull, with twelve thousand pair of eyes looking on in expectation of a bloody finale. It requires some nerve, and every Toreador must possess it before he can become an expert in his trade.

Armed with a permit, I penetrated to the little hospital for injured Matadors, where lay poor Manuel Rodas, the handsomest and most unfortunate performer of the day. There were half-a-dozen beautifully draped little beds in the room, adorned with the arms and crests of noble donors.

The dressing-room was crowded with "aficionados" (amateurs) and supporters of the bull-ring.

Many of these had the manners and speech of well-educated men. The bull-beef is retailed at an establishment adjoining the ring. Being killed while heated it is not of prime quality, and the price is (for Spain) very low—fivepence per pound.

My dreams that night were of the mangled bodies of horses, bulls, and men, and I awoke without any desire to witness again the inhuman spectacle. I felt that the best thing to revive me would be a trip to the mountains of Avila and the Escurial.

The dreary landscape around Madrid was not inspiriting, neither was the progress of the train, which took three hours to perform a journey of forty-six miles.

The Escurial is nearly four thousand feet above the sea, on a little plateau shooting out between the bold, bare peaks of the Guadarrama mountains.

It was a lonely, voiceless spot when Philip II. (husband of our "Bloody Mary") chose it for the site of his monastic home. But the silence has fled. The Escurial is no longer a solitary house, it is a town. A railway runs at the foot of the range. Tall chimneys show above chocolate factories, and streets of shops and private houses rob its claim for silence. Boarding-houses, hotels, and mansions make a bigger show than the great building itself. The Escurial is a great building, but it is in no sense beautiful or inspiring.

It is not, as so many affirm, built in the shape of a gridiron, but forms an imperfect square with a church and courtyard somewhere near its centre, and three towers running up from the façade. Rows of small windows along the dark grey granite walls give to the building a prison-like appearance, and the shrill, cold winds whistling around its corners add to the illusion. San Lorenzo—to whom it is dedicated—stands over the main entrance, holding a model of the gridiron on which he was toasted.

The Escurial holds many treasures of art, but, unfortunately for this wanderer, they were all locked up, this being the feast of San Lorenzo, and the church doors were alone open.

The frescoed roof by Giordano has a great reputation, and I found out for myself that the organ was splendid. The " vox humana " seemed to speak from heaven direct to the tired soul of man. The statues of Felipes II. and III.—father and son—by the high altar are very fine, and the effect is heightened on realising that one is contemplating a figure who swayed half the world and whom the other half held in dread. The old hermit king is gazing wistfully on the last scene he visited on earth, for he was carried into the church, a filthy mass of emaciation and rags, before closing his eyes for ever.

The Escurial is a wonderful building. It is vast, it is singular, and perhaps if I had seen all its treasures, I might write, it is beautiful. Its "popular" attractions show that it is "big." It has over three thousand windows, twelve hundred doors, eighty-six staircases, three thousand feet of fresco painting, and ninety-six miles of floor space. It cost millions of money, and, some have said, *enough blood to dissolve the stones that compose it.* In order to build it Philip robbed both rich and poor.

The insane bigot actually stuck a plate of pure gold in the highest turret, to show that his "white elephant" had not exhausted his plundered store. Surely such vanity and display cannot be acceptable unto God, who is not found in houses made by the hand of little man. The soul will draw nearer Him on the bare hill-top, in the lonely desert, or beside the babbling stream, or, better still, among the suffering brethren whom he can help and bless.

The Escurial is a great object lesson. The world is full of them to those who have eyes and ears. This Palace will go on heaping up legends and superstitions as stirring as the real tragedies connected with its past till the story will be more wondrous than the reality itself.

The feast of San Lorenzo brought visitors from all parts. Not only holiday-makers from Madrid, but half-wild, half-naked, and strangely clad men and women from the mountain districts. These peasants have the lowest type of head I have seen in Spain. They have round, pudgy faces, full mouths, and lips that curl back, exposing prominent, narrow, animal-like teeth. The cheek-bones are high, the eyes small and dull, the forehead narrow and slanting back to the crown of a sugar-loaf head. As the men slouch along they look like ugly bundles of flannel and leather straps.

The women are all head and hips. They turn their toes inward, as if from continually climbing hills.

Their short skirts are made of a piece of coarse blanketing drawn together round the waist by a couple of yellow cords. Their legs are bandaged with strips of flannel, and they wear on their feet leather sandals. Loose cotton blouses, and head-dresses formed by showy handkerchiefs, complete their attire. They were an odd-looking set. Madrid and its civilising influences did not seem to have touched them.

I got back to Madrid in time to dine with some

pleasant friends at the hotel made famous by "Pigott," and spent the evening among the gay throng who turn night into day beneath the trees and lamps of the Prado. The "crush promenade" is from 11 p.m. till 3 or 4 a.m., and this is the play-time of the Madrid children. The hot, enervating climate is the cause of these nocturnal habits.

In the company of an artist-friend I visited the institute for the study of fine arts, founded in 1869. It possesses few originals, but displays a fine collection of copies, and the floors are covered with the easels of industrious students. The introduction of fountains and masses of plants into these galleries seems to connect nature with art, and must add to the receptivity of those who work and study here.

The State professes to teach agri- and horticulture at a college in Madrid, but with very poor results. The Spaniards have more of the gift of conducting fairs and feasts than of producing the materials on which they make merry.

A big feast was taking place in one part of the city, and all the streets were decked with bunting, coloured lanterns, and oil lamps. Only the main thoroughfares were left open for wheel traffic.

The other streets had become dancing-saloons, show-grounds, and reserved spaces for all sorts of games, exhibitions, and bands. I walked through miles and miles of streets, and still fresh vistas opened before me, and the dancing, and bawling, and crowding still continued.

Fairly worn out, I went back to the society of my pensive widow and of my fellow-boarder, for I had learned to like her company better than that of the streets. She had large, dark, tender eyes, a sweet musical voice, and a tall, willowy form. What a life was hers! As a milliner she earned twelve pesetas a week by working eleven and a-half hours on week days and eight hours on Sundays. Her only day of rest was a rare saint's day.

I had made my last journey of inspection, had paid my widow her modest charge, and was sitting in my room waiting for the hot sun to sink a little before setting forth on my travels, when Clotilde, my landlady, rushed in, wringing her hands in terror.

"Oh, Senor don Carlos!" she cried; "oh, Madre miá! Maria este muriendo!" Beckoning me to follow her she fled from the room. I was coatless and barefoot, but I hastened after her. She led me to a small, dark room. On the stone floor lay Maria the milliner, her face white as the robe that covered her. She had slipped from Clotilde's arms in a dead faint.

I lifted her up and placed her on the bed. She looked the image of death. I had noticed that she often held one hand to her breast as though in pain, and it seemed that the kiss which Gregorio, her young lover, came regularly to bestow upon her was a little more than she could bear. She was very weak. When she rallied she cried feebly, and said she was "ill, oh! so ill." I told her that Gregorio must take her to the mountains—high up—in the cool sweet air, and that she would soon grow strong again.

"High up," she murmured, "yes, VERY high up—I shall soon be there. I am glad to go. Madrid is not kind; but oh! I wish Gregorio could come too. I do not like to leave him here alone."

Clotilde signed to me to leave the room. I busied myself with my final preparations, and then asked permission to see my fellow-boarder again. A doctor was with her. I saw at once that there was no hope for the fragile girl. Gregorio was bending over her, his face streaming with tears. I took the long white hand in mine, kissed it, and left the room. Clotilde told me all would be over in a few hours. The doctor said the poor girl had struggled on till a complete collapse of every enfeebled organ left no chance for recovery. I did not linger. My way is hard in Spain, and I dare not court sad scenes. Ah me! must it be ever thus? Must I, loving to see great things, be confounded by the simple incidents of every-day life? The memory of poor Maria Paz, the slave of the needle, will be fresh in my mind when all the grand sights of Madrid are faded or forgotten. The "song of the shirt" is being sung in all lands ; wherever men and women crowd, the weak are being crushed. Madrid is a "gay" city, but if you will enter into its houses you will find no dearth of sorrow there.

The sun was still shining bright when I left the Hostalza, though the shadow of death was over my sometime home. I never learned the sequel of Maria's story. I trust that she has met with true rest and a rich reward.

CHAPTER IX.

OLD AND NEW CASTILE.

AFTER ten days' diversion in "Old Madrid"— which, as every one who has seen it knows, is the most modern-looking of all the old-world capitals —I set out once more on my travels, taking the road *viâ* Aranjuez to Toledo. The road is fearfully bad. I had to flounder mile after mile through heavy dust lying several inches deep. My feet were soon skinless and sore, and I did not enjoy the fifteen-mile tramp before reaching a town. And such a town! Nothing like it can possibly exist elsewhere. Pinto boasts that it is the centre of the world! Think of that. To a Spaniard Spain is always "the world."

This place is, I believe, the exact centre of Spain, and in honour thereof the inhabitants of old perched a church on the nearest hill. It has become a shrine where Joseph and Mary are said to dispense rich and unrivalled blessings. If you stick up your walking-stick at Pinto at any time of the day it will cast no shadow, because the sun is always right overhead. A posada keeper told me this. I did not contradict him—I had other work to do—but I asked myself wonderingly how big a fool he took me to be !

The alcalde of Pinto gave me a shake-down at the posada. Anyone would know this alcalde to be a generous man. He has a family of nineteen children, some of whom are married, and their wives and children, making thirty-seven in all, living under his not very spacious roof. I went into the inner circle of this huge family, and all was peace and harmony amongst them. The allotted work of the day went on as if by clockwork—a wonderful domestic picture this, for old Spain. With so many mouths to feed it is fortunate that the alcalde is the leading baker of Pinto.

The parish church is a wicked-looking old place, standing on an artificial eminence, and surrounded by military ramparts. It had probably to serve as a fortress in bygone times. The pulpit is cut out of a massive column helping to support the roof, and covered from base to summit with delicately-chased figures in relief.

They boast a theatre at Pinto. It was, nay, still is, a barn. A few rude benches fill the pit, and the boxes are—just boxes, and nothing more. One can be hired for fivepence. This is the cheapest thing I have found in Spain—unless the entertainment be even cheaper !

One thing more in favour of Pinto. It is the cleanest town I have yet seen. All the houses are whitewashed within and without ; the inhabitants seem thrifty, and have a very neat appearance. Corn, wine, and oil are the chief products of the neighbourhood—unless, indeed, the harvest of miracles at the church on " the central spot of the world " rival them in richness.

Well pleased with Pinto—a tramp is always well pleased when he is well treated—I set out for Aranjuez. Passing over a miserable country carrying a few stunted olives and occasional patches of corn, I sighted the village of Valdemora—all mica and clay beds and olive trees. The road did not improve. Ploughing through the dust and scorched by the sun, I went on my way growling and choking by turns. All around me stretched wheat-fields unbroken by fences or hedges, and in the distance the bare, hot hills. My knapsack hung like a ton weight on my shoulders, and I was thankful to accept a lift on a mule car, which took me on to the big bridge, the " Punta Llargo," spanning the Jarama.

This was my second encounter with this river. It was on its banks that I met my first Undine. It had not lost by its journey, as so many Spanish rivers do. On the contrary, it had become a broader, deeper stream. And the bridge is a grand old fabric. The French knocked down the original structure erected many centuries ago, but the Spaniards built it up again in more impregnable and elegant style than before. It is now considered one of the finest bridges in Spain ; nearly a quarter of a mile in length, and built throughout of solid and massive blocks of stone. At both ends are broad square platforms, on which a small army of troops might be marshalled. Square stone columns rise at each corner, surmounted by heaps of finely chiselled armour and implements of war, guarded by an erect and vicious-looking lion. It is the bridge of bridges I have seen in Spain, and to be over it, what joy ! To be within the shadow of high elm trees—English elms too, for these mighty towers of green were brought here from our own land three hundred years ago to decorate the vale of Aranjuez.

What a difference vegetation and the sweet breath

of trees make to a land! It is fifteen miles from the Punta Llargo to the town, but amid so much sweetness it seemed but a stone's throw, and I quickly arrived within the sacred precincts of the country retreat of Spanish royalty.

It is a toy court, well suited to the wants of the present infant king. Aranjuez is a pretty little place, all palace and parterres and marble paths and miles of statuary and falling water. But nothing seems real. Here one may well reverse the original intention and exclaim : " He dreamed not of decay who thus could build." I forget the name of the king who, falling in love with the meeting of the waters of the Tagus and Jarama, founded Aranjuez on the dividing plateau ; but I shall never forget some of his fantastic notions. I shall remember the twelve roads all diverging from a circle a hundred feet in diameter, roads which for the most part lead nowhere in particular, eight or ten of them forming avenues,— the boggy flat on which, for the sake of being within sound of the artificial fall in the Tagus, the palace is built,—the miles of shady walks, margined by ugly stone walls over which no sheltering, softening mass of ivy has been allowed to creep,—the thousand and one ghostly statues peeping between the branches of evergreen shrubs and trees,—all these will be present in my memory when nobler figures have faded out.

The Casa de Vacas (King's Cow House) is now the racing stud of the Marquis de Villamajor. Here I made a call, to look for nothing in particular; but it is one of the glorious privileges of my profession that such visits are never out of order. I found what I did not expect—three fellow-countrymen, the stud groom and two jockeys, jolly· light-hearted fellows of the kind who love "taking of blackthorns and rattle of rails."

One of them asked me in a very humorous way to tell his dear mother that I had met her son in Spain, and that he was "doing well." "Yes," he said, "a mother always likes to hear about her son, but with all her love for him she likes still better to hear that he is '*steady*' and throwing his 'bawbees' into a heap." I believe my friend the jockey was right. Women can have an eye to the pocket even when steeped in tears. When a man is in great trouble he is reckless; when a woman is bereaved she can be most acute in mundane matters. My fellow-countrymen conducted me to a posada, and pressed me to breakfast with them the following day. A wanderer in Spain never neglects a chance of getting something to eat. If I were asked to name the greatest thing in the world, I should reply without hesitation—the appetite of a tramp! He of all men may best know "the art of taking a walk." The human world is not for him. He may not call the passers-by " brother," " sister ; " they will not own him as a member of the one great family ; and so, he ever turns to that broader, sweeter breast, the welcoming bosom of nature. This begets hunger. To look and gaze and stare,—to fear and dread and delight, and grow weary over the continually changing features of a land, is to grow hungry indeed.

I eat at all hours, anything and everything I can get hold of. A twenty-pound bundle and a twenty-mile walk will take all the bad qualities out of the worst dish prepared in Spain. Here is a sample day for you.

I have drunk a stiff glass of white spirit at four in the morning ; eaten a pound of hard bread without water at seven ; devoured a dozen tomatoes and cucumbers between eleven and twelve, and made the midday meal of half a gallon of lukewarm water ; luxuriated over a pocketful of dry crusts during the afternoon in a dry valley ; and in the early evening caught, toasted, and eaten four Spanish frogs ! Jupiter rains blessings on the poor, for the same night I enjoyed a six-course dinner, finishing up with cognac, coffee, and cigars !

I slept in the yard behind the posada, and in the early morning turned out to have a daylight view of

Aranjuez. It is not sweet in reality, but it looks it. It charms all who see it because it is a green valley, almost an unknown feature in Spain. There is a something about the place which makes it homely and attractive even to a stranger. I wandered up and down its many glades and groves, by its rushing watercourses and water-wheels, and sauntered on the banks of the black Tagus. It looked a river to fear rather than to follow—its waters seemed terribly treacherous ; and in truth they are. Fevers and epidemics ravage and at times almost depopulate the place ; and it is a case of

"Water, water everywhere, nor any drop to drink,"

nearer than the broad, sweet Jarama, two miles away.

I breakfasted in English fashion at the "Casa de Vacas," which has sheltered many a brave man and good horse in its day. Napoleon tried to burn it down in 1809, but finding it resist his efforts, he lodged a regiment or two in the stubborn old place. The following story comes down from this time, and is dealt out very soberly by the people of Aranjuez.

A ball was given at the palace for the Spanish and English officers. The French, offended at being left out in the cold, began an assault on the place. The servants appeared and desired the French to go away, adding that the English soldiers did not wish to be disturbed, and that they thought the action of the French *very rude*! Whereupon the French meekly departed. Does not this story do credit to all concerned?—to the Spanish, who say that the English, and not they themselves, frightened the French; to the French, who showed such profound respect for the usages of society--not to speak of their respect for English arms; to the English, who stood fast by the beauties of that hour, instead of rushing off to deeds of desperation and sacrifice, as so many did from the ball at Brussels to the field of Waterloo.

I was able to have a good look at the Royal Palace, a big square building, half of red brick, the other half of rough whitewashed masonry. Three rows of attic windows on the roof, and painted black, offered a strange, unsightly contrast to the white walls below. The interior is " gaudy, and expressed in fancy," but, on the whole, not " rich." The hall and staircase are broad and well proportioned, but the only embellishment consists of a coating of yellow ochre and brown umber. The " Cabinette de Arabe " opens from the first floor. It is a little bell-shaped chamber without windows or doors. The entire wall space is covered with a raised fretwork on six or seven planes, the whole presenting the appearance of a vast brilliant with a million facets.   Every tiny facet has a contour and colour of its own, and reflects the tints of some other.   As a matter of fact, the colours are only blue, red, and gold, with base lines of white ; but it is hard to believe this.   The carving is so minute, and the lights and shadows are so confusing, that the spectator cannot make sure either of colour or pattern.   The cabinette is in perfect condition, and is the best specimen of Moorish work I have yet seen.

The royal bedchamber is a plain room, with a full-length crucifix over the bed, and the ceiling shows some fine frescoes.   The windows command a beautiful view of gardens filled with statues, fountains, and bright flowers.   Beyond rises a little forest of trees kept in bounds by a hard, sullen hill.

The Queen Regent's boudoir is a pretty and spacious apartment, the ceiling covered with beautiful frescoes of winged cupids, gossamer butterflies, birds, and flowers.   The walls are hung with delicate mauve-coloured Barcelona silk, shot with pink roses. Reflectors and rich pieces of bric-à-brac help to beautify the scene.   This room has a charm rarely found in courts.   It is *restful*, and one is not tempted to moralise and grow moody therein.

Another room, called the " Buena Retiro," holds many lovely things, but the general effect is cold.

If all accounts be true, he who took such pride in creating the room and the name knew nothing of the latter. "Sweet retirement!" The title sounds sweet. But where is it to be found? Hardly in this cold and depressing chamber. I can only compare it to an enormous bell-shaped vase (seen from within), the sides and dome overlaid with china flowers, birds, and animals in relief. There is one set design moulded in various sections, but put together with such precision that the joints cannot be found. Nearly every tint and shade in the natural phenomena of the world is found here, yet the effect is chilling and inartistic.

The king's morning room is large and stately, containing many fine pictures—notably, five scenes in the life of the "Prodigal Son," by Conrado Bayen. "Orpheus and Apollo," "Bathsheba and Judith," by the same artist, are said to be of priceless value.

There are also lovely Sèvres porcelain vases in celestial blue, gold, and chocolate, and some with fanciful designs of flowers and creeping things. The dining-hall is crowded with curious clocks, collected from all parts of the world by Charles IV. and Ferdinand VII. Here mosaic figures, representing rural pastimes, and the arts, music, and painting, are scattered in glorious confusion over the nut-brown floor.

The ante-room, connecting the Regent's boudoir with the chapel, is full of small paintings by celebrated masters—landscapes and portraits by Poussin and Temmel, an exquisite female head by Mengs, and a Christ by Titian. A mosaic seascape, three feet by two, is the crowning triumph of this room. It contains I don't know how many hundred thousand pieces of stone, all of purely natural colours, forming a picture with every detail of light and shade admirably rendered. This work, executed in 1808, is valued at one million pesetas. The little chapel is also rich in pictures, not all sacred, and it contains some fine carved figures in ivory and silver.

The cabinette of Capo di Monte Porcelaine is, like the "Buena Retiro," a chamber completely lined with fanciful plates of porcelain in high relief. Blue is the prevailing colour, and the tone is so high that it jars on the sense, and almost takes the sight from the eyes. It is a gorgeous apartment, but not according to nineteenth-century conceptions of refinement and beauty.

My next visit was to the Royal stables, lately restored and presented by the Queen to her little son. Many a horse jobber in England owns better stables than these royal boxes. In the evening I took a last look at the gardens surrounding the palace, and started for Old Toledo. I had another six miles of shade, for the king who made this place planted trees up and down the valley, which, although it has always been held by farmers and market-gardeners, has the appearance of a private domain.

A thunderstorm overtook me on the road, and gave me what the boys call a "belltinker." After getting wet to the skin, and smothered with mud through falling on the slippery banks, I was thankful to reach the railway station of Castillejos, and there pass the night.

The station-master allowed me to sleep in the cloak room, but before doing so I shared a good supper with him, which had been sent down from Madrid by the night mail. Cheered by the presence of a good heart I slept soundly, and the next morning continued my journey towards Toledo—following the flow of the Tagus, but unfortunately not near enough to get a bath or a drink. The soaking of the previous night had given me a cold, but Nature came to my relief. I found the liquorice plant growing in great abundance, so pulling up an armful of roots I munched them as I jogged along, and towards evening I had fairly recovered. The Moor has left traces of his industry on this road. The river flats are irrigated by means of well water. This is drawn up in pitchers lashed to a circular belt, which revolves on a huge wheel, the motive power being a mule or donkey blindfolded and un-attended by any driver, which trudges round and round in a circle throughout the livelong day. These elevators, which are here in thousands, are called "Norias" (Persian wheels). It speaks volumes for the dusky Moor that the "Norias" are never found in any part of Spain which has been held exclusively by the Spaniards.

It was pitch dark an hour or two before I saw the lights of Toledo, apparently gleaming out from the clouds. I had lost the road, which since I left the shades of Aranjuez had been the merest track; so I took to the railway as the surest way of getting nigh unto the town. On the line I overtook a farmer-looking man. He was hopelessly drunk, and had all his work cut out to balance himself on his Jack donkey, which latter preferred taking the main way to walking on the track beside it. I felt bound to act as cicerone to the drunkard till I could see him out of danger. He put many questions to me, but as I was unable to answer him to his satisfaction he thought me more drunk than himself, and pitied me accordingly.

He said he knew of "a short cut" to Toledo. We took it, and found, like Pat, that it delayed us. We seemed to travel miles and miles without gaining a yard on the town. Perhaps we were "measuring the road." But I must say in my own defence that I had drunk no wine that day.

It was long past midnight when we arrived at the bridge which spans the Tagus and gives access to the famous city. For some reason the toll-keeper would not allow the drunkard to pass, and while the parleying was going on I sat down on my bundle and fell fast asleep. In the morning I was awakened by a fat old fellow in a white apron kicking me in the ribs and shaking a bunch of keys over my head. I discovered I had been sleeping in front of a kind of sentry-box, from which my persecutor sold fruits and cool drinks to those who passed over the bridge. He was naturally annoyed to find my untidy body lying in front of his shop door.

My companion of the night had flown. I was not sorry. Toledo lay before me. It has a fine old world look viewed from the bridge. It seemed to promise great things, but I cannot say that it revealed many to me.

The Tagus, still black and dreamy, takes a crescent course through a gorge it has made in a wild rocky range which dips into a small valley. Toledo stands on a hill cut off by the river from the parent range. The situation is most peculiar for an inland town, as it is nearly surrounded by water, and except by the bridge it can only be approached by way of the plain. In the old days when it was man's arm, not his ingenuity, that decided the victory, Toledo was well-nigh impregnable. To-day its strongest walls and ramparts could be taken by schoolboys. The city rises in a succession of terraces from the river.

Church steeples and towers shoot skyward in all directions ; some of sombre time-stained stone, others of check-patterned tiles in black and white.

The word " fantastic " does not convey any idea of the many quaint forms these towers and turrets take. As it was fair time a flag or strip of bunting floated from nearly every one of them. The morning sun had gathered up all the hazy fragments from the crags and crannies about the river, and in the blue vault above there was not one discordant shade or the vestige of a cloud. The ranges round are wild and bare. The only strip of cultivated land skirts the broad bed of the Tagus away in the direction I had come the previous night. I was sadly in need of a bath and clean clothes before joining the specially dressed throng who were crossing the bridge on their way to the fair.

But it will be all over with this tramp when he really stops to consider other people's opinion of him, so " rough and unbeautiful " as I was I made for the city. I wound round and round and round till I reached the principal plaza on the crown of the hill. It is small, and in no sense effective. The houses and shops are of quite ordinary design and appearance.

There are scores of towns in Spain far more antiquated and picturesque than the interior of this one. I am inclined to think that Toledo lives on its former reputation. The Cathedral is like many an ordinary woman—made famous because it has a dark history. Not being a great student of history, I own that I prefer things that carry the hall mark of superiority on their very front and figure head. The cry of the new American to the Parisian waiter, "*Give me something I can understand and digest*," is also mine.

This Cathedral is the most complex and bewildering I have ever seen. It has changed hands and beliefs so often that it is hard to know what end some portions are meant to serve. There are forms and figures and utensils belonging to the outside world of many centuries, rather than to the history and traditions of the Church. But I suppose "the Church" somewhat resembles myself on this pilgrimage, in that it is ready to take anything it may be offered. The ante-chambers of the Cathedral contain thousands of beautiful things, but the collection is marred by the presence of incongruous and ridiculous gimcracks—tin hearts and other frivolous offerings   The stained windows are superb, and I find no words to convey an idea of the effect of the gorgeous rays of light which they pour on the pavement of this great church.

The library contains thousands of rare and costly books and manuscripts, and the numerous chambers of the adjoining cloisters are clothed with pictures; some quaint and beautiful, others grotesque, hideous, and vulgar.

The re-tablo is sublime; the wood-carving everywhere of the highest excellence in art; and the choir-screen of wood, stone, and bronze is said to be unique. The most striking picture is a colossal figure of San Christobal—nearly sixty feet high—nursing a child. The anatomy is bad, but the herculean proportions make it effective.

The arches of the main doorway are deservedly famous. They are surrounded by chastely wrought figures of saints and sacred emblems. Although so hard and cold, the stone seems to shed the softest of tears and emit the sweetest odours from the sightless eyes and lifeless flowers which have lingered here through so many stormy centuries.

I confess to a love for neglected shrines. I may go further, and say I like most neglected things. A neglected garden speaks to me more eloquently than any well-tended parterre. And so it came to pass that I was attracted to the little noticed church and monastery of San Juan,* and held captive by its voiceless yet speaking stones.

There is but one popular attraction in the church —save its curious draught-board-patterned tower— and this is the recumbent figure of a saint (a bishop I believe he was) in white marble; a work of extraordinary beauty. I sat down to admire it.

Half-a-dozen sisters of mercy were kneeling round this figure, and one of them, evidently taking me for a *penitent*, urged me to kneel and ask a few favours from the saint, whose life, she assured me, had come "very near to that of the Lord Jesus." Unbelieving wretch that I was, I could not offer myself to this cold, dead thing in stone. I looked my thanks to the nun. I could have said a few words to her.

She was rather young, and had a sweet, good-natured face, and I'm afraid my looks betrayed more devotion towards her than to the saint in marble, for she distinctly blushed, and lost the serene, far-away look so common to women of this order.

Within the old white walls of the Hospital of

* " Hospital de Tavera.—Founded by the Cardinal Archbishop Tavera 1540, for the sick and invalids. The tomb is that of the founder, and is by Berruguete ; the latter died whilst working on the last details."—O'SHEA.

San Juan there is still opportunity to perform holy deeds, and I fancy that the quiet blue cloak and cowl may cover a purer, happier heart than belongs to many a prattling, commonplace woman of the world.

I often meditate and speculate about the mission of different generations of men, and I derive a peculiar kind of pleasure from the recognition that so few traces of the lives and works of countless millions are left behind. The yard of the above-named monastery is paved with enormous blocks of stone, and to look on it is to be reminded of a ruffled sea. Feet, human feet, have done this; have made impressions a foot or more in depth below the original surface; and the once round pillars supporting the balcony of the monastery hospital are worn out of shape by the friction of human hands and shoulders.

What a sentimental tramp I must appear—always mooning about in churches; but has it ever occurred to you that they are the only homes of the tramp? Here and here only he can lay down his unchristian load, doff his hat, and enter without fear.

Ah! we shall get rid of a good many time-honoured institutions before we unship our religion. Education will not "improve" us right out of it. Even an increase of the masculine qualities in woman

---extension of the franchise, open doors to the scientific laboratories, and all other of her heart's desires —will not make her and the sons she influences indifferent to all forms of faith. Men and women are kneeling, not only in the primitive fanes of Old Toledo, but at the Fountain-head of knowledge—in the Madeleine and Mayfair. Religions will change and have their ups and downs, but they cannot die. Man will continue to worship what he cannot comprehend. He peoples no known spot with the object of his devotion. Far away in the mysterious heavens he looks for light and life, and fancies, the white clouds which gather o'er the blue are the only barriers between himself and God.

When my tramping days are over I hope to find other walls to shelter me from the rude world. But at present the church is my only home, and the sight of a distant spire fills me with thankfulness. I have seen the grey piles showing over many a hill ; and looking down the long valleys, when the white, dusty roads offer neither shade nor rest, my only hope has been the distant haven built for God.

I was not sorry to bid farewell to the streets of Toledo. They are narrow, steep, and tortuous, and being pitched with enormous smooth stones, the wayfarer slips and slides and gets his feet pinched at almost every step. Toledo as a whole did not

impress me. It has taken to what Paddy calls
"*high notions*"; that is to say, it has new-faced,
and whitewashed, and slapdashed so many of its old
things that they look either new or ridiculous.

Towards night I prepared to leáve the town. As
I sat sipping a cup of black coffee in the principal
café, half the population crowded to gape at me.
Happily their attention was diverted by some other
attraction of the fair, and I was left free to con my
map before making tracks in the direction of Ciudad-
Real.

CHAPTER X.

OLD AND NEW CASTILE.

FROM the old bridge that had been on the previous night my airy-eerie bedchamber I took my last look at the black rolling flood, and struck the track over the rugged hill leading to Sonseca. I was sorry to say good-bye to the Tagus. It had not won my affections, but I have journeyed long enough to know the value of any river, and I knew that I should have to travel hundreds of miles before reaching the banks of the Guadalquivir. It was raining in torrents, and, crossing a cold wild moorland, I got drenched to the skin and almost perished with cold.

Hour after hour I trudged through the falling flood

—a dismal ending to my long day of sightseeing in Toledo. Only once did I get a drop of wine, at a solitary house on the moor. Late at night, fatigued and ill-tempered, I reached the "pueblo" of Bourgillias. The entire population seemed like myself—out of sorts with the weather. I could not get a shake-down anywhere.

There was no alcalde, no rest-house, no hospital; only closed doors, a go-to-the-devil expression on every face, and the rain still pelting down! At last I found a shelter—only a wet floor, and I was soak-ing. Nevertheless I stretched out and slept soundly till morning.

Then I went in search of a bakehouse, and bought a huge piece of bread. With this I took to the road. The sun soon dried me, and I felt none the worse for my rough night. I passed several hamlets before reaching Sonseca, a compact, clean village which lies somewhat low, and is a veritable oven.

The curious old brick houses are painted over with chocolate and sky blue, and on many of them are tracings of flowers, leaves, birds, and monsters.

A score of old crosses and stone columns mark an ancient burial ground, where donkeys and mules browse at their ease tethered to the old stones.

Half-a-dozen little chimneys rising above the house-tops betray the presence of some old mills, which have been turning out the best of Spanish cloth for more than a thousand years. I penetrated two or three of the dwellings, and some kindly women let me gaze my fill upon their old china, brassware, and primitive furniture.

They seemed to take a real pride in their pretty, quaint homes. The country around was all olive, corn, and vine land, hardened and withered by the sun to the same sad grey colour which is so depressing throughout Spain.

It was still early when I left Sonseca, and, as ill luck would have it, I was overtaken by another storm. Then the sun came out and laughed at me till I was dry, inside and out, and just as evening was taking big reefs in the broad plain, and shortening up the white, hot road, I got into the castle-crowned old pueblo of Orgaz.

I was just in the mood to make an impression on the Powers of the place. I was hungry! I put on the airs of a martyr; showed my scars (they are always and *only* on my feet); and then—expressed my admiration for the Spanish character!

The thing was done! The alcalde, the secretary, and another great gun promise that I shall be well cared for in their town. The alcalde accompanied me himself to a " posada " and ordered my bed, a real bed in a clean room, for the night.

After us came the secretary, bringing an acceptance paper for my signature. He had named me as he came along in the twilight, and this attracted an immense crowd curious to see the "Ingles." They were good-humoured folk, and I was fairly loaded with gifts—cigarettes and earthen cups of wine. They simply held a public meeting over me, and the clamour of tongues was prodigious. The gist of it all was that Orgaz was going to see great things now that an "Ingles" had deigned to honour (!) it with his presence. It was midnight before I could escape from the crowd filling the great yard of the posada, and go off to that sweet little bed surrounded by Spanish embroidery and white walls.

Who would not be weary for the sake of appreciating the simple comforts of a tavern bed?

I was tempted to lie long after daylight, only rising in time to attend mass at the old church. The altar pieces have some of the lovely wood-carving in which the Spaniards certainly excel. Here, as usual, the congregation was chiefly composed of women. They knelt in their black dresses and cloaks round the altar steps, shaking and twirling fans before their wrinkled faces ; while the men stood in the rear, dressed in their every-day clothes, ready to go to work in the Campo. They wear cord or black velvet faded to brown, black "fajas," dark-blue shirts, and hats of plush—in shape like a round bread-tray. Those who were independent of labour for the day sat solemnly contemplating the priest's movements. Some were old men, veritable patri-archs, in real old-fashioned Spanish cloaks, cord breeches reaching well over the knee and bell-bottomed, white cotton stockings and brown leather shoes or "espargots." The organ with its horizontal trumpet pipes sent forth lovely music, and the singing in this unknown country church was heavenly. I was so rejoiced that tears rushed to my eyes. George Herbert's lines—

> "Sweet day, so calm, so cool, so bright
> The world were dark but for thy light"—

gained fresh meaning for me on this Sunday morn-ing spent in Catholic Spain.

Four heavy walls are all that remain of the castle of Orgaz. I could discover no documents in that ready, convenient way some trippers do when in out-of-the-way and old-fashioned places. Neither did I break into any dungeon keep and unearth any distressed maiden seeking succour from my knightly arm, so I was forced to move on.

There is no escaping from our tasks. It is a *continuous* journey, this life of ours. Romantic youths and maidens—and some old folks, too—are inclined to believe that there are shady banks, rippling waters, and immortal flowers, by which many rest and escape the ravages of old Time awhile. But it is not so. I, at least, have discovered that there are twenty-four hours in every day, and, pass them where I will, there is a thorn or a chilling thought in every one of them.

After one of my customary fags of a dozen miles over open, plain land, I arrived at a bold range, which forms the extreme northern offset of the Montes de Toledo ; a steep-sided, wild, and waterless range, and the road scarcely discernible in broad daylight.

Having been to church in the morning, I was reminded of too many good precepts to allow my feelings to take shape in words, but I did want to curse that confounded hill for sticking itself right in my way. It took me three hours to climb up one side and down the other, and there was not a soul in the valley of Yebenes willing to compliment me for all my hard labour!

The inhabitants of Yebenes are evidently anxious to "go one better" than any of their neighbours, as they whitewash the roofs of their houses, and also make white lines across the cobble stones in the "calles," to show " *whos'n is whos'n*," as they say in Somerset.

From this small valley I had a good view of the
Montes de Toledo. The outline is not striking.
They are without any backbone.

The country is what geologists call "broken."
There is not a ridge or spine three miles in length—
nothing but easy cones, humps, and hollows, without
grace or grandeur. Valleys, dry dells, and basins
appear in the most unexpected quarters, and it is
strange that with all these natural catchment areas
no spring should find its way to make even a
solitary lake.

The few insignificant rills rising on the outer
slopes of the southern boundary are absorbed by
evaporation. The prevailing hue is a heavy rain-
cloud tint. It is a dreary, barren region. I should
not have ventured out of Yebenes without any bread
in my satchel had I not been assured by some
thick-headed fellows that there were "plenty of
houses near the mountains." So I decided to keep
my pack light, and jog on to some distant haven in
the black hills. Night came on whilst I was in a
long, dreary gorge. There were several little pools
of rain water, bits of quercus scrub, and pretty little
flowers of the crocus family growing beside my path.
But there was no sign of a human habitation. Towards midnight I saw two lights ahead of me, and
heard dogs barking. One light shone from an old

castle standing on a rocky promontory, the other from the cottage of a goatherd, who sat at his door puffing a cigarette.

On seeing my plight he placed bread and cucumber before me, and gave me permission to sleep in an empty hut.

In the early morning he directed me across the Montes to Nada—which I managed to miss, although I kept the given course over frightfully hot, desolate hills. In a dry valley I fell in with some goatherds tending a flock of two or three thousand brown-haired hornless goats.

No better examples of the primitive man could be found in Spain. Everything they wore was made of leather. Goatskin caps, shaped like an Etruscan helmet—the fur inside, and the outside black and shiny with frequent handling; shirts—also of goat-skin—tanned soft as chamois, and tied down the front with leather laces (instead of buttons); short jackets of dark brown leather, with fancy scalloped patches adorning the front, elbows, and pockets; buttons made of rudely-cut pieces of cow and goat's horn; and stiff, hard leather breeches. Leather sandals, and a score of green leather straps bound round ankles and calves, completed their attire. They were tall, hardy, dare-devil-looking men, and I was delighted with the strong picture they presented on their native heath. All their "kit" was equally primitive. They carried their meal (for making brown bread), their wine, and their water in skins. Oil, used for cooking and also for dressing wounds in their flocks, was held in a score or two of large cow-horns, with caps and spicket holes fitted over the large ends. All these horns were connected by links and straps, so that they could be carried over the shoulder as on mules' backs. A couple of old guns with the locks outside served to throw the picture into the long past. The blades stuck in their waist-belts were more like old reaping-hooks than knives. Rough and wild as these men were, they were very open-hearted. They offered me of their little store, and directed me to the best track across the mountains.

I learned from them that I should not come across a house for many miles. And they were right.

I must have walked twenty miles across this trackless maze of hills and hollows before I finally got away from them, and descended the long valley leading to Malagon. The small river Cambron, which waters this town, is subterranean in the summer. It is only in winter, when the storm waters come down from the Montes de Toledo, that its course can be seen ; but a subterranean stream of water which follows the open river bed is perennial, and serves to irrigate the low-lying country, which shows very sweet and green after the barren mountains.

I arrived at Malagon too late to lay siege to the alcalde, and being very tired I " put up " at a posada. In other words, I slept on the floor of the yard. In the morning I set out by the shortest road to Ciudad-Real.

Twenty-five miles—two little villages, a first view of the pretty Guadiana, an abundance of grapes, the death of two black snakes, and then the Royal City.   It is as flat as a bowling green, and very small to have such a big name.   This is the story of its origin.

Alfonso the Great, annoyed by the incessant appeals for aid made by the inhabitants of the old town constantly ravaged by malarial fever, came and looked at it and saw that it was bad.   He waved his strong arm in the direction of the dry plain. " Build and live over there," he said.

His subjects took him at his word.   They forsook the old town on the banks of the Guadiana, built as the king had commanded, and so came into existence the town and name of Ciudad-Real.

The Octroi is strictly enforced here ; but I passed through the big gates without even receiving recognition from the guard.   My clothes and person had become so faded and poverty-stricken that the toll-keeper did not wish to examine my load. I hold divided opinions about a tramp's dress and appearance. I believe that anything that awakens curiosity will do more for him than the small percentage of good souls who look on charity as a holy duty. A wretched, needy, even a dirty appearance claims the attention and support of many; but I believe a nimble-footed, bold-faced, quick-witted rascal gets most in the long run.

The town was musical with bells: deep-sounding and light silvery notes rang out from all quarters. This was the greatest day of the year for Ciudad Reál, the day on which the Virgin is brought out on a triumphal car (a veritable Juggernaut), and a gorgeous procession sweeps through the town. I was just in time to witness it. The Virgin wore a magnificently embroidered dress of emerald green satin and a cape of cardinal silk; a large and gorgeous crown on her head, surrounded by a silver aureole. The platform on which she stood was bright with valuable trophies and lovely flowers. Priests, gaudy as Chinese mandarins, marched on either side; and first behind the Virgin was the presiding bishop, arrayed in cardinal and gold, his hands folded in prayer, his eyes raised to the clouds. Four acolytes held up his train, into which women cast sweet-smelling flowers.

After the bishop came a band, and after the band what was called "the procession of the virgins," apparently all the girls of the town in white dresses, bearing flowers and lighted candles in their hands. Then the motley candle-bearers came—not a little band by any means; they were in pairs, and nearly half a mile long.

I have little inventive genius, but if I could invent "an economic candle," or one "warranted not to go out throughout the longest religious ceremony," I should make fortune and fame right away. I have seen enough grease run to waste in Spain to send this old orb of ours into space, if it could only be placed within a league of its axis.

And then the bad language that bad candles provoked! I have heard it, and I know. But perhaps even this is no misfortune for the priests.

Taken as a pageant, this procession ranks high. It is faultless in detail, and the remarkable feature is that all the actors and audience appear sincere. This procession of the virgins is not a travesty on some old-time custom; it is the old-time custom itself, brought down with all its original notions to this very day.

Here wave banners which were borne aloft before the centuries of our era were in their teens—sceptres which in former days caused vanity to grow into valour and lay down its little life on many a bloody field. This show is not merely a day's delight; it is a long page of history brought into convenient and attractive limits, and I for one could stand the like of it often and not tire.

Illuminations, bonfires, and fireworks wind up every Spanish show; and what a splendid fact it is that the people can go through all this excitement without getting drunk. A Spaniard drinks when he is thirsty; he is sensible enough only to sip, and that shyly, when he is not. If they didn't swear they would be the finest "crowd" in the world.

They use bad language—*very* bad language. It is not the sort of utterance that at times almost improves and dignifies an Englishman's remarks: it is low, filthy speech, not spoken in anger or contempt, but for the mere sake of saying it.

I was accosted in the street by a man who wanted to know if I was "the fellow he had read about." How could I tell who he had or had not read about? But it turned out I was "the fellow," and that a fellow-countryman was sojourning in Ciudad-Real. We met—we embraced each other. Spanish may be "the language of the gods," but the arrogant Englishman sticks fast to his own little language, and loves it dearly. There is nothing like a language for opening up and blending the sympathies of various members of the human family.

The men whom we like best are those who come nearest to ourselves. We are never quite close to those whom we cannot fully understand.

My new friend—my gratitude to him for the pleasant hours he afforded me compels me to record his name, Joseph O'Farrell—pressed me to put up at the "Fonda Pissarossa" (the leading hotel), and enjoy the current luxuries of the town.

I did not decline to do so. A clean bed, quiet, good food, and agreeable society are scarce items on a tramp's programme.

Have you ever noticed that they are usually thin men who sit late at table? I have, often—so often that I have but little respect for the fat porpoises who strut away early with a toothpick between their teeth, preferring a *tête-à-tête* with the maid in the passage to the story of the nations which may be served up after the last bottle has gone round. It may sound "big" to say "the story of the nations," but who is able to maintain that any place has never helped to swell the flood of history?

Ciudad-Real is a hotbed of old soldiers. They have but few clubs, but they meet regularly at the "Fonda Pissarossa," discuss their pet theories, and abuse the powers that be.

These ancient warriors admitted me to their round table, and I felt honoured to sit amongst them. They welcomed me because I was a curiosity, because, to use a favourite Spanish word, I was "caprichios." But they approved of me less when I ventured to pronounce an opinion on their country. One bluff old chap, a retired colonel of engineers, told me coolly that I knew nothing about Spain! I did not resent his candour. I am ever a student—I will listen to any man who offers to teach me. The irate Colonel went on, "It is easy for you travelling penny-a-liners to say what we are and what we are not, but to what end and purpose do you prattle and complain? Let us be fair. We ask you for nothing. Do not rob us of what we have now—the greatest thing in the world!" "What is that?" I asked. "*Peace*," answered the Colonel.

This remark gave me my cue for action, and we went off into a long talk on the subject of the conflicts Spain had waged in order to secure this blessed peace.

We agreed that Spain was not worth fighting for, and that being hard bound by natural conditions she could never advance and keep pace with the rest of the world. (This is in great measure true.)

Then, having pacified the old warrior by the adoption of all his opinions, I bade him good-night and went off to the Teatro Verano. I did not enjoy the performance, for the actors could neither play nor sing ; but a Spanish crowd is always entertaining, and, being fair time, there was a full house.

Ciudad-Real boasts nothing of importance in the way of old houses or churches. The Cathedral is small, modern, and bare. You may enjoy being reminded that "Tirteafuera,"—the birthplace of the priest who baptised Sancho Panza,—is within sight of Ciudad-Real.

I was introduced to the Canon, a fine-looking man, with a " fair round belly with good capon lined," and a rich manly voice. The cardinal cross displayed on the left breast of his flowing robe shows him to be one of the military knights of Almagro (of the old order of Calatrava). He welcomed me graciously. And so I had rambled so far without any certainty that I should benefit ? I replied that wherever my fellows are there is always interest and benefit for me. Some of the good and wise stay at home in shady, retired places, and these I love to discover.

" True," said the Canon ; " he who would know the world must go out of it as well as into it. We can only see things at a distance. The light must come between the object and the eye or it will only blind us. People who live always in the world know nothing about it, because they have never been sufficiently far off to see things as they are."

The Canon loves the English, on account of the riches they have given to his library. Shakespeare, Milton, Bacon, and Ben Jonson are his intimate friends. He delights in Bulwer, Dickens, and Thackeray, and considers Jane Austen, the Brontë sisters, and George Eliot the greatest women of genius in the history of the world. But his idol is Byron.

"The English are too near the North Pole to catch the heat and fire of his poetry. Only those who know the scenes and subjects he depicts can appreciate their marvellous fidelity. Even his objectionable passages are the greatest and gravest of facts."

The Canon lives very near to the real world, in spite of being chained to dreamy old Ciudad-Real. Like Emerson, he does not "build his castle high." He "embraces the common," "sits at the feet of the familiar and the low," and finds the simplest fact in nature an important part of the great whole.

On parting he commended Valdes (A. P.) to my attention, assuring me that I should read him with advantage, no matter where my hopes or feet may trend.

At the southern gate of the city I was able to look

on the battlefield of Los Arcos. It was a great day for the peninsula when that battle was fought; for the Moors laid forty-eight thousand Spaniards to rest in seven hours, and hoisted their standards on all the most valuable lands of Spain. The memory of that and many another great defeat will never cease to fill the Spaniard with hatred for " his eternal enemy," the dusky Moor.

My hospitable fellow-countryman filled my satchel with a store of good things, and, followed by the good wishes of as kind a heart as ever beat beneath an English waistcoat, I set out in search of fresh conquests.

CHAPTER XI.

OLD AND NEW CASTILE.

IN DON QUIXOTE'S COUNTRY.—LA MANCHA.—VALDEPEÑAS.—
ALMAGRO, THE LAND OF VINEYARDS.—A SPANISH FAIR.—
BOLAÑOS AND ITS SUBTERRANEAN DWELLINGS.—MANZA-
NARES : A GENEROUS RECEPTION.—ARGAMASILLA.—CER-
VANTES' PRISON.—THE CASTLE OF PENNAROYA AND MY DAY-
DREAM.—THE LONG VALLEY.—THE BATAÑES.

MY route lay across olive groves and vineyards.
I had reached the plain of Valdepeñas, the
famous wine district of La Mancha. It was an
extraordinary sight. Looking in all directions, the
eye met nothing but an unbroken stretch of vines.
All the plants were in full bearing ; big luscious
white grapes, little black bullety things, and fine
varieties of muscatel,—all were there. The soil is
a light red calcareous, over a shingle bed many feet
deep. Water can be drawn from any part of this
vast plain ; but as the vines do well without artificial supply no irrigation is required, and wells are
infrequent. It was dark before I struck a neglected

hut by the track side (there are no roads in any part of this great plain). Here I camped, and the next morning went on to swell the tramp population of Almagro.

It was fair time (it seems to be always fair or feast time in Spain), and I, being an independent tramp, went to the fair. I have seen so many that I seem to have placed myself under the obligation of saying something about one of them. The "feria" of Almagro is considered one of the largest and most picturesque in all the Castiles.

It is everywhere famous for the enormous number of mules and donkeys which are brought for sale. These being owned by gipsy dealers and by that peculiar population which haunt the Montes de Toledo and Sierra Morena, bring all the variety of colour and contrast which makes a country gathering in Spain so quaint and delightful.

The principal "calle" is the site of the fair. There are stalls, penny wonders, shooting and gambling saloons, much as we see in our own villages. The local industries are well worth looking at. I saw excellent copper and brass ware, cutlery, and silk garments. Almagro is also justly famous for its lace-making establishments and the quality of the material.

The "churro" stalls were thronged with customers.

This is a fine unsweetened batter, forced through a tube into boiling oil, which swells it to the size of a Bologna sausage.

The Spanish can enjoy no gathering without their "churro." It is licked and admired by large-eyed, open-mouthed children, carried round by mothers and fathers as a delight for those at home, or served up in little rush baskets to those who make a feast of the fair.

This dainty is served out by showily-dressed girls, who seem to win more attention than any other saleswomen.

A big trade is also done in hair. The dealers give two to four pesetas per ounce for good black hair, which they sell at treble the amount. The light colours are dearer. It was interesting to watch the girls with " their season's crop," all finely plaited and adorned with a score of showy ribbons, hawking the growing tresses to the different dealers. Satisfied with the offer, the scissors were applied, and a showy handkerchief clapped over the head kept the girl a beauty still.

Roulette tables were laid down in every corner, and the quarrelling and wrangling were at least audible! I was pestered to buy castanets by a girl who played them in my ears, and I was humbugged by scores of tramps and maimed and halt beggars, who did not seem to realise that I was a brother vagrant and one of themselves; but, best of all, I was taken for a *toreador*. To be compared to one of those gaily dressed and graceful forms is a compliment not to be despised, and I made up my mind on the spot to assume henceforth the toreador strut! A Mexican *Espada* had been announced for the bull-fight, and I, being the most foreign-looking individual in the show, was taken for that celebrity.

The plaza of Almagro is worth looking at. This is not a square, but a long open space two hundred yards by fifty, paved with enormous stones, and surrounded by peculiar old three-storey houses with projecting balconies, from which dangled green blinds and odd garments placed to dry.

Down the centre ran rows of umbrella tents, piled with pottery, glass, and chinaware. Tons of rock and water melons were placed at intervals, and coarse-throated men and women were yelling and bawling the merits of their wares. Under little awnings men and boys were beating out on anvils fixed before them all kinds of iron pots and pans. The noise was hideous: and consider—it never ceases! Who would choose to live in the plaza of Almagro? Whatever is in season is vended here every day of the year. The pots and pans and other hardy annuals are always in season, and never leave the plaza till they are sold.

They roll everything out at these fairs. Sacred dramas and bull-fights always go together. Then there is vending of corn, and wine, and oil, and crowding of mules, and donkeys, and goats, and pigs into every "calle," and all the country folk round coming in odd, and picturesque, and ridiculous clothing,—and Almagro itself with its mediæval plaza and customs ; all these varied elements make its fair time rich and interesting. Wherever there are fairs or "toros" I fare badly ! The biggest-hearted alcalde will not give up his annual feast to sit in the town hall for the mere sake of dealing out tickets and compliments to sturdy beggars.

Almagro had cost me several pence, and I was still without a place to lay my head. Cold floors under any roof would be at a premium on such a night, and the gipsies, who were there by hundreds with their dogs and fleas, would monopolise all the open-air quarters. I determined to sleep that night at Bolaños, which was but fifteen miles away. On the road I met a gipsy sitting beside a well and making lace.

I watched her busy fingers while she ran out a yard or two, and then I bought the piece for fivepence.

Bolaños is a small clean village, which, like most of the tidy poor, professes to have "seen better days." It boasts a ruined castle, a church without windows, and some curious subterranean Roman dwellings, which have been inhabited for two thousand years by the successive occupants of Spain. These little beaver-like mounds, rising from a perfectly flat plain and emitting little columns of smoke, have a most singular appearance.

There are two communities here, the cave dwellers, and the villagers living in decent stone houses with girls sitting at every door working at lacemaking. I slept at the posada, and started early the next morning, still surrounded by the green sea of grape vines. The sun was scorching, and I found little water to refresh my way. Night came upon me when I was still surrounded by the interminable fields of green.

It was soon pitch dark, and no house in sight. I soon got off the narrow track leading between the vines, and blundered on mile after mile, quite uncertain as to the direction in which I was moving. I decided to sleep among the vines. I had just unrolled my bundle and prepared to stretch out when a dog barked, and betrayed the presence of a vine-dresser's hut. I made for it, but the owner was a surly brute. He told me there was plenty of room on the plain, and on the plain I slept.

On waking I saw before me the town of Manzanares. It was but four miles away, and, refreshed by the cool morning air, I soon put that distance behind me, and got into the old plaza just as the stalls and their contents were being hidden away and their owners were crowding into the great church to hear mass. Whilst I was taking a rest and writing up a few notes in the plaza, a tall, good-looking priest came along, and without asking me the nature of my mission, nationality, or creed, he threw me *a penny!* I took it! I could not thank him, but I shall remember the rich benevolence of that man's face for many a day.

At the "Casa Consistorial" the powers were wondrous kind. The Ciudad-Real newspapers had informed them of my existence, and they all agreed that I was worth supporting. I did not attempt to deny it! A new world seemed to open. People were not merely curious, they were generous, and all day I was invited hither and thither and richly entertained. One man insisted on putting me up at the posada, and the mayor gave me letters of introduction to the alcalde of Argamasilla de Alba, whither I was bound.

Manzanares is a small compact little place, which manages to squeeze in a population of sixteen thousand souls. Before leaving, I visited the great "cuevas" (cellars) of Messrs. Jimenez and Lamothe, and saw the rich juice trodden out by men's feet from the tons of grapes hourly poured on the great floors. One cellar owns nineteen enormous pipes, eighteen feet by fourteen, each containing thirty-six thousand litres. In another cellar are thirty-six clay jars, each holding one thousand two hundred gallons of wine. Throughout this vast establishment, the most primitive methods of wine-making exist side by side with the most modern inventions. Brandy distilleries, a chemical laboratory, and the electric light are found here.

Woe betide the tramp who puts his confidence in the man who shows him the " short cut."

It is only twenty-six miles from Manzanares to Argamasilla, but I went round by the " short cut," and got there in thirty-nine ! Such experiences are of little use. I confess that I was able to express myself in Spanish in a clearer and more voluble manner than ever before, but the words were of a decidedly common order, and only suited to such occasions. I think they would look somewhat out of place here. Thirty-nine miles through the great vineyard, with only grapes for food, no water, and a sweating sun, sent me a mere crawler into the very first posada of Argamasilla. I was almost too tired to take anything, but after I had managed to eat some bread and eggs and drink a good jug of wine, I stretched out on the hard floor and slept for thirteen hours before I awoke ; and then it was not a fair wake, for the people of the posada made such a stir around me that I "came to" before I was properly refreshed.

A white elephant would not be a much greater novelty than an Englishman in Argamasilla. Half the population accompanied me with my letter of introduction to the mayor's house. After partaking of his hospitality we set out to visit the prison of Cervantes. It stands in the "calle" bearing his name —an ordinary two-storey brick house, with nothing of the prison about it. But as it possessed the only cellar in which a criminal could be safely incarcerated, the honour of holding Cervantes captive fell to its lot. Argamasilla cherishes the memory of Cervantes as Stratford does that of the immortal Will. Although not daring enough to claim it to be his birthplace, it omits no incident of the old soldier's life. All his career, even his fighting at the battle of Lepanto, occurred here—in this very cellar, if I am to believe the local story. But I decline. As a matter of fact, Cervantes passed but a very short time here. The opening sentence of " Don Quixote " shows that it was in this narrow cell that he conceived the character of the immortal Don, and wrote his earliest exploits. But the greater part of the story was written after the author had regained his liberty.

The cause of his incarceration is still a disputed point in this hotbed of Cervantine criticism. According to the most trustworthy tradition, Cervantes came from Madrid to collect the king's tax—an odious exaction which all endeavoured to resist. The mayor, incensed by his importunity, charged him with the embezzlement of the moneys collected, and it was on this count—now believed to be groundless—that Cervantes was thrown into the dark cellar which has shed so much smiling light over the romantic land of Spain.

From the small entrance hall five steps lead down to this long narrow cellar—thirty feet by nine, and seven feet four inches from floor to ceiling. A tiny oriel-shaped hole admits a faint ray of light from the entrance hall. There was once a second light hole in the opposite wall, but there is no evidence to prove that it admitted light in Cervantes' day. There is now a second cellar adjoining, but this is quite modern. Part of the original door, well protected with iron clamps, is likely to enjoy many more years in its honoured position. At the back part of the house can be seen the window where the first chapters of " Don Quixote " were thrown by the prisoner's guard to those who waited below. The house, which is fast tottering to decay, is used as a dwelling and shop by a shoemaker. It is also the post-office:

letters slipped into a square hole in the wall fall into a box in the cellar. It is unfortunate that no effort is made to preserve this house, which has as much claim to protection against the ravages of time as any in the land.

At the old church, whose ruinous state leads one to infer that people here are not over fond of worship, are two or three old paintings, reminding one of the illustrations of the "Don" and the "Licentiate." (It is generally accepted in Spain that Cervantes drew his great character from the Mayor of Argamasilla.) There is, in fact, an oil painting of the mayor who caused Cervantes to be imprisoned, which is reproduced in the Spanish imperial edition, printed at Barcelona 1851-1852, and copied into most of the illustrated English editions.

Spanish pilgrims to the cellar prison are almost unknown.

True the town has no attractions. Seen from the broad and, save for the grape, bare plain of La Mancha, it is a rude, uninviting place. But I must not forget the hospitable nature of its inhabitants!

I lunched, dined, sipped, and supped with them in the space of a few hours, and the Mayor, ex-Mayor, and other dignitaries walked out of the little town and put me on the right road for the Castle of Pennaroya.

The weather was threatening, but a self-respecting

tramp never stops at threats; and who, not being a tramp, can feel sure that it is wiser and safer to stand still than to go on? The rain did come, and the thunder and lightning made merry at the loneliness and helplessness of my position; but with fresh interests just ahead I felt half indifferent to the force of the storm.

I took shelter in a solitary house with a lot of children who had been picking grapes for the wine press.

Whenever the lightning flashed they crossed themselves and said, "Protect me, Mary, Mother of God," with very pretty simplicity. It grew dark before the storm had ceased, and my castle was still far away. The track leading to it, hardly discernible by daylight, could not be seen at all. The owner of the cottage kindly pressed me to stay the night, but I determined to go on.

It was a hideous walk—an up-and-down journey over rocky mounds and down into little basins filled knee-deep with the storm water.

Trusting to the long grass growing in the marshy bed of a little valley, I endeavoured to cross; but I got bogged in the centre, and for a long time found it impossible to extricate myself. This was La Mancha!—the land of Quixote!—surely yes! None but fools and dreamers would venture here. I told myself that I was a more harebrained clown than he whom Cervantes drew so largely and yet so well !

Of course I went the way of all flesh ! There was no help for it. I reviled everything pertaining to Spanish romance ; and well I might. I was plastered with mud from top to toe, and it was not sweet mud either.

After an hour's trudge I came to a deep gorge. This raised my hopes, as Pennaroya is said to be on the confines of a gorge. I picked my way along a winding path by pools of black, turgid, uncanny-looking water, surrounded by sighing rushes and bounded by steep rocky walls. At times the path narrowed, and I was obliged to creep warily under the overhanging cliff to avoid slipping into the water. At others it crossed tottering plateaus of spongy bog, which moaned and croaked as I shuffled along, and yawned audibly when I reached the firm shore and left it to itself again.

There was no moon. Dark clouds covered the sky, and here and there between them showed a few leaden-eyed stars. The rain had chilled the air, and there was a " creepy-creepy " covering over everything in sight. Positively lonely as I was, I confess to having the most intense pleasure on realizing my position. The old story that had charmed my boyhood came back with the freshness of yesterday.

I knew that I was actually looking on the valley that had been the delight of many early hours, and that the dream of twenty years was at last changed into solid—though in this twilight questionable—shape.   By-and-bye the grand old castle showed out against the sky line.

It seemed to be almost over me, but I had a long fag before I reached the winding zigzaging path which leads up to it from the valley.   Of the castle gate only two rude piles of stone are left standing. There was nothing to prevent my marching in and taking possession of the central court.

Here I saw the strangest night picture I have seen in Spain, and it set me dreaming.

The moon has risen, and the black veil lying over the land has disappeared.   The high wall, which once connected the two wing towers on the edge of the cliff, is no more, so, standing in this court, I can look down the long valley of the Guadiana, over the lands which tower above it on either side, and away to the line where the river seems to meet the clouds and is borne up in fragments of filmy vapour.

In the strong white light the hills look ghostly and uncertain.   The cork-oaks and other little trees show as bottomless pits scattered over the white ground ; and, wherever high peaks cause long shadows to be thrown, the broad landscape is divided into mimic islands, surrounded by nothing more substantial than yawning chasms.

Perched here many hundred feet above the valley, it seems an easy thing, with the help of the deceptive moonlight, to float off among the lights and shadows of the cliff, and touch lightly down on the silver streak which rests so beautifully still below. I cannot persuade myself that there is no river,—only those little black pools and mud flats, and swaying grasses, bulrushes, and bull-frogs. With the moon the mists have risen and concealed that black ugly bed, and now it is a soft inviting couch, covered with a tapestry of silver grey, restful and sweet to look upon.

The old castle towers which flank the scene rise like gigantic sentinels into the still air, and on one of them an old owl sits and " whoa's " and " whoo-oo's " —melancholy, low—and a rickety belfry sways and creaks in unison with the dismal bird of night. The white, square stones which pave the old yard are stained and embroidered with weedy growths, and many shine like deaths' heads looking up beyond the old walls to the stars above them. " It is in solitude that we are least alone." Every spot is peopled—every object is a human form.

It's always the way! A man can never have his dream out. I had sat myself down on the edge of the cliff, letting my legs dangle over six hundred feet of void space, and had looked up and down the valley and at the old castle and the mopy owl, until I was in love with it all, and felt that I could fall asleep amid its quiet and repose, and then dream it all over again and see how much was truth when morning broke. But it didn't turn out like that :—I made a noise, and a dog up and barked at the intruder.

I looked round, expecting to see an enchantress or a belated Dorothea, but instead, an old man in snowy-white night clothes, and armed with a loaded gun, showed through one of the doorless portals, and demanded an explanation of my presence within his gates. He was not Giant Despair, so I was Hopeful. I told him that I was a pilgrim, and being tired had fallen asleep in his grounds. Then he hauled his old gun down from his shoulder, and bade me come in.

He was the caretaker, and lived with his pretty old wife in two dungeon-like chambers of the castle.

These old folks made a bed for me on the floor, wished me a good night's rest, and left me to go on with my dream.

In the morning I finished my contract with the loaf of bread I had brought from Argamasilla, and then, in company with the old man, went over the castle. Save the little chapel, which is held in high esteem by some local magnates, all is ruin. There are some beautiful gems in a basket on the altar, and a silver effigy of the Virgin, numerous brooches, rings, and scarfpins of value, and some trashy trinkets—without which no Spanish shrine would be complete !

Alas ! with the morning sun the long river and the ghostly islands had disappeared, and nothing was left but a marshy hollow with now and then a sullen pool showing through the green. The witching landscape had vanished—and with it my dream !

Descending into the valley, I tramped the whole day, meeting with nothing worth looking at save the "Batañes" immortalised by Cervantes in his undying story.

These "batañes" are beaters* and troughs into which newly-spun and greasy cloth from the old-fashioned looms is thrown for the purpose of washing out the oil and dirt. Strings of mules and donkeys, laden with cotton and woollen stuffs from the far-off mills of Albacete, deposit their loads here and browse around till the washing and drying are over. They are then reloaded with the clean material and left to pick their way homeward over the hills.

Near the "batañes" are dozens of little clay pits.

* Fulling-hammers. See "Don Quixote," Chap. xx. "The Adventure of the Fulling-Mills."

partly filled with water. The cloth is thrown into these pits and trodden by barelegged workmen into the clay. When thoroughly smeared, the cloth is drawn out and allowed to dry in the sun. The clay, which has absorbed the oil, now peels off, and the cloth is almost clean. By way of a finishing touch it is now placed in the " batañes," " dumped " for five or six hours, then re-dried, rolled, and placed on the mules' backs, ready for the warehouses of Albacete.

The "batañes" consist of long troughs made of very thick, strong wood. These troughs are fixed side by side (from two to twelve in number) over a pit similar to that made for a water-wheel. Throughout the length of this pit a large spindle, carrying as many wheels as there are water-troughs, revolves by means of water falling on powerful wheels at each end. Over the troughs stands a kind of gallows (two uprights and a cross beam), whence depends a shaft connected with a transverse piece resembling the head of a hammer. This hammer, which is forced backwards and forwards by the revolving wheel, draws in from the stream at every blow three or four feet of cloth and " dumps " it against the end of the trough. By this means the dirt and ravellings are pressed out and the cloth freed from all impurity.

I sat beside many of these "batañes," and was rocked and splashed in turn by the jolting beams and spluttering water-troughs. Maidenhair fern and other shade- and moisture-loving plants almost hide the substructure of some of the old works. Belts of lilacs, poplar, fig trees, and wild vines confine the scene. The simple fellows who conduct the industry are so primitive in their dress, and so limited in speech, that one can readily believe no change has taken place since the day of Cervantes.

CHAPTER XII.

OLD AND NEW CASTILE (*continued*).
DON QUIXOTE'S COUNTRY.

JULIEN, THE RURAL GUARD.—A PRIMITIVE SUPPER TABLE.—
THE CASCADE OF LUNAMONTES AND RUDIERA.—THE LAKE
DEL REY.—MINE HOST PACO.—A JOVIAL EVENING.—ANGEL'S
SONG.—MY GUIDE AND HIS DONKEY.—THE LAKES OF
RUDIERA.—THE CAVE OF MONTESINOS.—A DANGEROUS EX-
PEDITION.—ST. PARTRIDGE'S DAY.—MY LAST LOOK AT OLD
PENNAROYA.—I AM HOSPITABLY ENTERTAINED AT ARGAMA-
SILLA.—MANZANARES WELCOMES ME BACK.—CONSOLATION.
— VALDEPEÑAS.—THE MARKET-PLACE.—THE SIERRA MORENA.
—FAREWELL TO CASTILE.

THE Mayor of Argamasilla had given me a
letter to a rural guard living in this valley,
directing him to entertain me for the night and to
conduct me to the Lakes of Rudiera and the cave
of Montesinos. The guard was not at home, but
his sweet young wife bade me enter and await the
return of "Julien." He soon arrived, accompanied
by some fellows who had been out rabbit and
partridge shooting. They brought home a good bag,

and while " Dolores " prepared a giant dish of the lately deceased rabbits for the hungry hunters we sat drinking aquardiente and smoking cigarettes outside the house.

The party was augmented by a couple of " guardias civiles," and we were soon seated round an enormous bowl filled with rabbits, partridges, strips of bacon, and tomatoes. There was not a vestige of a knife, fork, or cloth. A huge loaf of bread and a big skin of wine lay beside the bowl, and each in turn " whacked " off a piece of bread, dipped it into the bowl of meat and tomatoes, and " wetted " his throat from the wine-skin without further ceremony. I wanted food badly, for I had tasted nothing since morning. My kindly hosts seemed eager to give me of their best, and I passed a pleasant evening listening to tales of sport and local news.

The next morning Julien and I set out for the great cascade of Lunamontes and Rudiera. For an hour or two we walked up the narrow valley past batañes and cornmills, till we reached a place where the hills closed in on either side. Here stood some old masonry, showing the remains of walls and vast cellars below the ground level. Julien could tell me nothing about them, save that a certain Infanta had made a journey from Madrid to see these simple ruins. Shortly after leaving them the cascade appeared before us, and a beautiful sight it was. The valley of the Guadiana is fully a quarter of a mile wide at Rudiera, and, running across it from cliff to cliff, is a natural bar of ironstone and sandstone between forty and fifty feet high, which, damming up the waters above and forming the Lake del Rey, produces one of the most exquisite cascades that can be imagined.

Being summer time the flood was not great, but the little torrents and falls of snowy foam, showing here and there between the fern-clad cliffs, and gleaming through the branches of the tiny fig trees and other green growths scattered along the ridge, produce a lovely soft picture which is worth a little pilgrimage to see.

In the centre the water dashes through a rift, worn eight or ten feet deep in the rock, with such force that it takes a clear leap into space and falls, a boiling, seething mass, into a basin fifty feet below. Sitting on the cliff above we distinctly felt the vibration caused by the falling water. It was, for Spain, an unusual scene. The Lake del Rey opens out to more than a mile in width, and shows clear and beautiful for a couple of miles up the valley. In the clear water the hills are reflected in softer, prettier colours than they really wear, and the filmy fragments of cloud floating overhead are seen resting on the great blue sky which seems to form the bed of the lake. The little hamlet and tall palace of Rudiera were perched in a sandbank to our right, and away below, in the long valley we had lately traversed, loomed the rich streak of green betraying the subterranean course of the Guadiana.

This extraordinary river occasionally sinks completely out of sight, taking an underground course for many miles, and then reappearing as a strong flowing stream. A Spaniard usually appears indifferent to the charms of nature, but Julien was fully alive to the beauty of the scene. "It is without fault," he said proudly.

We gathered fern fronds, flowers, and scented leaves, damp mosses from between the crags in the ridge, and then walked slowly back to the little old hamlet, which appears to crouch submissively at the foot of the palace. All the gunpowder used by the ancient kingdoms of Castile used to be made in this out-of-the-way place. The waters of the Lake del Rey worked " polveros " (powder mills) in Rudiera, and the palace was inhabited by a high military official, who directed the manufacture of the gunpowder.

The old mills still stand, but instead of mingling that "villainous salt petre" and its allies, the villagers grow fruit and vegetables within the walls. Arrived at the only posada of the place, Julien handed me over to the host, with directions to guide me safely to Montesinos, and to put me up while in the district. This was welcome news. When I carry a letter of recommendation I cannot be sure whether the contents are favourable or not, but these notes from Manzanares and Argamasilla are lifting me out of my tramp's position, and making of me a tripping tourist!

I wanted to start at once for the cave; but Paco, my new mentor, had no guide at hand, so I had to wait till the morrow. I passed the early part of the afternoon on the edge of the lake watching its constantly changing beauties, and, later, I joined a party of sportsmen, composed of the two "guardias civiles" who had come up from Julien's house and a couple of engineers who were taking the levels of the different lakes.

My name being decreed unpronounceable I was dubbed *Quixote*! and, though trusted with a gun, every one of my fellow-sportsmen kept at a very respectful distance from me. We had plenty of work and not much luck, and on returning to the posada we dined together, and spent the evening right merrily.

The younger engineer, Angel Candelas, was a splendid-looking fellow, tall, well-made, a handsome face, glossy black curls, and great, melting eyes. Moreover, he had an excellent voice. When the last dish had vanished Angel called for a guitar, and after twanging and thrumming it for a few seconds he sang to his own accompaniment the following song, which I roughly translate :—

ANGEL'S SONG.

" Night's breeze, dawn's glow, or evening's chill,
    May change this flower of love, but cannot kill
    An immortelle.   No frosts nor blasts can stay
    Its growth, nor sharpest blade its beauties take away.

" By all the world adored, despised, maligned,
    All powerful for awhile, by all resigned,
    This I must hear, but cannot prove,
    For by my joy I live, and all my joy is love.

" Come, bend thee,*—list!   For though my song is old,
    My heart is young, and in its purpose bold ;
    From me thou wilt not learn that love's a lie :
    My heaven thou art—the world for which I sigh."

Every word came from the heart of the singer, for he was in love. He had confessed to me during a few moments when we were thrown together whilst rabbit-shooting out on the wold, that he hoped soon

* "Come, bend thee " is an appropriate appeal in Spain, as serenaders woo their loves from the street, and the fair ones must bend from their balconies to catch the sweet whisperings of their " Angels."

to marry a beauty from the Guadarama. Apart from his passion, Rudiera might have seemed a sorry place ; but love peopled it with visions which were a thousand times fairer than the eddies of crystal water babbling round it.

The sergeant (guardia civil), who scorned all sentimental singing, tried to break the spell Angel had cast over us, by thumping on the table with his fists and roaring out a comic ditty, highly diverting to those who understood Spanish idioms and subtleties—which I did not.

Then I asked Don Luis, the old engineer, for a song, little thinking of the turn his talents took in that direction, for his face was rather grim and pessimistic ; but when he had puffed to the end of a cigarette, looked into all corners of the room to make sure of his audience, and ordered Demetria, the domestic, to bring in more wine, he ran his fingers very softly on the strings, gave the old instrument a friendly hug, and sang to a plaintive air this song :—

DON LUIS' SONG.

" In youth came a wondrous longing for a something distant far,
It spoke of the word ' ambition,' of a ' goal,' and ' hickory-star,
And I thought as a child to follow up—up to the source of
　　light—
Would bring me a golden harvest of knowledge pure and
　　bright.

"Then I dreamed of love and living for one who crossed my
 way,
And I felt that man's 'great ambition *is woman's heart to
 sway;*
So for *her* did I breast the current of life so wild and strong,
But the love of my youth has left me,—there is nought en-
 dureth long!

"Now the night is closing round me, and the death winds, chilly
 and wild,
Proclaim the end of the journey, and laugh at the dreams of
 the child,
Am I forced to the sad conclusion,—that all our hopes are
 but dreams,
And the brightest joy we inherit is but as the rainbow's gleams,

"Which come between the shadows and storms of a long, long
 day,
Giving birth to hopes that will never come true, in our wished-
 for way.
There is nought but loving and losing—I have proved it near
 and far ;
There is nothing left but music, no friend save this old guitar."

I would gladly have reproduced a brighter theme
than this, but I must deal with things as I find them.
Doubtless Don Luis experienced a kind of happiness
over his regrets; I feel sure he did, for, as Angel
afterwards informed me, the old man was always
at his best for a day or two after giving vent to his
favourite song.

Between the singing and playing of the two
engineers and the "sergeant," old Paco, the host,

chipped in with snatches of Gitanescos and Sevillanos, till, having proved himself a singer, he was forced to give us a series of short couplets, all telling of the old, old, and universal story.

His post was no sinecure, for, standing in the doorway, he had to divide his time between singing, applauding, and giving directions to the servants in the kitchen.

He was a real country host, fit for a Hogarth or a Rembrandt to portray. Unlike the ordinary Spaniard, he had a very red face, which was also unusually round and flat. He wore over corduroy trousers a bull-fighter's jacket of blue cloth, tastefully faced with scalloped goatskin. A black faja partly covered a clean white shirt-front, and from his narrow collar hung a mere line of emerald-green silk. His merry, good-natured face gave courage to the peeping, half-shy Demetria, who awaited orders by his side.

This local growth in no way resembled the Demetria of stageland: she was only, to keep up the lingo of the stage, a "baggage," wearing her clothes bundled like a life-belt about her hips, and her open bodice revealed a white neck open as her heart to all the winds that blow. This, and a red and yellow striped skirt and short yellow stockings, made up her costume. Her jet-black hair was coiled in heavy rolls round the sides of her head, her eyes were black, half-wild, half-shy in expression, and her hands "beautiful as May." Spanish women possess the mysterious art of keeping their hands soft and white while doing the roughest work. Demetria sometimes leaned on Paco's arm, which was stretched across the doorway, and seemed to regard him more as a father than a master. Such is generally the case in Spain : there is very great respect but no distinction. The poor expect the same attention as the rich and powerful, and they usually get it.

Between songs, and stories, and much puffing of cigarettes, the evening passed quickly away, and after partaking of a peculiar local dish composed of breadcrumbs, chopped raisins, and sugar, fried in olive oil, we bade each other good-night.

At daybreak, an old man, Solanos by name, came to offer himself as guide to the Cueva of Montesinos. The magic of the word made me wide awake at once, and I was soon dressed and at the door. Solanos had provided himself with a strong and almost jet-black donkey, very appropriately named "Carbonero." As for myself, I had to use "shanks' pony." But what of that? The charm of the journey would outweigh every discomfort. I was treading hallowed ground,—ground peopled, glorified, and idealised by the greatest master of Spanish romance and song. When I thought over the past night, I grew baffled and uncertain as to how much was fact, how much fiction. My new experiences seemed more extravagant than the old diversions attributed to the place, and I walked on as one in a delicious dream.

My guide was a dear old fellow, with a mop of bristling white hair falling over a smiling, sheepish face. He wore a blue shirt, short black jacket, blue knickerbockers, white cotton stockings, and a red handkerchief round his head. He coaxed and *persuaded* Carbonero to " arrie " (get up !) with a stick almost as big as a clothes-prop.

The journey from Rudiera to Montesinos is about twelve English miles. The road skirts the " Lagunas del Rudiera." There are thirteen of these lakes, three small ones below the cascade of Lunamontes, and the other ten above, all of considerable size and some of indescribable beauty.

It is a daring statement that " the world is full of song." It may be nearer the truth to say it is full of beauty, but we know it is not. Nevertheless, these lakes of Rudiera form one of the most lovely and impressive pictures in the world. One must be careful to avoid bias in Spain. A little luxury is very apt to go a long way. Spain, as a whole, is ungenerous, ugly, churlish, brutalising ; and he who sees it in its fulness, remembers few natural glories.

The lakes of Rudiera are a splendid exception.

The short day spent wandering on their shores, gazing on the encompassing hills, drinking in the sweet, pure air, and gloating over the delicious pictures, will never fade from my memory.

The first lake, "Del Rey," is much larger than the others. It is shaped like a Y, and a low ridge of rocks, which cross it at the junction of its three arms, divides the ancient kingdom of Castile from Albacete. As we trudged along its banks we met a few peasants, more showily dressed than any I had seen before.

At a "batañe" by a rushing stream, which ended its bustling little life in the clear lake, two or three women showed as bright as a May meadow: all stripes and strips and splashes of colour from head to foot. Domestic, clean, and shy, they were pretty accessories to the lake shore.

As we advanced, the hills reared to the height of mountains. We passed batanes and corn mills, surrounded by wild vines, and hedged in with belts of poplar and fig-trees. Our path lay along strips of narrow shoreland, covered with rushes and other aquatic growths. Here and there a nook was turned into a primitive garden for water-melons and corn.

Noisy, yelping boys, high up among the rocks, were gathering "esparto" grass, or tending herds of red goats wearing bells which clang and clatter down the valleys and around the sharp peaks and spurs, till distance softens them to sweet musical notes. The water of the lakes is faultlessly clear. Any dark object thrown in can be watched falling, down, down, down, till it appears a mere atom resting on the white pipe-clay bed. A stone no larger than a horse bean was distinctly visible in fifty-six measured feet of water.

As the hills closed in and we traversed mere ledges jutting out over the water, the scene became extremely grand. The hills are of sandstone and pierced with fantastically distorted bands of iron. The winds and storms of ages have fretted away all the sandstone where it has been exposed, and the ironstone rusted and softened by the elements has become as vari-coloured as an artist's palette.

Bands and splashes of chocolate, yellow, and ferruginous red, fleck the giant walls, and the brilliant hues are faithfully reflected in the still waters below.

Lake Redondilla is the gem of all. It is about three-quarters of a mile long, and sharp turns in the valley shut it in by its beautiful self alone.

The waters have treated the shore as the winds and rains have served the rocks above. The soft sand has been laved and licked away by the kiss-kiss of the pure waves, and the entire circumference of the lake changed to a magnificent piece of fret-work.

Imagine a wall twenty feet high, honeycombed, wormeaten, waterworn into a ravishing circle of embroidery. It bears more resemblance to a splendid wall of coral; but here there is more daring treatment, more diversity of design, more superb colouring, and it is surrounded by more seductive waters than those which wash the shores of the coral islands. To see this lake in its wondrous home is to see the perfection of nature undisturbed. The rocky platform, along which we passed, projects forty or fifty feet from the cliffs on either shore. It is undermined by the lake, and here and there are holes through which one sees the water below showing green and wavy as it trembles in the soft shadow thrown by the rocks above.

The wild outline of hills, the brilliant colouring, the clear skies, the pure air and sweetness of all around, combine to make the rocky shore of Lake Redondilla one of the most heavenly resting-places I have yet encountered.

Old Solanos, born and bred among these scenes, failed to understand what charm they could possess for one who had seen other lands.

I could have lingered a life away by this enchanting lake; but other and more famous places were beckoning me on.

At the head of the last lake stands the ancient

village of San Pedro de Martel, which boasts two old corn mills, a "batañc," and eleven houses all told. The population consists of about twenty men, women, and children, and a dozen donkeys. There is neither church, cura, schoolhouse, store, nor wineshop—not even a venta where donkeys may be fitted with shoes, so that it may be said to be a quiet place, not much given to politics or reform, or likely to cause much trouble to my host Julien, the rural guard.

The lakes *above* Rudiera are :—

Del Rey.	Lingua.
Colgada.	Redondilla.
Batanes.	Seneca.
Santa Marthiana.	Conseca.
Salvadora	Blanca, or San Pedro.

Below :—

Cueva Mounella.	Collayo.
Thesapho.	

Lake Blanca gives place to a green valley or morass where the source of the Guadiana takes its rise. A faint track forms the donkey road from San Pedro to Albacete.

About a mile along this track, and then another mile off to the left over an open heath, lies the cave of Montesinos. Solanos and I found it without much trouble, though no one accustomed to cave hunting or exploring would dream of looking for a cave in such a place. The rocks around are of a hard iron-stone composition, and show no signs of having been disturbed by any volcanic force.

The cave is entered by a large hole on the side of a slight depression on the open heath.

It is about twenty-five feet across the mouth of the cave, and, on looking down, a deep, black shaft with perpendicular sides became visible. I had brought a line with me, but this was not necessary, for the projecting rocks render it possible, though somewhat dangerous, to get down to a platform some forty feet from the surface. The daylight falling on a part of this platform is thrown back into a large chamber which opens to the left as one descends, showing dull red stone sides streaked with lime. This is the only part of the cave which resembles the description given by Cervantes. But the fact that he places the chamber on the *right* and not on the left, and that he is wide of the mark with regard to the geographical position of the cave, leads me to believe that Cervantes never saw the place himself, and described it on the strength of hearsay. Coming back to the ledge a great eerie cavern yawned below, and on throwing a few stones they bounded over an incline of wet slippery rocks, and then splashed into water which gave off deep and chilling sounds.

By the aid of a candle I managed to scramble on to the slippery incline, and holding on to the rocky projections let myself down backwards for about a hundred feet.

Solanos was afraid to accompany me, so I had to make the survey alone. As the angle of my descent removed me from the mouth of the cave the daylight was cut off, but I was compensated by finding the grade easier. Leaving the wall, I walked to the centre of the cavern and lighted some paper in order to view the formation. It was all ironstone. Below me, huge rocks were piled and jammed against each other, and between them black motionless pools of icy water. It is here about thirty feet to the roof, and about sixty wide. Climbing over the loose rocks I plunged into a large mound of soft, quaking mud, which stuck to me like glue. Beyond this mud heap the cavern narrows to about twenty feet in width, and under the left wall flows a deep, dark stream. I recognised that my position was a dangerous one, for, were I to slip from the smooth, slanting ledge on which I stood, I should certainly be carried by the water under the opposite wall of rock, and here no power on earth could save me from drowning.

I made no lengthy stay there. Creeping slowly along, I got among loose rocks and stones which fell splash into the water below, at almost every step I took. Perched on a safe retreat, I tied a stone to the line and let it down in the stream. It measured about sixteen feet before touching anything, but if this were the bed of the stream or only a projecting rock I am unable to say. Farther on the cave resembles a coarsely hewn tunnel, nine to fifteen feet wide, and twelve to twenty in height. Bits of wood, twigs forming torches and pieces of charcoal, showed that others had explored the cave, probably the local people. The bed was still composed of huge rocks with the stream flowing beneath.

By dint of much climbing, and jumping, and crawling, I managed to get safely to a little shore of shaly stones, where I rested, for it was hard, hot work. On setting off again I got into the only opening visible, a kind of tube about four feet high and two to three wide. I crawled down this tube for about six hundred feet, and then found myself confronted with a pool of still water, and beyond it a dead wall of water-worn stone.

The bottom of this narrow way was composed of coarse, broken stone, and I feel certain that this was not the true bed at all. The water had probably worn its way down to a lower level, leaving the passage high and dry. I took all possible care to note the length of the various sections, and to see that I overlooked no openings or caves running above the present water level. I cannot be sure, but I believe I have traversed all the Cueva of Montesinos.

It is about four hundred yards in length, and from the bottom of the perpendicular shaft it takes a crescent course, and, as its slowly moving waters show, well-nigh at a dead level. This is the source of the Guadiana, whose waters find their way through the breach in the rocks to the green vale lying before San Pedro de Martel.

I am the first "estrangero" (foreigner) known to have visited the cave. I saw no band of sirens, witches, or goblins, no angel dispensing immortal life, no Merlin to remind me of death. All was cold, clammy, and ghostly, but Don Quixote's band did not appear.

It was a comparatively easy matter to get back to daylight. Beyond the plunge into the mud heap I had suffered no mishap, and I think poor old Solanos suffered more terror than I, although he never saw the inside of the cave. "Carbonero" had been enjoying two hours' rest and the flavour of some Spanish thistle, and Solanos had puffed out the contents of his tobacco box; so both donkey and rider were willing to turn towards home.

The sun was sinking fast, and, by the time we regained San Pedro, had dropped behind the hills

But every now and then, as the valley turned westward, a flood of warm, red light fell upon the sapphire and emerald waters of the lakes. The clear morning air had not revealed all their beauties; at every turn there was some new delight, and the twelve long miles that they might elsewhere have been were gone, and the lakes of Rudiera with them, before I was half tired.

Paco welcomed me back and provided me with much needed food and drink. Then I took leave of my generous host, and, accompanied by Solanos, I returned to Julien's house.

Julien and Dolores entertained me that night, and in the morning sent me off with a good breakfast and the assurance that I was—*faultless!* Would that it were true!

On the way down the valley of the Guadiana I fell in with some sportsmen, who invited me to join them.

It was September 1st, "Saint Partridge's Day." By what strange irony of fate was it decreed that I, a mere tramp, should shoulder a gun and go after partridges on the first day of the season?

It was a pleasant day. There was not much to shoot at, but plenty to eat and drink.

Having bagged a couple of rabbits and three or four doves, it was lunch time.

A fire was made, the rabbits were skinned and cut up, the doves were plucked, and the lot fried in a pan which had been brought for the purpose.

Spanish sportsmen display all the attributes of the true "pot-hunter." They will shoot anyhow and anything, and eat it as soon as possible,— probably fearing that delays are dangerous in hungry Spain.

With the rabbits, doves, tomatoes, melons, and grapes, and an abundance of very good wine, it may be said that we lunched well. Perhaps it was more than a little rough, but not less sweet on that account.

The "hungry hunter" is well known : in this case he was combined with the hungry tramp. Only those who have played both parts at once can know what a delicious thing it is to satisfy the needs of the inner man.

Afterwards we wandered away over the great limitless heaths, getting but half-a-dozen head of game for our pains. Then night began to fall. All but one of the party decided to camp at a hut and resume sport on the morrow.

The other, who turned out to be the veterinary surgeon of Argamasilla, offered me a drive in a little tilted cart behind a good mule. We passed under the cliffs on whose crown rests old Pennaroya. The night mists were gathering round it ; it was just going off to sleep, and we left it to its rest.

At Argamasilla I shared a good dinner with the "vet." and his family, and then was shown to a soft white bed.

In the morning my host gave me a valuable book, and wished me, in the gracious Spanish manner, "felicity through all my days." Words, only words, but oh! how precious and helpful are kindly words none but a homeless vagabond can ever know.

They cheered me during the long, heavy journey to Manzanares, where I was most kindly welcomed back.

Being Saturday night all the clubs and cafés were in full swing. In company with an Englishman, I went the round of them, and saw how lightly Spaniards pass their time. A cigarette, a cup of coffee, a soft seat and a soft companion make their ideal world.

The typical Spaniard is seen in Mazanares. The streets are full of graceful figures, with long, narrow heads, high foreheads, and chins cut to a point. Great black eyebrows, intensifying the flashing black eyes, and the fierce moustache twisting upward from the curled lips, have a fitting companion in the Vandyke beard.

Pale skins, fine even teeth, and beautiful hands

are their common property. But—no rose without its thorn—they are vicious in temper, self-indulgent, and indolent.

On the morrow, after taking leave of many generous acquaintances, I started for Valdepeñas.

There is practically no end to what a tramp may find! Here, in old Spain, with all its wants and ills, I have actually found *consolation !* and in most substantial and lasting form. This is the name of a hamlet in the vale of Depenas, in the province of La Mancha. It owns a few shabby old houses, and an old church, which has grown so thoroughly disgusted by the world's indifference to the gift it has been holding out for centuries, that it has unshipped its old tower and part of its roof, and stands a tottering ruin in the attitude of abject despair. "Consolation" is small, and stops short.

That is common! I was not in the least "consoled" by having to travel over ten or twelve miles of a newly stoned road, from which there was no escape, as it was all vines and olive trees on either side.

Valdepeñas is a town with a population of, report says, 18,000 souls. It is pretty, singular, and interesting.

Its houses, style of business, and inhabitants are all old-fashioned. I paid a real to sleep in the porch of a posada overlooking the plaza, which at peep-o'-day was crowded with market people vending all that the heart of Valdepeñas could desire.

Men and women took up their places in rows, working at their trades, and children stood in front hawking the goods.

Women sat working at house-linen, lace-making, darning and patching clothes, while the customer waits coatless or shirtless, as the case may be. One fellow was earning pennies by instructing mule drivers in the art of making safe and fancy knots.   Another, vending frying-pans, pipkins, and braseros (foot-warmers), was making his presence heard by knocking out a lively tune with two brass or copper spoons on the head of a frying-pan. Women were selling "fry." Some sell nothing but ears ; others feet, tongues, or *eyes*. They slight no digestible article in Spain.   I bought a bullock's eye. It was very good, though the idea was not pleasant.

Others displayed baskets full of crawling, slimy snails.

Girls stood behind tables covered with cool drinks, groceries, and sweetmeats.   Bread, flour, vegetables, and fruit were piled in rows along the ground.

Old men, women, and little children, dodging in and out among the crowd, fastened greedily upon the bad fruit and refuse thrown out by the stall-keepers.

Two young pleasant-faced nuns, with large baskets

on their arms, begged for a scrap from every store, in order to support their home for orphan girls.

Donkeys stood still as death, with flat boards fixed over their panniers, containing the produce of a garden, poultry run, or pig-stye. The vendors were of all types, and the blending of oddities makes the daily market in the plaza of Valdepeñas a real show. A great church, destitute of windows, as is so often the case in Spain, and lighted by a row of half-moon-shaped holes under the eaves, forms one side of the plaza. It is said to contain some rare relics. There are bolts, and bars, and padlocks enough to help out this assertion, but I looked in vain for anything rare.

Valdepeñas bears the reputation of being extremely wealthy. The old town is said to be completely undermined by cellars and store-houses holding millions of "arrobas" * of wine and oil.

Traditions, legends, and superstitions run out like water here, and a novelist would soon find some excellent and original materials for a romance.

From Valdepeñas to Santa Cruz the country is very fine, from an economic point of view—easy undulating lands of fair quality, all cultivated and producing excellent samples of wine and oil, besides red wheat and a great variety of fruits and vegetables.

* An arroba is twenty-five pounds. Liquids are sold in Spain by weight.

Santa Cruz de Mudela is a small, neglected looking town, existing, like its neighbour, on the products of the local soil.

The alcalde sent me to a horribly dirty house, where the owner, after carefully inspecting the egg boxes, told me I might sleep in the fowl-house. This privilege I declined, and on making a second and very plaintive appeal to the alcalde, he sent me to a decent posada.

My next tramp was to El Visillo, a little hamlet up on the high tableland which lies on the Castilian side of the Sierra Morena.

It afforded me nothing more than a sleeping-place on the floor of its posada, and a good elevation from which I could take a last look at Old Castile.

From this slope of the Sierra Morena I could look away to the eastern end of the Montes de Toledo, with the great plain of La Mancha filling the intervening space as a vast, misty sea.

I have not found every Castilian to be a gentleman ! I have not found them of such good quality as their rougher and more industrious brothers of the north.

New Castile is a vast tract of land embracing all classes and types of character. North of Guadalajara the natives are little less than brutes. They have harsh, vulgar tongues, with manners as uncouth and depraved as their speech.

Madrid admits of no criticism. Like all capitals, it is a compound of its provinces, with a strong leaven of foreign blood to affect and perhaps strengthen it.

South of Madrid there is a marked change from the north. Cleanliness becomes more general, the home instinct is keener ; and the farther one journeys south this becomes more and more apparent. The increase of sunshine forces the inhabitants indoors, and they endeavour to make their interiors attractive.

The Castilians appear to dread the heat as much as the cold. I have seen whole communities hide themselves in the shade from ten or eleven a.m. to four p.m.

With the sun comes indolence. Although in most districts, when the soil is favourable, it receives attention, it is evident that much more might be done by ambitious and willing hands. " As much as my father did is enough for me," is the general remark. Where a weed or bad blight appears it is cursed and talked over and allowed to take the field. No sensible system, no downright effort is apparent in agricultural matters, though, such is by nature the true industry of the country.

Much of the bad land might produce a little, all the good land much more.

With the Moors upon its surface Castile would soon become a green lawn. Its present barrenness is caused neither by climate nor poverty of soil. The poverty and indolence of the "Castilian gentleman" are the true causes of the miserable condition one sees to-day.

I cannot agree with those who are always asserting that Spain is "the most magnificent country in the world."

I go flatly against them, and declare it is by nature one of the worst, and it is allowed to become perhaps the very worst in the world. What do its admirers mean by a magnificent country?

I take it that such a country should be capable of feeding and clothing, instructing and comforting its children from its own native store. This Spain does not do now, and I have no ears for what she was! All lands were great when man was little. If Spain ever had a hundred millions of people, she starved them; that's all!

To-day her seventeen millions—two-thirds of which are shamefully underfed—are not supplied from her native produce, and the blame is not entirely to be laid to the door of the Spaniards.

Where is her timber, and where her coal? and where is the quantity of water that a country so vast, at such an elevation, and under such a sun, requires of necessity to sustain and develop vegetation?

Let us take a look at the country as it really is—

sce it in fallow, in seed-time, and in what should be harvest. Let us look at the pros. and cons., and run our fingers carefully down the return sheet of this sweet land !

I am neither for nor against the Spaniard or his country. I am only anxious to show what they really are to-day, so far as I am able to understand them You cannot gauge Spain by the Spaniard's opinion of it. He loves it ; this is natural. He will tell you it is the world. But it is his pride that confounds him.

His " Rio Tintos," his " Bilboas " are sending off clouds of " smoke," and enriching every square foot of the Peninsula—and still he starves !

But the wind blows cold from my elevated perch on the Sierra side. I ought to look back with a grateful heart on the many warmings and square meals the Castilian sun and sons have bestowed on me.

Adieu, Senors, adieu. *Felicitie*

CHAPTER XIII.

ANDALUCIA.

I SAID good-bye to Castile some hours before I was fairly out of it, for the road slopes down to Andalucia, miles away from the frontier line. The great breach in the mountain, the Cañon of Depeñasperros, is so deep that a strong stream, which takes its rise on the Castilian side, flows through this gorge and forms a tributary of the Guadalquivir. A railway winds along this valley on a level with the stream, except where it takes short cuts through several little tunnels which pierce projecting rocks.

The scenery, though wild and churlish, is not without charm. The deep valley helps to give effect to the great bare towers of cold stone shooting up to a dizzy height on either side.

The road lay a thousand feet above the railway and the foaming stream, which tumbled along in very good imitation of the bustling train which now and then shot past it. From the narrow coping running along the edge of the cliff bordering the road-side, I could get lovely little peeps at walls of rock showing masses of lichen and gaily-tinted moss, while from the crevices spring tiny mountain daisies, carnations, and harebells.

At a sharp turn in the cañon—so sharp that no way out is visible—one seems to stand within an enormous ruin, ivy-covered, damp, and silent. This fancied relic of man's making is almost perfect, but it is only fancy. Far away on the highest slopes, little scrubby growths of wild olive, native oak, and of wood and broom swayed and bent to the wild winds, and, still farther up, on the lone, dull grey peaks, the misty clouds were scudding and gathering as they flew.

The Sierra Morena is nothing extraordinary to look upon. It is a great rain gatherer and little more. The road through Depeñasperros ("the dogs' stones,"—literally, "too bad for a dog"), in spite of being the recognised road connecting the two kingdoms throughout all known time, is as bad as it could possibly be. It is composed of rough, loose stones, over which one blunders and slips at every step. An occasional mule car and a regular stream of overladen donkeys are now the most important patrons of this road, although in pre-railway days—if but a mean percentage of its tradition be true—it was a busy and dangerous path.

Depeñasperros was for centuries the fastness of the most bloody banditti in all Spain, and the long record of crime has taken such a hold on the minds of the natives that, even in these peaceful days, they shrink from any mention of "the dogs' stones."

A girl whom I met some miles below the pass told me that another foreigner had passed that way a few weeks before. He was an Italian bicyclist; but he couldn't bicycle Depeñasperros! He had to carry his bicycle over six miles of those lovely loose stones, and, said my informant, "he didn't seem to like it!"

Every Spaniard swears by Andalucia (and everything else he can lay his tongue to).

If you have not seen Andalucia you can know nothing of natural beauty. From the Bay of Biscay to the southern boundary of Castile, I have heard of no other place where the perfection of nature is always to be found. If so, I certainly made a bad beginning. From midday to dark I fagged over bald, bleak ridges, down craggy paths leading to narrow gullies carrying nothing more remarkable than a dribble of dirty water and a few weeds. No very excellent discoveries so far! Perhaps by-and-by?

"By-and-by" came, but it brought no better results. I ascended high hills, from which I could obtain views of enormous stretches of country, as bare and wild as that I had left behind. To the south-east the Montes de Jaen presented a noble appearance, but even that perhaps was due to distance.

After passing through miserable villages where all the inhabitants seemed to be languishing for want of something to do, I found myself on the crown of a bold ridge, whence I could see signs of life and activity ; but it was not Spanish activity. The tall chimneys which tower above Linares and La Carolina proclaim the existence of silver and lead mines which English, French, and German enterprise have made paying concerns, as well as sources of eternal complaint to the lazy Spaniard, who, to give him his deserts, is very industrious with his tongue !

Travel not only brings strange bed-fellows, but strange beds, and they are liable to be more uncomfortable than strange. After the long day's walk, I felt that I could endure something more downy than cobble-stones and wet earth, but these formed the share of earth's luxuries provided for me at La Carolina. At No. 1 posada the posadero didn't like the look of me, and wanted the money down before I turned in.

I was tired and out of temper with the world, and this latest hit of the posadero didn't please me. So after exchanging a few lusty compliments, I took myself off to the Posada Del Ville.

Here the posadero was more discerning, and, seeing no roguery in my eye, he showed me to a dark corner where I could sleep. After I had lain some time, I woke to find that I was very damp, and on examining the floor, found that I was lying on wet and foul earth. I made a move, but it was a change without much benefit. The posada floor was in part pitched with large round stones, and I must choose them or the wet earth. I chose the stones and got some sleep, but when I woke in the morning I had a terrible cold brewing, for my rug was wet through, and I had been lying all night in a thorough draught. I paid the posadero his real, and started off before daybreak without seeing any more of La Carolina.

It looks old enough to have nursed the giant babes who fashioned old Rome, but as a matter of fact it is a modern town. I have no doubt that every guide book will tell you that it is one of the towns built by and peopled with the Germans, imported into Spain by Charles III., with the view of putting an end to the brigandage and plunder so common in his day throughout the land. I think these Germans must have done their work thoroughly.

The little of the Teuton that is left in La Carolina nearly did for me !

They can make soft bread in Andalucia. Thank Heaven !

This is no idle remark : I am truly rejoiced to record the fact. Bread is but an item with many. With a tramp it is his first and last course, his three meals a day and supper at night ; and hungry as he always is, there is a sense of monotony and dryness about his fare which makes him long for a slight change. I began by disliking Spanish bread, and in less than a month I had grown to detest it !

Had I been permitted to choose I might have fared a little better, but the " beggar's crust " is always a hard one, and the smile of the loveliest Dulcinea in Spain will not soften it to my liking.

The Spaniards always kiss the bread they are about to give away.* I have seen many a dirty hand and unwashed face meet on the bit of bread I was going to make a meal of, and if by chance a white

* The poorest Spaniard will offer to share his crust even with his social superiors.

hand carried the morsel to a rose-bud mouth, and luscious eyes looked down upon "the gift for God," it did not make it any softer! Truly the Spaniards love a crust. They cut and slash their thin, flat loaves till they expand in baking to the appearance of a batch of rock cakes. Spanish bread is not a common thing. In soup it is delicious as the finest biscuit, and has its place in the tureens of the highest in the land ; but the same bread without that good soup is as mustard without beef, and if it is ever your lot to eat as much of it in a month as I have done you may wonder that I could speak so moderately of such hard fare. Spanish bread is leavened by means of a piece of sour dough which is kept over from day to day. This is a very wholesome method, and deserves to be widely known.

With the daylight came a warm clear sun, and I soon got rid of the effects of my wretched night.

I tramped nearly all the day through olive country, in some places thriving and well cultivated, in others neglected and decayed. Occasional patches of vine land and cork oak broke up the scenery. Only one thing was lacking—water. If this were conjoined with man's industry the district would be very rich.

I got into Bailen just as it was growing dark. I don't like the official world, it is so confoundedly bumptious, and the lower the grade the higher the nose is jerked. One of these little gods told me to be off about my business. This only incited me to humbug him the more.

I muttered a few spirited anathemas in the face of this limb of the law, and then I left him with his hand on the sword which a local bye-law prohibits him from drawing.

The alcalde was in the Campo, and "won't be home till morning." There was an empty treasury and a general dislike for vagrants, and I was again invited to take myself off. Two notices to quit might be enough for some people. But a tramp makes his own laws, and acknowledges few others. I had decided to occupy "the boards of Bailen"—"for one night only." After much curious enquiry from a group of young men, I was, by way of variety, taken to the prison and recommended to the gaoler as an eligible party for a night's lodging.

The gaoler proved kinder than the other un-informed rascals. He gave me No. 4 cell, and a sack of straw to make my bed. His wife gave me some soup and pitied me—at least she said she did— and then I went to sleep, happy in the thought that I had defeated the town guard and mayor's clerk, and found some kind hearts in Bailen.

But daybreak brought sorrow. The gaoler's wife found me mourning over a broken pitcher—reduced to a pile of æsthetic grey chips—and a pool of cart-wheel dimensions.

The pitying creature of last night became a fury. She was big and powerful, and her voice towered far above her capacious chest. I am a match for many people, but not for a Spanish woman in a battle of words. In the language of those who support the manly art, "She knocked me over the ring and the ropes, and the belt was given to her."

I am always "a Roman in Rome," and after such a desperate encounter, I felt as a sinner who would be happier if forgiven ; so I bundled my wallets and walked off to the principal church, a substantial red sandstone edifice with singular and artistic decorations in carved stone and wood. The expression of the face and the animation of one colossal figure was quite extraordinary : wood has rarely seemed more alive. Lamps, icons, and candelabra of solid silver were to be seen by the hundredweight. The sacristy held fine old carved chests of splendid workmanship. The carved wooden frame of a mirror is valued at three thousand "duros" (£600), and five thousand have been offered for a similar frame at another local church.

On passing through the plaza I saw a Spanish fight. Two market men were having a noisy battle over a rascally donkey which had devoured some of the fruit and vegetables exposed for sale in the plaza. It was a most amusing exhibition. Perhaps the Spanish are the only people clever enough to fight one at a time. The owner of the vanished viands made his grievance known to every mortal soul within hearing. He cursed the donkey and its owner, then he cursed the owner's mother for giving birth to such a rascal as he declared his enemy to be. He raked up all he could against the offender's family, and cited other cases in proof of his negligence and the greedy appetite of his donkey, and then, by way of compensation, he demanded five reals. All this time the owner of the animal stood like a sheep, modestly submitting to all that was said against his fair name ; but no sooner were the last words out of his assailant's mouth than he lifted himself into a more defiant attitude, and went for the vegetable man like a shark—but of course only in words. There were no fisticuffs, no brandishing of blades : only with so many statements to contradict, and so many accusations to make in his turn, he soon got out of breath, and so gave the other a new chance. He accepted it with alacrity, and like a wily lawyer debated and repudiated all that had been uttered against him, and thus, having made his sheet clean again, he doffed his hat to the crowd and redemanded his five reals. But the other was in readiness, and replied in flowing speech—that not a real or a cent had he for the pocket of a rascal who lived by fraud, deception, and even worse crimes.

This brought louder and stronger speech from the vegetable man, and cheers and cross compliments from the crowd. Both men took their turns and fought desperately for twenty or twenty-five minutes, yet there was no blood or even the sound of a blow. When they were too tired to say any more they dropped the subject, and so the fight ended. If the donkey ever came to the rescue with the lost vegetables, or any money changed hands, I am unable to say, but I am of opinion that the fight paid the bill!

Bailen is nothing but warfare. Even I have been engaged in it: I have seen others at it, and I am told that it was here Napoleon waged his last battle on the Peninsula.*

And in those days when Bailen was besieged, the men, and the women too, fought with more substantial weapons than their tongues. For sixty-seven days the city was besieged by the French and defended by only five hundred Spanish soldiers and the inhabitants, who were eventually starved almost to the very last man. It was in the summer of 1808. There

* This is not at all correct, but I record the local story of the siege of Bailen. The Spaniards defeated the French under Dupont.

was very little water in the town, and in the heat of
the dog-days it became foul and the cholera broke out.
The provisions were exhausted, and all chance of
fresh supplies cut off. The French troops lay round
about and shot down all who dared to show in sight.

In desperation, little bands sallied forth to fight
the foe. Women stood side by side with fathers,
husbands, lovers, sons ; and history records that they
laid many a Frenchman low. The love of life made
cannibals of the desperate population. The wounded
were put to death, their bodies quartered like sheep,
hawked through the town and devoured. When Bailen
capitulated she was dead. Wounds, starvation, and
disease had destroyed her brave people, and the army
of Napoleon made its entrance into, not a city but
a pestilential sepulchre.

To-day Bailen is poor, very poor ; but compared
with bygone days it is well off. Better its sleepy
silence and groups of idlers, better its wordy
battles over broken pitchers and lost turnips, better
anything than such a year as 1808.

On leaving Bailen I had to do battle again, this
time with a hard road, made harder by the fact that
I was stockingless and frightfully footsore. It is
well that I can look round and see others as poor,
perhaps poorer than I. Misery likes friends, and
there is no dearth of misery (if poverty be misery) in

Spain. It may be true that there is "no poverty but ignorance," but that proverb was probably written by a lucky sage who never felt his backbone grate against his waistcoat buttons.

The little river Campana was a treat I could not afford to pass lightly over. I had a much-needed bath. Then I washed all my clothes, and sat under an arch and waited for them to dry. And I had to wait.

The clouds came up and blotted out the broad blue sky, the thunder boomed, and then came a downpour of cold rain.

This was comforting! I was half naked, and the balance of my clothes were "in the wash."

I sat under the arch all the afternoon, all the evening, and half the night! Then I put on some of my wet clothes, rolled up the rest, and started on the dark and lonely road.

Never talk hastily about the "charms" of "walking tours." There are charms, but there are also discomforts which will bring bad temper and bad words out of the most docile of men. A couple of hours' sharp walking warmed me, and brought me to the ventas of San Antonio. God bless him! I don't know anything against him, and if his good deeds inspired some one to build this house, then he is worthy of praise.

It was long after midnight, but I managed to wake
up the sole occupant of the house—a little woman
—got a stiff glass of white spirit from her, and went
to bed on a heap of harness which lay upon the floor.
The morning broke fine and warm, so I dried all
my clothes, munched my pennyworth of bread, and
started on a long, narrow road bordered with olive
trees.   Early in the afternoon I reached Andujar,
where I found fair time : feast time, posadas full
of good paying patrons, and posaderos quite independent of vagrant tramps.   I was relegated to
the shade of a gloomy stable, with nothing more
agreeable than a few million mosquitoes for company.
This was not pleasant; still I confess to liking
Andujar.   It is clean, prettily situated, full of old-
fashioned buildings and old-fashioned people with
old-fashioned customs.   It has a history long, strong,
and noble, and many mute memorials of an extinct
race who camped here in the early days of the world.

To-day Andujar, which has a population of twenty-
three thousand souls, lives by the same means (oil
and wine) which gave it sustenance nigh twenty
centuries ago, when Julius Cæsar came and took it,
and built a castle and forts, and strong walls, and
a bridge over the Guadalquivir, all of which stand
to this day.   Then the Goths (so famed for destroy-
ing) built some habitations which show here and

there in the high and narrow "calles" which the
Moors reared.   Andujar is a big and pretty piece of
patchwork, made up of Roman towers on Phœnician
foundations, Gothic windows in Roman towers, old
Spanish balconies and defensive ironwork round
Moorish windows and doorways, and stucco and
carved stone effigies, arms, and crests over half its
giant portals.   Its "calles" are quiet, yet full of song.
In no town in Spain have I seen such pretty windows,
fashioned for pent-up Dorotheas and Dolores to peep
from, or sit a-listening to "delire and delore;" or
finer illustrations of the prowess of the chivalrous old
knights of Spain.

In nearly every street stands some curious device
in hand-beaten ironwork, depicting a feat of arms
or Lochinvar type of gallantry.

The casque with flying plumes, supported on
crossed swords and breastplate, with spurs and hand
shields lying round, is a favourite device.   One displayed in addition two flower-pots containing representations of the rose and carnation twined over the
armour.   These things are all very finely worked
and exceedingly rare.   Some of them have become
so rare that they are not to be found in Andujar
any more, and the owners of others have been forced
to remove them from conveniently low doorways and
place them slightly nearer to the stars.

The main entrance to the parish church displays seven different styles of architecture, each said to have been executed in its respective period. Accompanied by the town clerk, I went up into the tower of this church, and got my first glimpse of the Guadalquivir. I wonder why this river is so famous. It is known to all people, and usually in song. Many who cannot pronounce the word bring it into their story—which is generally of the heart. What Horatius, or Leander, or Perimele of the Moors —for it is a Moorish name—did this old river bear up that it has grown so great? Looking down from my perch the waters showed as a shiny satin band, twisted, twirled, and coiled among the unending forest of olive trees. Its banks are irregular enough to please the most fastidious of lovers, but as love does not walk out in Spain what purpose can they serve? Near the town silver poplars and aspens produce a slight variation in the grey monotony of the olives, while mountains east and west guard and limit the vast scene. From below came the sound of music and merry-making.

Andujar is as conservative as it looks.

The people delight in keeping up old customs, hence the "feria" of this town is one of the most charming in Spain. I found a friend in the "secretario," and we went to the fair. It is one of the prettiest things of the kind imaginable: not made up merely of gaudy caravans and gipsies, coster-mongers, and showmen, screeching and canvassing for customers.

It was held on a fine, broad, natural terrace, bounded on one side by an old Roman wall and on the other by the Guadalquivir. The long open space was transformed into a veritable summer "City of Delight." A double row of tastefully designed and well-built kiosks, dancing-rooms, cafés, and "salons de musica" lined a fine promenade. Between these stand neat little stalls filled with curious "dulces" and "bebes."

The town clubs transfer their quarters here during the "feria." All classes are represented. There is the fashionable "Circulo de la Pearl," the "Liceo," the "Primativa" and the unassuming "Ordinarios," and even one more, the "Solteros" (bachelors). Each has its ball-room, its band, its working staff in fanciful uniforms, and a pretty display of bunting. Every night a fine programme of dances is gone through by senors and senoras in plain and fancy dresses, while music and games are provided for non-dancers in the ante-chambers, besides which there is the charm of promenading in the "pasco."

Rows of lamps and bright-coloured lanterns flood the promenade with light, revealing a series of ever-changing pictures as the merry crowd moves up and down.

Flowers (in pots and tubs) are packed in thousands to form parterres, banks, and grottoes round specially made fountains ; and all these hues and sweet odours, mingling with the dresses and perfumes of the wearers, make the evening air heavy yet refreshing.

The knight and his steed have passed away, hence there can be no riding a-tilt for lady's love from the high crupper of a caballo. To-day the Andujar knights win their ribbons on—bicycles!

The beauties of the town—and they are many —furnish handsomely embroidered silk and satin scarves, which are placed at regular distances on a long horizontal bar, each being attached to a silver ring. The modern knights, armed with little canes like a conductor's baton, ride at a dashing pace under the bar, and each endeavours to " ring " the scarf of the girl of his heart. At least let us hope he does. A large stand, fixed near this seat of love's warfare, was filled with the beauties of the town. Not one man dared show himself among them. I own to standing a very long time before that stand. It was a picture—not all loveliness, but still a picture.

The finest women I have seen in Spain were in Zaragoza and Madrid, and here in Andujar.

Every girl had a new frock and fan, liberty's free

smile in her eye, and a bunch of pale pink or yellow roses or carnations in her hair. If her beauty was that of youth, her cheek wore a faint colour as delicate as her assumed shyness. But those who are forced to " make up " for time's ravages are powder-puffed and besmeared in a most hideous manner.

This practice does not annoy Spanish men. They say very idly, " It is a *costumbre* (custom), nothing more." Be it to their credit or otherwise, the Spaniards are not exacting in the matter of female dress.

Of course the ordinary attractions of fairs were here—shows, merry-go-rounds, theatres on wheels, organ-grinders, and a big circus.

The Spanish clown is a sad dog—at least he looks it, for wherever I have seen him he has been dressed in funereal black ; and to make the contrast complete, his long, loose combination robe is relieved by white bats, tarantulas, frogs, cockroaches, and other little monsters of the night.

His dress is the only thing strange to English eyes. He wears his hat on his hip or his elbow, puts his tongue out, and turns his toes in, just as our Grimaldis do. He poses with one hand resting on nothing at all just above his thigh, and lifts his straight, black eyebrows till they mingle with his forelocks in the good old-fashioned way.

He even has the same complaints, cries in the

same key, and pinches his finger under his own foot, as we have so often seen him do before. He is master and lackey at the same moment, a miserable failure in every useful art, and yet capable of bringing the house down at a " bound." And in one other particular he is essentially " homely," for when he is " off " you may be sure to find him at the nearest canteen, as merry and ready to drink your health in a glass of grog as any clown in England would be.

The patrons of the fair are the population of the province. They come from the Montes de Jaen, the broad valley of the Guadalquivir, and the slopes and dells of the Sierra Morena. They are of all stations and estates, and their varied dress and manners make the great crowd motley and delightful. From the peasant of the plains and the mountains to the beauties who are dressed in the latest Paris fashion is a long stretch, and all the little fancy and quaint touches which come between make the assemblage one big masquerade extending over the styles and fashions of three or four centuries of sluggish time. This fair takes place during the first week in September, and if you should ever visit Cordoba or any famed place near, you would do well to include it in your programme.

I varied the charms of my long and pleasant

evening by making my bed in the fore-mentioned stable.

The mosquitoes nearly skinned me, and I soon lost the little respectability I might have brought to Andujar.

In the morning I met an Englishman, and we went together in search of novelties. We found and looked over old houses, old churches, old monasteries, the market, and the Plaza de Toros. We visited the gaming tables (in the upper stories of a convent), and won five reals over a " spec." on " Monte," and then we went to lunch with a Spanish lawyer.

I mention him to show how the generality of Spaniards live at home. The lawyer was married. He had a beautiful wife with fair, golden ringlets, and around her clung nine little sons.

He was an educated man, as the phrase goes (it too often goes for nothing), and welcomed us with an air of genuine good nature. The meal was in readiness. It consisted of one course only, and there was no wine or coffee. It was the " puchera,"—a very good puchera of " garvanzos," rice, cauliflower, and bacon all boiled together.

The bacon was cut in little strips like dominoes. There was no tablecloth, no napkins, no plates, no knives, forks, or spoons. We ate from one dish— host, hostess, nine little boys, the Englishman, and myself (thirteen at dinner and no bad luck followed us). The mother used her fingers, as forks seemed to be scarce. The father pressed me to eat freely, assuring me there were tons more in the kitchen (though there was probably not an ounce), and picked out dainty bits of bacon with his fingers and tossed his hand before me,—as one would a bone for a dog to catch,—that he might poke it into my mouth. I took all his baits, so did my fellow-countryman, and we felt none the worse for what we had eaten.

This was rude simplicity and no mistake! At what period of civilisation does Spain now stand? She certainly represents a bygone age from our point of view.

The guardian of the city purse is a generous man and a progressist. He wants to see Spain opened up, colonised if you will, and her position better understood by the outside world. He will support any man who will travel on and say that Spain has a chance to be vastly superior to what she is, and with the belief that I shall fulfil his desires he helped me on my way and bade me "go with God!"

This is the record! I put a red cross against the town of Andujar, prayed for long life for its discerning (?) "secretario," and shouldered my bundle.

Barring the mosquitoes, I had been treated right well.

The sun was on the wane when I crossed the Guadalquivir on my way to Marmolego. I was assured, as usual, that it was quite a short distance— a mere lover's walk. So I found it. But I have heard of lovers taking very long walks. By the way, they make love very modestly in Spain. I wonder how an Englishman can ever win a Spanish woman. The process would kill me, even though I were as hardy as old nails.

A man can get used to most things, but what Britisher would have patience and strength to look up at a third-storey window through the day, and content himself with making gestures and grimaces at his love, under the light of the street lamp or the fickle moon, through four or five hours of every night? Lord John Russell wrote—

> "The women of old Spain can scarcely spell a letter,
>> But then, their mirth's so unconstrained one loves
>> them all the better!"

Spanish beauties rarely send love-letters; the reason is as simple as it was in Lord John's day— they cannot write! There are writing shops where the letter can be moulded in the latest fashion and in the most exalted language for the modest sum of one brown penny.

I reached Marmolego about midnight, having taken the longest and the worst of two bad roads; and after a short night's rest on the floor of a posada I set off to visit some thermal springs bubbling up on a hillside sloping towards the Guadalquivir.

These springs used to be famous. Everything used to be famous, if we can trust to local tradition. It was all better in the old days, and when we were younger, and looked up, up, up, to the great world which we now look down upon with so much disdain.

Whatever travellers' tales may be told about Spain, there is one indisputable fact, that it is " sunny Spain." It can blow and snow and be downright cold when it likes; but taking it all in all, it is a very sunny land. I have spent weeks without seeing anything which might truly be called a cloud. Flaky mists and gossamer remnants, too delicately transparent to cast shadows, lie along the sky at evening, and celestial worlds of ether reveal themselves at morning if one is up in time to see the faint dews vanish from the scanty herbage.

I was glad, at the end of a long, hot, scorching day's tramp, to come in sight of the old city of Montoro. This is the Toledo of Andalucia. The site is not less secure or imposing. It is perched on a high, bold, triangular mass of rock, and the river flows round two of its three sides.

Seen from the river on the northern side, the picture is most charming. The houses are piled one above the other, the foundations of those above appearing to rest on the roofs of those below. It has a crazy, past-hope appearance, and even the showy-tiled towers of its many churches cannot redeem it from the look of despair which seems to show on every crumbling wall.

The Moors made Montoro one of their strongholds. Its fine position rendered it a safe retreat. Kings held court here, and there was once a beautiful Alcazar for the king's favourites, and fine gardens and arbours on the banks of the river. These have disappeared. Montoro knows nothing of kings and of court beauties now. The people are sober-sided as the old houses they inhabit. True, they have their bit of pride, but it is in a good living cause. Montoro is surrounded by four million olive trees. The oil is pressed out in four hundred different mills. The industry gives employment to eighteen thousand souls, and an annual average return of thirty-four million reals. The inhabitants rejoice over this fact, and I do not think them vain. I should like to see more rejoicing over what Spain produces. If her people would only believe that a hard hand is a badge of honour, they would fare much better, and soon increase their store.

Good luck seldom dogs the heels of a tramp, but curiosity is frequently my salvation. I was followed by an inquisitive crowd, which caused me to attract the attention of the town guard. I was marched off to the Town Hall, and asked to explain the reason of my intrusion within the sacred precincts of the old town.

The Mayor was extremely civil, and offered to succour me with two pesetas. I told him that I did not need money. "Never mind," he said, "so much the better. Take them : a fat purse is a good passport !" (Think of this in official "Bumbledom" at home !)

A beggar on horseback does not always ride to the devil !

Although so well off, I paid but twenty-five cents for a bed on the posada floor, and a twopenny loaf went for supper and carried me over the next day.

As my journey lengthens so does my strength, and also my weakness. I find it easier to deal with the people ; but I grow daily farther away from that world of which I have usually felt a part.

Nature is neither very beautiful nor very busy in Spain, and her votaries are few. To live down to Spanish customs is not refreshing, and I grow poorer as I learn more. Spain is too much of a "sleepy hollow." There is a great deal of work to be done and I want to brush along and do some of it. It is rarely a long road for a Spaniard. He mounts his mule, goes to sleep, and wakes up at his destination. When he has had a row or an argument with some wayfarer, he turns in and sleeps again. Spaniards of more than one rank sleep in their clothes. The countryman and small "middle man" are usually without any bed or covering when on the road, and even in their homes a pallet of straw or heap of grass suffices them.

While turning over these manners and customs in my mind, I wound my way through the narrow "calles" of Carpio. It is a big village, nothing more, scattered over a conical little hill, situated about a mile from the Guadalquivir. A fine Moorish town on the summit is conspicuous for many miles around.

This is not the only trace of the Moor's handiwork. A tremendous weir lies across the bed of the river, and ponderous water-wheels (eighty feet in diameter) lift water far above the river level and distribute it over a large plateau, which was in Moorish times a vast and beautiful garden. A few badly kept orchards and fields now occupy the ground.

It is not difficult to get into society in Spain. You have but to appear odd and "todas el mundo" invites you at once. I am not going to divulge all my experiences in Spain, so I shall not say what particular virtue made me welcome at the palace of Carpio. Enough that I was welcomed by a kindly Britisher, and under his, or rather the Duke of Alba's roof I found the best bed and board I had hitherto encountered in Spain. A ducal palace is enough to embarrass and overawe a real tramp, and set him wondering if he is awake or dreaming! But there was no doubt about it, I found all things too substantial for dreamland, and some heart pangs which I would gladly have felt only in dreams. I was pressed to stay at the palace to enjoy a rest, a square meal or two, and, when it pleased me, to unfold the story of my wanderings. I agreed, and a day or two passed pleasantly and quickly.

My palace home had more of interest than luxury about it. It has for centuries been the home of the Dukes of Alba, which is shown by the rare circumstance that thirteen dukes (two of whom were archbishops) lie side by side in a vault below the little church hard by. The present Duke is Charles Stuart —who claims to be heir to the throne of Scotland, and nephew to Napoleon III. and the Empress Eugénie. The house is small, inartistic, and very much out of repair, and without any of the charm of age.

The Empress Eugénie has often graced Carpio with her presence, and many of her bits of furniture

and other treasures are stowed away here. How
much these musty things might tell! The Albas
possess the most precious private reliquary in Spain.
Among its treasures are two silver and crystal
cabinets containing skulls and bones of the eleven
thousand virgins ; another holding some bones of
St. John the Divine ; another a nail of the true cross.
Two quaintly fashioned silver coffers filled with the
bones of saints and pious martyrs are dated 1643.

A statuette of San Francisco is a remarkable work.
It is about twenty inches in height, and said to be
carved out of a solid piece of wood. The saint is
dressed in the garb of a ragged pilgrim, his sandals
and robes patched and cobbled in true penitent
fashion. The patches, stitches, and everything else
are of wood, and I am asked to believe that the grain
of wood shows the required colour. But I have proof
to the contrary, for I picked out one of the wooden
stitches which had been so neatly let into the patch
it is supposed to hold in place. But admitting this
hard fact about San Francisco, he is still a very
artistic and faithful model.

But the unique treasure of the reliquary is a hair
of the Virgin enclosed in the perpendicular column
of a level crystal cross. It shows a light brown
colour, and is fine in texture. I do not give these
particulars about this relic on account of any great

respect for it ; but perhaps there are a few who would like to know of its existence. Besides these very valuable relics there are many others, all venerable enough to satisfy the most devout and antiquated tastes. Viewed as a whole, the reliquary is a pretty little work of art.

In one of the side chapels of the church stands the gorgeous effigy of Santa Theresa. Long ago, so runs a story, when a Duke of Alba died in Naples his body was enclosed in this figure, and thus brought to Carpio in order to escape the taxes levied on dead bodies passing through Italian and Spanish towns. Santa Theresa had never been heard of as a substantial figure before ; but ignorance does not stop to think.

The people came in crowds to help the Saint over all the bad roads to her final home. A throng of priests attended her from stage to stage, and she and her burden arrived safe at the little church. Then they laid the dead duke beside his fathers, and set up Santa Theresa in the chapel ; and even to-day men and women kneel before that impious fraud, and I verily believe feel the happier for having done so. I saw a young girl with her hair cut off close to her head. The lost tresses hung from a peg in the wall of the church. A boy friend of the girl's brother was ill ; the brother said an offering to Mary might restore his companion to health. The maiden was poor : she had nothing but her hair : a beautiful plait of great length and glossy blackness. The boy did recover.

I saw a hideous figure splashed with blood and covered with gaping wounds, which is a sort of rain-fetish in this district. When it will not rain and the people are too poor to pay the priests for any big effort, they sally to the church, bring out the rain-god, and have a kind of masquerade through the streets. They say the rain always comes afterwards!

Ignorance is everywhere the lash that whips us all ; but he who is in search of downright super-stition and blind idolatry should go to Spain.

My host was married, and had a sweet little boy. He fell ill suddenly. An old nurse came to see him. She stood with her hands crossed over her breast looking steadily at the child. "He cannot live," she said slowly. "Why?" asked the alarmed parents. "Some one has cast an evil eye on him," replied the old woman. Her words proved true. In spite of all our efforts the child passed from this world. When it was known that the little one was dead, the villagers came to offer their sympathy. According to custom the parents stayed in their private rooms, and the fulfilment of all the necessary duties fell to stranger hands.

Acolytes in red and white gowns came with enormous candles, and awaited the arrival of the strangely dressed babe. It wore a white dress covered with bows of white and orange satin, and ornamented with rich gold embroidery, white leather shoes, a crown of pink and white flowers, and a gilt spray in its right hand. Thus adorned it lay in state all day. Women came dressed in rusty black, with lace mantillas, and after viewing the little body, and kneeling before a candle, would sit in solemn silence for an hour or two and then depart.

As the solitary companion of my host, I was called on to represent his family and Old England at the grave-side. Of all the sad hours I have known in Spain this was the saddest. I was the last of a large crowd of mourners. When the little coffin had been placed in a niche of the cemetery wall (they hold no service at the grave), and the mourners all filed past it, I had to stand and listen to expressions of sympathy for those who were spared.

The crowd hurried off through a misty rain, and I was left alone. The evening shadows were gathering over the land, the sun was low and reflected a few rainbow tints on the dreary sky. I was glad they were rainbow tints. Without them what would life be to us all? I walked back to the palace, my cheeks wet with the first tears I had shed in sunny Spain.

Carpio had offered me a change of scene and of subjects. It had been as the world is—all things by turns. Standing by the dust of dead dukes and of a dead babe I had felt anew that humanity is one. Surely there is no escape from sorrow. Wander from east to west, and assume what character we may, wherever humanity's voice is heard will come the notes of grief and pain.

CHAPTER XIV.

ANDALUCIA (*continued*).

I LEFT Carpio at 6 p.m. on a fine sunshiny day. After my rest the road was light, and I arrived at Alcolea (seven and a half miles) in less than three hours. Extremes are always meeting! After sleeping in a palace, I had to content myself with sharing a chaff loft with three other tramps.

In the morning I went to view the battle-field of Alcolea—dear to every Spaniard because it is of recent date and about a woman! Here Isabella, with her insurgent troops, met her foes and took a beating from them in very good style. How every man fought and bled I dare not pretend to know. The story is so variously told, that I might add to the

complications which already exist. Only this—
the battle lasted a day and a night. A fine bridge
over the Guadalquivir was held by the imperial
troops in a manner which has brought forth poetry
as eulogistic as that which tells of him who kept the
bridge "in the brave days of old."

It was a very hot morning, and I soon pulled up
at a roadside ventas. Poor starving country as
Spain is, you can get anything you may care to
order, or at all events an imitation of the genuine
article.

The owner of the ventas had neither wine nor
aquadiente, and the water was bad. Did I like
coffee? Did I not! So she broke up a handful of
maize-corn between two stones, clapped them in a
large brass ladle, and placed it on a tiny fire. When
the corn was heated and browned, she poured it into
a jug, added boiling water, and then went to the
door, calling, " Nee, nee, nee,—Cabra, cabra, cabra—
Benga, benga, benga." Up trotted a skinny she-
goat, and propped itself ready to be milked. Though
the goat was thin, the milk was rich, and, without
sugar or a silver spoon, my coffee so rudely prepared
out of maize-corn and goat's milk was a delicacy I
could enjoy when no more a thirsty tramp. Soon
after leaving the ventas I ascended a little hill, from
which I could see the big dome of the famed

cathedral of Cordoba, and an hour's steady walking brought the old city full in sight.

To the visitor who has "dreamed" of Cordoba, the first impression must ever be disappointing. It is huddled together over an uneven piece of ground beside the Guadalquivir, and presents an array of angles and odd corners, crooked, tortuous "calles" and parti-coloured masonry, which must be a delight to the class of beings who love " patch and crazy " work.

Every one knows Cordoba is old, and it looks it. Its plazas and its people echo the language and sentiments of centuries long dead, and should a modern fabric show in sight, it is but a gaudy intruder, which mars and disfigures the scene. In order to know Cordoba one needs fancy, imagination, a fine memory, and the keys of the town, and then it may become a delicious dream. I have none of these advantages, so I can speak of Cordoba only from a tramp's point of view. While moving up and down this old-fashioned place I lighted on the English Consulate, and having the usual wants and audacity of my class, I appealed for such assistance as every Britisher abroad feels it his privilege to expect from these worthy men. The Consul proved himself " a man and a brother " by inviting me to become his guest during one delightful week

Having found a home I became an independent member of society, and could take my walks abroad with the air of a man who owned something and needed a place in which to store it. The Consul was in search of a house, so we went "house-hunting" together.

It is a grand scheme! If all others of your own invention should fail, and you want to see a lot of old houses and people "at home" when visitors are not expected, go in search of a house. It is easy to be pleased and admire everything, and equally easy to decline making any bargain before first consulting some absent body. Had I not gone house-hunting, my acquaintance with Cordoba would have been small indeed, but now it seems that I lived there through centuries of changeful and eventful time.

Cordobose houses are not mute memorials of the historic past. They speak aloud, and with eloquent tongue. They tell of the life, and power, and learning, and glory, and victory, and defeat, and death of great people and great kings. Although "change and decay" are written on all around, the air is alive with the spirits of departed souls. This sometime "fount of learning, arts, and religion," the "ornament of the world" and "wonder of earth," is now all dead or dying, and yet it speaks in feverish tones of the transitory nature of all earthly glory.

Cordoba has had a good many royal palaces, but only one remains. It is called the Vièja Alcazar, and is to let. We went and saw it. It is a tiny bijou palace, standing on a pretty flat beside the river. The house seems to have been built for two lovers to play hide and seek. Inside, it is a miniature Hampton Court maze, odd little chambers and passages with tiny windows and dark-stained glass, which appear to have been made to shut out, rather than let in the light of day. The front of the house is ablaze with showy coloured enamel tiles, let into white porcelain cement. Round its balconies and verandahs cling old-fashioned climbing plants, and a marble fountain, which stands before the principal portal, is pressed out of shape by the many hands which have rubbed against it. The fishing and bathing pools are surrounded by natural flowers, and rich ornaments, and floral wreaths, in cold stone.

The garden is sweet with the scent of orange blossoms, and there are shady, inviting rest-houses where the court beauties of old may have confessed their romantic loves. We can take this palace, garden, and all the story of it for £20 a year! And the tax collector shall not trouble us for another cent. We went to another house under the eye of the prison and the fine old bridge,—a stupid, comfortless old place, without entrance hall or corridors.

The rooms themselves formed the passage, and the amount of doors to be opened and closed on making a short journey through the house was too much for the patience of any Britisher. In the bedrooms, curtains composed of solid masonry hung from the ceiling round the space convenient for the bed.

The kitchen was at the top of the house, another proof, if it were needed, that "modern inventions" are somewhat old. As this house did not suit our requirements, we went to that of a noble marquis, who, being possessed of but a small family and still smaller income, wished to let three-quarters of his establishment and content himself with passing his days in attic modesty, and spending his nights, and the rent, in the salons on the "Gran Capitan."

The Marquis was a plain man, and not above doing a little business if it meant money.

He welcomed us to his little den (it was a den), and commanded us to sit down, and as he was in his shirt sleeves we did not hesitate to obey.

There is really no moral reason why a marquis should not be seen in his shirt sleeves, and, as the weather was hot and he was fat and juicy, we forgave the negligence of his attire, and proceeded to question him about his house. He would take four thousand reals (£40) per annum, and he called in the Marquesa to bear him out that the place was worth the money.

Both these noble personages were horribly dirty, and all about them miserably wretched and unclean.

The pedigree of the Marquis looked well as it hung from the time-stained walls, and even his own sheet may be free from crime ; but we could not feel that it would increase our self-esteem to share his house, so, after seeing little more than its inmates, we " try again." We came upon a lovely little abode standing within great gardens which once afforded delight and retirement to the beauties of the Moorish camp.

The house was shut out from the rude world by a labyrinth of grape vines, pomegranates, oranges, and other luscious fruits. The air was heavy with the scent of flowers, and all around was so rich and sweet that Nature seemed to fairly overflow.

A portion of the old Roman wall stands in this garden. We ascended it by a flight of stone steps, whence we got a grand view of this old-world domain.

We were in the heart of Cordoba, yet we could see nothing but greenery, shady arbours, fruits and flowers. Here were quiet and rest ; and to him who finds nothing but fatigue in the bustling world, how much that word contains ! At the end of the old wall stands what was once the principal Roman gate of the city. It is now, alas ! changed into an impromptu stye for two Spanish pigs. We saw other houses, other gardens, all overflowing with that indescribable charm which now hangs round the cities of the past.

I went to the cathedral without a guide-book, for I am a refractory tramp, and do not like to be led up to things or beliefs. Here are my notes : " This cathedral has impressed me more than any building I have entered in Spain, and yet I can say nothing about it. I have been mooning around it for two whole days. I have wandered up and down its many aisles, round and round its hundred shrines, pondered and dreamed as I have leaned against nearly all its four hundred marble columns, till I have grown weary and bewildered by the thoughts it has aroused. I know nothing of its history, nor do I feel I need to. It is a great living force which speaks out a world of infinite variety."

Powerful as this fabric is, it does not inspire any religious reverence. I think " Christians " must view it as a great pagan temple. It is essentially an earthly temple, but though made by my fellow-men, they have invested it with a something which baffles and is above my understanding ; and that something may be the voice of the Moslems' God. Priestly vestments, always attractive in Spain, look out of place here. One expects Moorish robes, turbaned heads, yellow sandals, and jewelled scimitars on the forms which glide about its silent courts.

But these have had their little day, and the less gaudy priest is the only coloured object one looks on now.

The choir and chapel which the Catholics have fashioned in the centre of the building form a splendid monument of Spanish art, though they are condemned by all who would view the Mosque Cathedral in its original form. The retablo and screen are of wood, carved and polished till they look like massive copper. The white ceiling adorned with cherubs and other angelic creatures, with faces all as natural as life, yet perhaps a little too pure and beautiful for this world, holds one entranced and happy. Time counts for nothing in this building. What one sees is too vast for treatment, what one feels and delights in is not to be got rid of in words.

I cannot presume to say what is the wondrous charm, or wherein lies the beauty of Cordoba Cathedral. Gloomy and profound, it must arrest and fascinate the lightest heart, and push its way into the head of him or her who is already over full of this world's glories.

There are six hundred priests in Cordoba!

Cordoba is bankrupt—nothing less ; but it tries to keep its head up and indulge its light loves. It pays for big toros and keeps scores of cafés and gaming-houses going, and the patrons of these resorts claim to be highly respectable and very much alive.

There is not a single art or industry in force here. The people boast of their beautiful silver work; but it is only what is known as "Cairo work,"—silver wire, plaited and twisted into cheap trinkets. The "Gran Capitan" is a fine "pasco," but it is not an unmixed blessing. Cordoba is not so large that she needs big lungs. If her people would turn out and cultivate the silent hills which lie in idleness and neglect around them, theirs would be a better life than such as they can obtain in the "Gran Capitan."

This city, which was once looked up to by the whole world for its magnificence, learning, and power, is now all that is poor and low. It needs but a shower of hot dust and ashes, or a high tide in the old river, and it would consent to be crushed out of being as certainly as Pompeii and Herculaneum.

My pleasant week came to an end, but the memory of it will live long.

I slip into harness and proper company with great facility. No sooner had I left Cordoba than I fell in with two other tramps: one a Frenchman bound for Cadiz, the other a little Spanish cripple, who was going to Melilla to fight the Moors.

Every Spaniard thinks himself big enough to fight his "eternal enemy," and this little chap—much

under five feet in height and a miserable cripple in
both legs—pegs along right cheerfully, for he is sure
he will be accepted as a volunteer and get a stripe or
two before the war is over. The Frenchman is not
so philanthropic. He is going to Cadiz simply because
a tramp must always be going somewhere, or he
would get no support. He can speak Spanish, but
" he doesn't intend to "—he profits by his ignorance.
Three tramps in company are all too much on a
Spanish road ; starvation or blackmail is inevitable
unless we part. After my week's rest I was fresh,
and,—their news-bag exhausted,—I took them at a
pace which soon grew too hot. One by one they
lagged behind, and I have not seen them since.

A walk of some hours in the darkness brought me
to a tiny village, sleepy and still as death. I could
find no stable or barn-door open, so the only bed
left to me was Mother Earth. The night was
bitterly cold : a sharp white frost, and when morning
broke my limbs were so stiffened and sore that it
was some time before I could muster strength enough
to continue my journey.

At Carlota, which is the sister town to La Carolina
built by Charles III. and named after his two
daughters, I fell in with an Englishman, who treated
me with much frank generosity. I passed a day and
a night under his roof, gained some practical advice

about local and agricultural matters, and was accompanied by him for some distance on the road towards Ecija.

The " temperate clime " was now behind me, and palms and other subtropical vegetation began to show themselves. These growths indicate a change, nothing more. The country is still as monotonous and wild, and water scarcer than ever. This dry monotony is the dominant characteristic of a Spanish landscape, but no doubt it has a fascination for the native born. Spain is ever a land of wide horizons. From the farthest hill one looks down on a wide world. The air is usually so thin and clear that tiny objects can be made out at a distance of miles. Where mountain chains are in sight one may be certainly interested by the lights and shadows, clouds and colours which the winds and sun cast around them.

From the roadway I could see the famous old castle of Almaduna, which is perched on a high peak rising near the bed of the Guadalquivir. Beyond the castle runs the Sierra Morena, all glittering and sparkling in the evening sun. The space lying between the Sierra and the road is filled with olive trees. These throw a grey, sad shadow over the landscape, and lend a tinge of melancholy to the scene. The olive mills and occasional dwellings—

all snowy white—show through the dreamy ether, and nothing speaks of active life save the hope which enables this tramp to push on.

At Ecija I found a pleasant change. The river Genil is large, and its banks carry a broad margin of shady trees. I cast about me for a modest posada suited to my needs. A tramp is always in need ! " That eternal want of pence which vexes public men " must have been the plaint of a tramp ! I found a very crowded posada, where for a penny I got a bed in the chaff-house amongst fully a dozen other wayfarers. They left me very much alone, for I heard them whispering that I was a spy picking up information about Melilla—a topic which was sending the country folk mad with fanatical notions.

Ecija by daylight is a really pretty old town. The Spaniards have it that one Austin or Astor founded it immediately after the destruction of Troy (by this the Spaniards profess to have a much better knowledge of the Asiatic city than we), and it has gone on distinguishing itself ever since. It resisted Romans and Moors, and sent its bravest sons to wage the siege of Granada.

But she worked too hard. She gave of her children, and her wine, corn, and oil, till she became very poor ; and now, Spanish-like, she has nothing but her pride to soothe and delight her. She has

no trade and no industry save—politics. The
"secretario" tells me they do a big business in this
article,—that matters took an upward tendency last
evening, and that "there will be a grand revolution
to-night!" . Won't I stay and see it ? No, thank
you. I am not in love with revolutions over matters
which I do not understand.

But I can understand the plain fact that Ecija is
overtaxed. Its people refuse to pay a "consumos"
duty equal to two hundred per cent. on all that
comes into it, and to-night they mean to fight the
authorities and make a tariff which the Governor
will have to accept as final. I hope they got
their rights without much fighting. They are a
tidy people to look at. Ecija is very clean, and its
inhabitants ditto—a population almost unique in
this respect. I didn't see anything of "the thirteen
boys of Ecija ;" doubtless they are all in their graves.
The "trece Ninos de Ecija" were an old band of
robbers who haunted the roads of Central Andalucia
for many many years. The circumstance which
keeps their memory green in the heart of all Spain
is the singular fact that they were always thirteen
in number ; though occasionally broken up by the
police and shot down by civilians, whenever they
reappeared it was always as thirteen. They were
not cold-blooded rascals, and were well spoken of by

all (except their victims) for their extreme humanity and their care for a few old monks who were fed and clothed almost entirely from the spoils of the boys of the road.

Excepting this little blemish I know of nothing against Ecija. I don't stick up for it because I got any great assistance from it, for I did not.

I called on the "secretario," and he spurned me with the most contemptuous frown he could call into his smug little face. He was an old man, and could be caustic without any downright effort.

He told me that Spain was for the Spaniards, and not for English tramps.

Then he asked me how long it would be before I had completed my plan for an attack on Spain (by the English), and if I should enjoy a few months' solitary confinement in their little prison previous to bringing me up for public justice to be done.

I assured him that this was all very interesting. It was so new, so unlike any experience I had ever endured before, that I begged he would continue in the same strain. The sun shone so fiercely, and the nights were, on the contrary, so intensely cold, that to follow him in fancy to that pleasant retreat where none but "guardias civiles" and town guards come, was quite refreshing, and looked more agreeable than many of my actual experiences have been.

There is not a man on earth who can stand against a natural fool! The "secretario" was convinced I was of that order, so he told me to be off, and "the devil look out for himself if he fell in with me."

I didn't go to the devil. I went to the alcalde, who was a very different man, and regretted his heart could not swell beyond his means. Ecija was under a yoke. "But if you should come round this way again. . . ." "Now, really, I don't think it likely that I shall, but thanks all the same!"

I carried the order he wrote for me to the "secretario," and on beholding me for the second time, the look of surprise and disgust which overspread his face far out-did the expression it wore when I first addressed him. He saw he had made a mistake. He owned that he was blind as an owl at midday. He begged me to excuse the slight he had offered me.

Of course I would! I, a tramp, not willing to be charitable when I expect all to be charitable to me! I assured him that there was "no faulte," and his shrivelled-up little face relaxed into a bland and generous smile which hung fire there during the time I was in his company. "He blossomed in an hour," as the song says. He took me by the hand and said I was . . . ! He told me where to go, and what to see, and finally he gave me a book as a lasting token of his eternal respect!

Ecija is as full of colour as a circus waggon. Its churches, palaces, and houses are nearly all striped and splashed with showy colours, and although the hands which laid on these curious traceries were not highly skilled artists, the effect is decidedly picturesque. From a gentle hill near the town I looked down on seventeen tall towers, all painted from summit to basement, and presenting a very rare and effective picture.

The road from Ecija to Luisiana was dull and monotonous. I slept in the stable of a ventas, after sharing with the kindly family their evening meal of boiled chestnuts, olives, and bread.

My way now lay through rich but sadly neglected country. The soil was deep and rich, but it yielded no crop. Such neglect in the presence of such want as I had left behind me in Ecija showed all too plainly where the fault lay. It is not more law, but more individual effort that is wanting in Spain. The people have lost their self-respect. There is no longer any honour in labour or any dishonour in laziness and indifference to probity and justice. On the road I was subjected to a rigorous search by three "guardias civiles," who overhauled everything I possessed, and took copies of such notes as I had in Spanish. They were, as ever, very respectful, and set me wondering what system of discipline makes this body so different from all other Spanish officials.

Satisfied that I had a clean sheet, they let me go, and before evening I reached the loftily situated town of Carmona. As it was Sunday, all the world and his wife were promenading in the principal "calles." "Un poseo" (a walk) is the great luxury of poor Spain. To stroll and look at other strollers is a never-failing source of delight.

Carmona is an attractive town. It shows fine arches of Moorish construction, a large old castle and many Moorish houses. The church of San Pedro has a beautiful painted tower. It is of great height, and possesses some fine carved stone-work. I took pot luck at a very good posada, where every one was raving about Melilla and too excited to notice me. I slept in the chaff-house with other tramps, and found the bill all the lighter for having done so, for while a tramp gets his "doss" for a penny, a traveller's bed is a "real."

There is nothing but parasitism in this district. The people live on each other, and the only working force is the poor donkey or mule. If I ask what they manufacture, they say flour ! A flour mill or a press that gives out a few hundred gallons of oil is quite a big industry, and sufficient to satisfy a town as large as Carmona (16,000 souls).

The cultivated lands around it do not total ten square miles, yet there are hundreds of miles lying waste. I longed for enough Spanish to curse these lazy rascals to their face. But there, what is the use of grumbling or swearing at a Spaniard? He likes both, and enjoys a wordy row as much as his dinner; so I must hold back my bad language for another occasion.

Just beyond Carmona the Giralda shows in sight, and I felt inclined to rush on, but my bundle was no lighter, and the tramp who hurries loses ground. Twenty-five miles stretched from Carmona to Alcala de Guadaira, and as the sun was hot, and the way was dry, my day was not an easy one. From the open ridge which the road takes, I looked over a great black valley. The earth is black with white houses showing here and there, so that it looks like a wintry sea flecked with white sails.

I ought to be well-nigh purified and fit for "Happy Land" by this time, for I have drunk hogsheads of holy water since I started on this journey. Nearly every well and fountain yields up its cleansing flood in the name of "Our Lady" or some saint, and why the Spanish public should remain so worldly in the presence of so much grace is another of the problems which remains to be solved. Here at Alcala is a precious flow said to be the direct gift of San Joachim to the people of the town.

In the morning I had a big wash of clothes that I might make a decent entry into Sevilla.

At Alcala are the remains of a Moorish castle and fort, forming one of the largest ruins in Spain. It is over a thousand feet long, and broad in proportion. It occupies the crown of a hill projecting itself towards a half-circular vale, along whose bed flow the clear waters of the Guadaira. Nothing more than bits of outer walls and towers remain, just enough to show its former size and strength. As I wound along the road by the river-side I got a fine view of the old place. On the western side thirteen towers shoot towards the clear sky, and behind them, on what was once the courtyard of the castle, rises a little church, whitewashed and lively looking in comparison with the decaying towers—as if the Christian shrine were gaily crowing over the downfall of the Moor. Nearly everywhere the triumph of the Spaniard is marked by the substitution of a church or monastery for the Moorish castle or fort.

The Moors were great engineers. Their systems of raising and conducting water are known and appreciated by the whole world. There are large tracts of land in Spain on which the Moors introduced water, and made the scheme profitable, and yet, in spite of the progress of science, modern engineers are unable to deal with the same localities, or understand the extraordinary success of the Moors. Here, from Alcala to Sevilla, a distance of ten miles, the Moors made an aqueduct to supply the latter with pure water. They raised the water to high levels by means of enormous wheels, bored through hills of rock and sand,—erected bridges and flumes over streams and canons, and brought this great volume of water into Sevilla in a manner that must ever compel the admiration of the Spaniard who hates them. There is an elevated aqueduct nearly four miles in length. I tried to count the arches, but grew tired. Three or four miles are enough to speak for themselves.

CHAPTER XV.

SEVILLA.

I HAVE read that the approach to Sevilla is always beautiful, but it showed nothing very attractive to me on my entrance. The situation is good from a commercial point of view, as all Sevilla stands on a flat by the river, but the "calles" being narrow and crooked, one rarely gets a view of more than a couple of hundred yards in extent. I had been taught to believe that the Sevilla streets and houses are all quaint and beautiful, but this is not the case. Some of the "calles" show some lovely dwellings, but the vast majority are poor and uninteresting.

Taking it all round it is not "beautiful old Sevilla." It owns some rare beauties, but there is no hard hunting necessary to discover blots and imperfections, which tell heavily against its boasted perfection.

I must confess that Sevilla did not receive me well. All Spain was just then mad over the last row with the Moors, and the Sevilla street arab was undiscerning enough to take my light baggy knickerbockers for the costume of his "eternal enemigo." The cry of "Une Moro!" was raised, and I was followed along the narrow streets by hundreds of boys and (shall I call them?) men, who threw stones and garbage at me, forcing me at last to take refuge in a tram. To have fallen so far below the English standard as to be taken for a miserable "rifeño" was hard indeed, and I ceased to be vain of my appearance as a tramp. Policemen do exist in Sevilla, but they have their own private and important business to attend to. Large and noisy as was the mob, no "active and intelligent officer" came in sight, nor did I hear a solitary remark in my defence from any street passenger. Sevilla is famous for its bull-fights, and, consequently, for its brutality.

Clear away from the mob I found a home, a "happy home," in the Calle Genova. The name, "Fonda Alegria," spoke for itself!

Here I found blissful retirement, and when I chose to break the silence, some pleasant moments with a very strong and singular character in the person of a Russian naturalist who, like myself, was a despised alien in the town of the Giralda. The next best thing to a fellow-countryman is a fellow-stranger.

There was a marked resemblance between the Russian's life and my own. We had both rebelled against that crowd which is called "the world," and yet we imagine that, like lesser Newtons, we pick up grains, and shells, and sand, which afford us truer joys than are known to the vulgar mob hurrying along the street outside. My friend could afford to speak lightly of "degrees." He boasted of nothing save the need of knowing more.

After taking high honours at the University of Kieff, an insatiable love for the simple things in nature set him roving. He had made a complete tour of the coasts of the cold Black Sea—throwing his grappling net for the salt weeds and "curled darlings" which shroud the rocks submerged around its shores. Then journeying down to Marmora he had studied a phase in the lives of the innumerable wild fowl which cross that sea in their migrations from Lower Poland to their winter quarters on the brackish fens of Asia Minor and the Persian valleys.

He had culled rare lichens, zoophytes, and fine fossils from the rocks and reeds of tiny islands of the Levant; and then he had gone on to Smyrna, Galilee, and Egypt, and,—without venturing into

" Shepherd's " of Cairo, or the seductive cafés of Alexandria,—had found more real and substantial pleasures in the small still life which blooms and fades without a name on the low hills beside the far-spreading Nile. What an innocent life! His worst crime is the slaughter of some little creature that he may study its structure and provide, maybe, a new antidote for the suffering world.

I believe that Platon Koulakoff is storing up little by little knowledge which will one day be eagerly welcomed by the students of science.

At the end of three delightful days my Russian comrade set off for Madrid, and I was left to find new interests in old Sevilla. It holds many attractions, but the greatest of all is the Alcazar.

Could the nations of the world see this one triumph of the Moors, I think they would subscribe a fund large enough to keep the remaining stock in affluence, that they might teach future generations the lesson of beauty which the religion of Mahomet inspires. The Spanish say that "the truth and the roses have thorns," and accordingly some faults are to be found with the Alcazar. Let them snarl! There is still more perfection here than is crammed into any similar space on this planet.

The heart is quickened and grows faint by turns as one moves shyly within its gorgeous apartments,

till the surroundings grow into an Arabian nightmare,
and one awakes to find oneself all the poorer for
having seen this poetical mosaic.

Who can describe, who can presume to say what
this palace is like, how it is ordered and what it
contains?   I can only say that it is faultless in detail
and equally perfect as a whole.   One grows by
custom indifferent to the choicest things, and the
most delicious sweets are the quickest to cloy; but
who ever tired of the Alcazar?   It is usual to worship
where we cannot understand, and who can understand this wonderful palace, even though it be the
work of an inferior brother?

I asked an Englishman wherein the secret of its
beauty lay; and he answered, "In its reality! The
Alcazar is not a toy. You recognise a convenient
and sensible dwelling into which it is a positive
sacrilege to trespass."

The main entrance opens on a courtyard flanked
by the palace walls. A long and splendidly decorated
corridor penetrates to the centre of the building.
Here is a large, open "patio" surrounded by white
marble columns which support walls and balconies,
overlaid with intricate mosaic work in every variety
of colour. The spectacle, though dazzling, is yet soft
and harmonious. The state rooms open from this
"patio." No two are alike in shape or in decoration,

and there is not one in which it would not be a joy to be kept a prisoner for life! They are all ablaze with rich coloured embroidery-like tracings, and, although entirely destitute of furniture, the very floors must seem a bed of roses to all who are privileged to rest on them. The gem of these apartments is the "Salon des Ambassadors," situated at one end of the beautiful "patio," and next to the room in which the deposed Isabella was born. The "salon" is square, and the walls run up to form a dome. From the marble floor to the crown of the ceiling the entire wall space is ornamented with the finest hair lines and touches of colour, the most prominent being celestial blue, orange, crimson, ivory, and gold. But it is not the mere painting of a smooth wall surface. Every inch has been first carved and chased in the most exquisite and varied Oriental designs, and the touches of colour seem to have been literally breathed into them. The softest hand would be too heavy to paint these lilies.

There is a meaning in all these tracings, hiero-glyphics, and fantastic masses of colour, but the key to the wondrous enigma is lost. But you do not want to reason here; you do not want knowledge; you only want *to be*, and, given breathing space, you will be as happy as the wisest of earth. The Alcazar must be seen; it defies description. You are a prince of the pen, and you are a queen of song, but neither of you can sing the praises of one square foot of this enchanting palace. Presumptuous man aspires to many things which are above him, but here he is compelled to bend humbly before the work of his fellow-man.

As the Alcazar is the offspring of many minds and hands, it may be that no one man will ever be able to convey more than a vague impression of the magnificence of the whole. All the floors are of the finest marble or enamel work. Arches of exquisite mould give access to the rooms. Look, wander where you will, all is loveliness. It is the shrine of shrines for artistic effect. To stand at the northern end of the "patio" and look towards the Salon des Ambassadors is, I verily believe, the sight of the world. It matters nothing that it was restored by a cruel king.

All the virtues find a footing here. Patience, industry, love, beauty, strength, wisdom, hope, faith, charity, religion, are embodied in these walls, and it is a living testimony to the intelligence and dignity of the Moorish artists and artisans. Bear it in your memory and make a little pilgrimage to Sevilla that you may not quit this life without having seen the "ornament of the world."

After the Alcazar, all the other sights of Sevilla

are poor. They must be seen first or they cannot charm.

The tower of Sevilla, the Giralda, throws its shadow over the Cathedral, which is of splendid proportions and beautifully decorated within and without. The " Guardian Angel " and the " Vision of San Antonio " (Murillo) are its " popular " treasures. The latter is surrounded by fresh interest from the fact that it was recently stolen and taken to America ; but the Church authorities scented out the sacrilegious rogues and brought their idol back and set it up in one of the chapels, where it now hangs protected by strong iron bars.

I did not see the " beauties " of Sevilla at every turn. Perhaps they were making the most of a late summer at San Sebastian or Trouville. I went to the tobacco factory, where I was told I should see the Sevillana in all her glory. I saw her, but not her glory ! It was a wet day and she probably felt " dumpy," and not inclined for the accessories of dress, scent, and powder. About two thousand women are employed in this great national tobacco factory, and a plainer or more unkempt lot it would be hard to find.

The Sevillana whom young men sigh for and old men talk about is not a real beauty. She is as far removed from that hand-on-hip, coquettish damsel, with short skirt and showy stockings, white lace mantilla and pearly teeth, as is the veriest blackamoor from Old Guinea.

She is just a black-eyed, sullen-faced, thick-ankled, and dowdily dressed baggage, who, if she does laugh, does it without much show of reason.

If I were asked what the face of the Spanish woman most regularly lacks, I should say GOODNESS. One rarely sees a good face in Spain.

The women of some provinces are clean and thrifty, patient under pressure, and thoughtful for the home-coming of the bread-winners from their labour ; but that indefinable something which shows out of the eyes and comes forth from sweet lips in soft, but strong speech, and which we know as goodness, is non-existent in the Spanish woman.

The Spaniards say their women are " virtuous and brave." An idiot may be both and not call for our special respect. I have looked closely at thousands of women, and the wise counsellor, the woman who sees what is wrong and would help do what is right, the woman whose love imposes obligation, is still unknown to me. When I have seen a good face it has usually been passive. There was restfulness in it, but it was not marked by sufficient spirit to increase the good of the world.

The Spanish woman is always shielded and protected, because she is not supposed to know or do anything. She is more than half a Moor in her indifference to progress, and is so much in need of grace to sustain herself, that none can escape for the benefit of those around. I consider the absence of a good type of woman the greatest calamity of Spain. The woman must mother the world, or it will decay. The Spanish woman is not motherly. She is distinctly unconscious of the importance of her office. The man who calls her to be his wife is her only example, and, be it bad or good, she draws but little from it. She loves money and hoards it as the means to purchase salvation for her soul, and this ignorance, born of fear, binds her and keeps her a low, unaspiring thing.

I remained in Sevilla eight days. Each day I took my simple meal alone and sought my dessert out of doors in the sights of the city.

Only on one occasion did the dessert come to me. My room in the "Fonda Alegria" was at the top of a six-story house, and the Fondero and his wife, being rather bulky people, seldom came to know if I stood in need of anything. A little, beady-eyed damsel with a deathly pale face came each day to make my bed and leave the food I had ordered, and these offices performed, she was seen no more till the morrow. But a day or two before I left, she appeared at midday with some fruit, and asked me to accept it. It was a dull, dark day, and the world—my world —seemed very gloomy, and perhaps the maiden saw that I was not too happy. At any rate, she said "Pobre caballero," looked kindly at me, and wiped a very human tear from her eyes.

Poor little soul! she would have done much for poor me—I know she would; but ere I could tell her that there was no cause for tears, she had gone, and in place of the brief ray of sunlight came the shadow. Sevilla was dull, and my attic was dull. I often recalled the experiences of Beranger and Balzac and Thackeray in their attic homes in old Paris. I, in old Sevilla, was even more alone, less talented and more friendless, and yet my gentle consoler had the power of brightening my world for a moment as did theirs.

The local press said that I "preserve a sympathetic appearance," and that " I spoke generously of Spain." (This is kind, and much to my credit, considering the ungracious reception I received.) But do they mean it? In a land where you can buy and are expected to sell "truth and justice, religion and piety," for the sum of a penny a bargain, I am slow to accept words as facts. However, I think it politic to say, " Mil gracia, Sevilla and thy people ; fare thee well !"

There is nothing, after all, like the road for a tramp. It is his proper place. He forms a natural part of the landscape, and the people he meets there treat him more humanely than do those of the crowded towns.

CHAPTER XVI.

FROM SEVILLA TO GRANADA.

I HAVE got down in my note-book, " The road from Alcala (just beyond Sevilla) to Arahal is a vile brute," and I am not inclined to alter the statement.

The land is good and in some places well cultivated, but the road is flat, bad, and uninteresting. A few wretched houses showed here and there, but I could get no bread anywhere, and the number of times I was told to " go with God " was all I had to sustain me till I arrived at Arahal, a walk of nearly twenty miles. As it was the time of olive-gathering, the roads were thronged with men and women of all ages, journeying in search of work in the groves and mills. Many of the women were dressed in male attire, and it was only by their softer faces that they were distinguishable from the men. The object of the male dress is to facilitate tree-climbing, standing on ladders, and creeping about to pick up the olives. They all smoked, and their bad language was coarser and more frequent than that of the men. The Spaniard who stays at home thinks those who journey about as olive-pickers are a bad lot. This is probably true, but although I met thousands of them between Sevilla and Granada, they always treated me with courtesy.

At Arahal I was overhauled at the posada of the "Sun" by the guard, who, on finding no treason about me, instantly turned friendly, and offered to present me to the dignitaries of the place. Arahal has but four thousand inhabitants, but no town is too small to have its share of great men.

The village Hampdens were assembled this night in council to hear and consider the pleas of certain poor widows and others who objected to their sole supports being sent to wage war against the Moors in Melilla.

I saw these widows, and other poor and helpless people, crying pitifully, and telling sad tales of their distress, as I was ushered into the council chamber of the town.   About a dozen of the fattest men I have ever beheld were seated round a board.   Evidently the people of Arahal think that brains and bigness go together.

A very fat and ruddy-faced priest, who was one of their number, acted as spokesman.   On learning that I was interested in agriculture, the great and august body warmed and proceeded to welcome me as only fat men can.

They pressed me individually and collectively to give them my opinion of agriculture in Spain.   I was glad to be able to tell the wise men of Arahal that they were in the midst of great national wealth, which they appeared to be making sensible efforts to increase.   Of course this pleased them, and they left off praising me, and went in for praising themselves.   They told me what quantities of corn and oil they grew, and how fat it had made them.

I could not deny this!   Furthermore, they confided to me that since they had found that energy meant success, Arahal had been daily growing in wealth. This was so far removed from ordinary Spanish talk, that I found myself wondering what manner of men these could be, and from what source they had derived their simple wisdom.

Their generosity turned out to be as great as their size, for they gave me a pocketful of cigars and cigarettes, and ordered a good supper for me at the posada of the Sun. Meanwhile, the poor women and a crowd of curious idlers were kept shivering in the street. It was a sight to make one shiver, for Arahal stands high and much exposed, as there are broad plains all around it.

At the posada a crowd of young fellows were held captive by a few rural and provincial guards. These raw recruits seemed to think they would be able to mate with whom they pleased, and be expected to lead an attack before they had been in red trousers twenty-four hours. I heard them making compacts and promises to stand by each other in life and death, and to send relics to the lonely old mother or pining sweetheart they were leaving behind, though it was more than probable that they would be ordered back to their wooden ploughs as " misfits " before they got out of their native province. We sat late round a tiny fire made of corncobs which smouldered in a *brasero* on the posada floor. The recruits told many simple human tales about *Mi casa* (home), and the old days—both of which seemed to have gone for ever. When the fire had burned out, and the last tale had been told, I went off to the chaff-house, where I lay and shivered till morning. Arahal's last gift was a cold, and I had to walk my hardest to get rid of it before night. I struck across a long uneven plain, whose bed was well-cultivated corn land, and the little rising ground was capped with olives and cork oak.

The towers of Carmona and the peaks of the Sierra Morena showed away to the west, the plain ran up to the horizon on the north and south, and, far away to the east, rose the snow-capped Montes de Maron, and still farther off the peaks of Antequera.

Towards evening I got away from the plain and struck a road shut in between long stretches of grape country and forests of olives. Now and then a snowy white house showed from a strip of garden filled with lemons and oranges. The *Pinus maritima* shoots up here and there, and the smaller cabins inhabited by the peasants are thatched with its fine branches.

I managed to buy a bit of bread and fruit on the road, and this kept my heart a-beating till at last, footsore, I arrived at La Puebla de Cazalla.

Have you ever been so varied in your thoughts as to wonder if a tramp may have thoughts of love? I really believe he has. I have heard the most ancient and miserable specimens chirp very hopefully about certain maiden and widowed hearts, who sigh for them. I, too, have had my love passages.

Passing a posada, I saw three very pretty girls sitting in the doorway, and they saw me. What then? Why, I saw that I was welcome and went in. The place was full, but room was made for me.

One of the maidens darned my stockings, another put some stitches in a shirt, and one sensible minx prepared a good bowl of soup. If you feed a man he will love you, and I cultivated a liking for my ministering angel right away. The other two were beauties, but what had they done for me?

Two of the girls had made a little journey in the world, and they fell to telling me what they liked best in Spain, which was of course the Church. Spanish women never tire of hearing of the histories attached to their sacred buildings. In the course of our talk I learned that a carpenter of La Puebla was the carver of those wonderful doors which are to be seen on the Church of San Francesco in Madrid.

I soon found a man willing to accompany me to his little home. Truly genius crops up in unexpected places. Edoardo Martin is an ordinary-looking little man, but he is a true genius, and one who will take no honour to himself. He showed me his chests containing thousands of steel tools, and he tells me that all the virtue of his work lies in them.

He has certificates and complimentary letters signed by royal hands, and a few engravings of his best works hanging on the walls of his simple home; and I know of no other possessions which could prevent his feeling very poor. The doors of San Francesco were the work of two men, Antonio Varela (an Italian) and Martin. The former is dead, and Martin may be looked on as dead to the world. His roof shelters a strong character, who once yearned to pull down what his host loves to build up. Hypolito Pauly was a member of the Carlist band in Spain, and of a Radical Association which flourished in France under the late Empire. He has now lost his belief in a change of rule as a panacea for all ills, and is a calm, kindly man, whose sole ambition is the improvement of those around him. He has long since proved that he can do more good by preaching peace in the village of La Puebla than by noisy denunciations of the powers that be on the banks of the Manzanares or the Seine.

Teaching is his occupation, and the schoolmaster and his scholars formed a delightful old picture—he in his black silk skull cap and long cotton gown, they in clothing of all colours, shapes, and states of decay. The little chamber with its white instead of black board, and charcoal instead of chalk, and its oil amps hanging round walls on which the rudest out-lines of maps were roughly drawn, looked like a school that might have held its own against the storms and threatenings of a thousand years.

La Puebla being Spanish to the core, is strictly

conservative, and although the teacher has seen London and Paris in stirring times, "his new fangled notions" do not make way with this self-satisfied public.   He told me of the "pomps and vanities" he had witnessed in various capitals, described Bismarck's laugh in his young days as something between a bark and a sneeze, and spoke in generous praise of the Empress Eugenie's singing.   He was honest enough to admit that he had been the servant of rich, vain clowns, who were flattered and deceived by his telling them what he knew they wanted to hear.   To-day he is doing better work, and although his average income is but a shilling a day, he is a happier man. Beside the little fire of his artist friend, he told me some pages of his early life, and I can but hope that he may be long spared to instruct the dull boys of La Puebla.

Martin and Pauly took me to an oil mill, built after a Roman design, which has been standing for many centuries.   I cannot attempt to explain the mechanism of this big old thing in wood and stone. It is said to pay just as well as any modern invention, and therefore why complain?

I returned to find the posada crowded with a motley throng of olive pickers and lavender sellers. The latter owned a mob of donkeys, laden with sacks of the sweet herb, which they were taking to Sevilla.

There were also a man and his wife who would certainly have to watch the wind, or it would carry them away, for they were draped with hundreds of yards of cream-coloured sausage skins which they were hawking round to the butchers' shops. The women were all busy cooking oil broth and an endless variety of soups over the little heaps of charcoal hissing and sighing on different parts of the posada floor. Tired out, I went to sleep on the cold floor in the close neighbourhood of the lavender sellers, and of the man and his wife, nick-named " The Balloons," who sold the sausage skins.

When the time for starting had come, Francisca, the daughter of the house, who had prepared the soup for me, came to my side, and, stretching out her hands so that I might take them, said, " You are the first Englishman I have seen, and I don't want you to go away! How different you are from the Spaniards!"

There was that in the girl's voice which forced me to take the words as a compliment. I told her that I did not pretend to represent the Englishman at home.

" Will you ever come here again?" she asked.

" No, never."

" And is England far away?"

" England is quite close, as I count distances, but

my only home is where night finds me, and when I leave Spain I shall go right away to the other side of the world."

The maiden hung her head, and could say no more.

Just then her mother, a woman with a beautifully calm, sweet face, came to tell me that a mule car was starting for Osuna, and I could get a lift. I thanked her, pressed the hand of her gentle daughter, and, after stowing my bundle and myself amongst a lot of flour sacks, Francisca and La Puebla were soon lost to sight.

As the driver of the mule car was a dull customer, and the country no better, I lay under the broad awning, musing over the incidents of my stay in the village, till Francisca appeared the very embodiment of Byron's " Haidee," and I fell to wondering what her future would be. Judging from the life around her, it would be simple, and if anything more, hard.

I have heard it said that Osuna has " a great name and little worth," and there appears to be some truth in the remark. One really wonders how the town exists. A rich piece of country to the south of it carries nothing but occasional patches of corn, and as there are no manufactures, one is left to wonder how such a big stomach as Osuna is fed. True, it knows nothing of fashion or luxury, but its common needs call for more than it earns.

It is rich in churches and in open spaces, some of the latter carrying a few stunted trees, and others bare of everything but dirt!

The mule car halted before a very clean posada, and I decided to stay at the same house for the night.

I found an excellent fire—a luxury in a tramp's life—and after I had eaten a basin of bread soup, I sat in amongst a knot of scissors-grinders, umbrella-menders, bird-cage and trap makers, and other tramps, and listened to tales of the road!

Those who were known at the posada were allowed to sleep round the fire, but I, being an alien, had to share a chaff loft with a rascal who ground his teeth in such a hideous and savage manner that he kept me awake the whole night.

In the morning I paid the posadera for my bed and board, shouldered my knapsack, and was marching off, when I was asked to pay eight reals as the fare between La Puebla and Osuna.

This looked like blackmailing, and I indignantly refused to be detained on the plea of such a debt. But I had to yield to superior strength.

The scissors-grinder and umbrella-mender came

to the aid of the posadera, and between them I was made prisoner. I was offered my liberty if I would give my sleeping rug in payment of the fare. As I had not the slightest intention of parting with my only comforter, I insisted on their sending for the guardia civil. But the cunning dogs sent for a municipal guard, a local rogue who favours those he knows. This worthy appeared, and with great pomposity he summed up the case before hearing the evidence! Taking his long sword in one hand, and grasping an old horse pistol, which he carried on his hip, in the other, he informed me that Osuna was no place for me to try my little game. The posadera told her tale, and the guard said, " Clear." The scissors-grinder testified to the desperate nature of the arrest, and again he said, " Clear." The bird-trap and umbrella-makers gave corroborative evidence : " Clear ! " The mob who had gathered round seemed anxious to lynch me, and to all their vicious remarks the guard responded, " Clear."

There was nothing that was not clear to this Dogberry, save his own obtuseness. Would I pay the debt (the posadera was the owner of the car and mules) or go before the " beak " ? I told them that I would go before forty beaks before I would give up the only thing that had kept me alive o' nights.

As it was Sunday, and the Casa Consistorial was closed, I had to be detained till the morrow. My enemies took me to a stable and turned the key on me. During the day I was given bread and olives, and at night I was brought forth like a chained tiger, and allowed to toast my legs for ten minutes in front of the fire. Then I was led back to my manger bed; and although I was a prisoner in a strange land, and the world of Osuna was quite ready to hang me, I could afford to go to sleep in the belief that to-morrow would not be the worst of all days to me.

In the morning, leaving my knapsack as security, I was allowed to go in search of some one to defend me.

I went to the Town Hall and gave *my* version of the case, and the alcalde and the secretario found it to be "clear." They apologised for the treatment I had received, and sent a guard to fetch my baggage from the posada.

When I had got my precious bundle once more on my back, my old enemy, the municipal guard, hove in sight. How pleased I was to be able to look that limb of the law in the face, and show him that he had been badly beaten on his own ground! Then I looked round for the road to Estepa. I was so disgusted with the clear-sighted guard, and so unpopular with the street idlers, that I was glad to make the shortest way out of the town, without entering any of the many churches and disused monasteries, or visiting the pantheon of the dukes of Osuna, which the alcalde told me was remarkable for the extraordinary beauty of its architecture.

At midday I crossed a small river bearing the name of an adjacent village—Aquadulce, though just then it was Aqua-rubia, for its waters were blood red.

The country near the river is rich, and in places quite pretty. The village rests in a hollow, and just then the hills around were golden with the dying leaves of the poplar trees.

Between Aquadulce and Estepa, a mountain of white chalky stone rises abruptly. I had been told by the mayor of Osuna that in a basin on the crown of this hill are the remains of a Roman theatre.

As night was coming on, I did not see this curiosity with my own eyes, but on making inquiries of a friend whom I afterwards met, he endorsed the mayor's description, adding that there was strong local evidence that the Romans must have been very numerous in the province, and attained to a high degree of civilisation.

Estepa, which is built on a slope of the great white hill, forms an exceedingly fine picture, and commands one of the most generous views I have seen in Spain. The landscape is composed of hundreds of square miles of corn, and wine, and oil, intersected here and there by dark irregular lines indicating water-courses, and there is actually one little lake reflecting the sunlight. Estepa was a stronghold of the Moors. A fine tower, and some massive walls forming the ramparts of a citadel, still stand as memorials of their presence. Some of the old Spanish houses are of great beauty. One, in the principal *calle*, has a façade of polished grey marble; its Attic windows and porch are supported on spiral columns of the same, while a knight's arms and floral trophies on a shield form the keystone of the portal.

From Estepa eastwards the country is very hilly, and the narrow road winds corkscrew fashion in order to avoid the hills. In a tiny vale, with high limestone cliffs shading it through half the longest day, rests the sleepy little hamlet of Laura. The valley is well watered and the soil good, so that fruit trees and garden plots are abundant. The changing tints of autumn were over it all; wherever the eye fell it rested on golden-bronze and rich brown hues, and as coloured foliage and babbling waters are rarities in Spain, I found it pleasant to halt here for an hour, and gather a few wild scents as a memento of the sweet little spot.

New experiences awaited me at Casariche, where I was arrested and dragged to the Casa Quarte on suspicion of being a spy. I had to reproduce my signature to show that it tallied with those on my passport and health certificate, and I was cross-questioned about the whys and wherefores of my journey till I fairly lost patience. My tormentors pried into my letters, papers, and note-books, wrote down all I said in my own defence and obliged me to sign it, and then with very solemn faces and half doubts as to the wisdom of the proceeding—they let me go!

It was nearly ten miles from Casariche to Alameda, and I had to find my way through half wild and neglected country. The road, which had gradually been growing narrower, now ceased altogether to exist. As there had been much rain, the heavy clay soil made the walking greasy and heavy.

From midday till night I trudged over the un-peopled space, and it really looked like putting in a night on the cold ground; but, with just enough light to guide me clear away from some straggling olives, I discovered Alameda a couple of miles ahead, showing as an extensive farm building in the midst of a vast stubble field. I was so dead beat that I made for the first posada that came to hand, though it had a miserably tumble-down appearance.

The posadero took me in, for she says tramps are her usual customers—and so it seemed!

There was certainly a goodly number of the fraternity here this night; rough antiquated old chaps most of them, and, by contrast, the girl-wife of a blind guitar-player. He was a tall, dark-skinned, sullen-faced man of twenty-eight, and looking much older; while his wife was a tiny, red-haired, blue-eyed girl of seventeen. She had a pretty face and figure, and looked in every way too good for the life she had been called to lead. Doubtless the poor blind Gonzalo needed a cheery companion to make up for the terrible loss of sight, but how he had been able to woo and win such a genial and faithful little attendant it was difficult to imagine.

When the house had been locked up, as is customary in Spain at nightfall, the musician began his songs and tales, and the wife her canvass for coppers. I was surprised to see how liberally the wayfarers gave from their little store of centimes and crusts. As for myself, my mite was reserved till morning, as I did not wish to increase the curiosity of my comrades.

Before going to bed I scribbled a few notes by the light of a torch which a girl held over me. As the sleeping places in the posada were few I was relegated to the corner of a small loft with Gonzalo and his wife, when in spite of the noise they had made all the evening with their songs and jokes and tales, I found them quiet room-mates.

Rain was falling heavily when I left Alameda, and it poured steadily all day, though by pushing along through heavy country I managed to keep warm and fairly comfortable till I reached Archidona. Here, aided by the attention of a kind woman and a good fire, I soon made my things dry and clean again. I was entitled to some comfort after a climb of two solid hours up a road which ought to be a flight of steps, before reaching the town. It is scattered along a terrace on one side of a great hill, magnificently wild and rugged. Far above the town, on what look like inaccessible crags, stand an old castle, a church, and some fragments of defensive walls.

Archidona though drowsy is said to be rich. And it ought to be. There is some splendid land in the valleys below, and the climate is good enough to satisfy the most fastidious farmer.

Although the posada was dedicated to St. John it was not a paying concern. A pedlar and myself were the only patrons, and the pedlar having nothing interesting to say, I went to bed early in my little chaff-house. With the morning came more rain and no prospect of its clearing, for I was daily getting into a more mountainous country, and the winter season was drawing on apace.

It so happened that a man whom I had met some days before in another town came along with a troop of donkeys, and he promptly offered me a ride as far as Loja. Of course I accepted, and after priming him with a deep glass of "Spanish delight" (aquadiente), I mounted my humble steed, and we jogged off through the little town, much to the glee of some street urchins.

We journeyed many miles through a valley carrying a small river, the mountains running up shaggy and terrible on either side. After leaving the river we made a miserable climb over churlish, stony hills, entirely destitute of vegetation and everything else, save a few look-out towers and heaps of stones, apparently of Moorish construction.

Beyond these hills dipped another valley and a stream aptly named the "Cold River." So we found it.

At a solitary house near the fording place we fortified ourselves with more "Spanish delight," and then made another long climb, happily the last, for, on gaining the top of the hill, we looked down on the rambling, picturesque old city of Loja.

I was not allowed to enter it unmolested. The "guardias civiles" were as cautious and painstaking as ever, and, in spite of my being wet and cold, they held me for some time, till, satisfied that I had not come to blow up Loja, they gave me a glass of wine and my liberty.

The donkey-man had gone his way, and I was left alone, very much alone, for no one would take me in. Doubtless the rough weather had roughened my appearance, and I was told that the " next " and the " next " posada was the place for me, till at last there was no " next " left, and I had to show my colours and insist on being taken in. The posada where I elected to stay was full of a very mixed crowd. There were a couple of well-dressed commercial travellers, several hawkers of a lower grade, and a great many unclassified rascals like myself! One or two of the faces would have enchanted an artist in search of a villain. The Spaniard is usually seen at a disadvantage. He professes to be clean shaven, but it is only once a week or fortnight that he visits the barber, and then for the day he looks clean and manly, after which he drops back into a blackguardly ruffian. It takes a very good face to show through a black growth a week old ; hence it is in a great measure the beard that makes Spain so full of bad and repulsive faces.

The posada fire was made of almond shells. A little heap was lighted early in the evening, and when it had burned low, the posadero collected the halfpennies from those who patronised it and put on more shells.

All the house fires burning in Spain would not make so big a pile as you may see on a 5th of November in the Bishops' Close at Exeter or Bridgewater. A "candella" (fire) in winter is a Spaniard's most precious luxury.

Being a stranger I was questioned about England and the way we live there, and when I said that "garbanzos" (chick peas) are unknown, a young fellow wanted to know what on earth we lived on!

The "garbanzo" is to Spain what the potato is to Ireland, only more so. It is served up in company with a little oil or bit of fat bacon, and such bits of green vegetable as may be in season, three times a day from the cradle to the grave of two-thirds of the population of Spain. The "puchara" is the dish of Spain ; it varies in its composition in the different provinces, but it is always wholesome, and a keen appetite prevents it becoming stale. Although the Spaniards are more than vulgar—they are hopelessly indecent and disgusting—at table, they still find cause to complain of the defects of strangers. The meanest beggar in Spain will ask you to share his crust, even though he sees you partaking of much better fare.

It is considered a compliment to be fed with the fingers of another, and yet if, in supplying a light, you don't offer the fiery end of a cigarette to a Spaniard, he regards you as an uncivilised brute. The commercial travellers at the posada promptly told me there was " something wrong with my education," because I did not ask them to share a hard crust I was trying to get my teeth through. Fortunately, I am a thick-skinned tramp, or the many shocks of this kind which I have received would have " settled me " long ago !

Here is an illustration of the value of money in Spain.

In the course of the evening the posada was turned well-nigh upside down, and every one made to look like a rogue, about a penny which the posadero had lost through a hole in his pocket.

It is impossible for pen and ink to convey an idea of the downright excitement raised by this missing penny. It led to searching everybody and everything in the house ; it led to scores of tales about other lost pennies, and peculiar ways of recovering them, or their eternal disappearance, until a long evening passed in what might truly be called a " Penny Lecture." The posadero appeared to be very well off, but that made no difference ; the penny was lost—clean gone—and she wanted to know the manner of its going. The penny was not found before I went to bed in the chaff-house, and the sad faces of mine host and his wife on the morrow told me that the rascally " brown " was still absent from the bolso (purse).

I had thought Loja pretty in the rain, but it was sweet in the sunshine. The valley was so full of autumn colour and richness, the river made such poetic windings, the town was so old and hoary, and the hills around it so wild and defiant, that it made a beautiful old-world picture, with just a strip of railway and a tunnel's mouth to remind one of the new.

Loja is Lucerne—without the lake, the Glacier Gardens, the Lion, and Tell's plateau ; yet it has many features in common with the Swiss town. I dare make this confession in face of the fact that Loja is known as the hell of Spain !

But I enjoyed my glimpse at the infernal regions— at least, the Inferno of Loja. It is not a hot place, for it is formed by a fall in the river. There is a break in the rocks at the lower level, and within this breach lies a great rock, shaped like an egg-cup. The waters from above empty themselves into this hollowed stone, and then rush round boiling and foaming in a most fantastic manner. A surrounding wall of water is constantly forced back by the torrent falling from above.

It is a strange and original little scene, and in a land where natural wonders are scarce the Inferno of Loja counts as a big thing.

The town guard was at his post, and not anxious to conduct me to the guardian of the city purse. But I hit him hard by dealing out my usual thrust—that he was only a town guard and not the alcalde. Once in the mayor's presence I was warmly received, and regaled with such coffee and cognac as might tempt a tramp with a bad memory to say nothing but kind things of Spain. ·   ·

Take my word for it, Andujar and Loja are good towns for English tramps! You may get a first night among the mosquitoes or in the rain, but, depend upon it, you'll finish well!

It is customary for tramps to "post" all the good places, and I want to whisper it very distinctly in your ear, that if you should ever be hard up in Spain (and God knows who may not be hard up), you must try and make round for Andujar or Loja ; and as I left both places with the sweet word " Felicitie " sounding in my ears, you may believe I was not in bad odour, and that it might do you no harm to mention my name.

I cannot omit mention of the horrible sights I saw in the principal church of Loja. The real hell was there! A series of pictures representing souls in torment, showed all the miserable agonies and writhings of which the human form is capable. Limbs and fragments of bodies were painted with a ghastly realism which well-nigh sickened me. These were the gems of art in Loja! It shocked and saddened me to realise that there can exist to-day in Europe a religion which offers such incentives as these to faith in an all-merciful Saviour.

Loja good and bad kept me till long past noon, and then I started for Granada, thirty-four miles away. It was a very good road and a pretty one. It lay beside the Genil, and the stretches of land on either side were well stocked with fruit trees, extensive tracts of sugar beet, and garden produce.

Towards sunset I came to a tributary of the Genil, which, as the bridge was broken down, I was obliged to ford. As it was a cold evening, and the bed of the river was covered with sharp stones, I did not enjoy having to strip and carry my bundle and clothing across on my head. By the time I had dried and dressed myself it was nearly dark, and I knew that the nearest village was many miles farther on the road. Close to the river stood a solitary house, a ventas, at the door of which stood two women, who called to know where I was going, and offered to put me up for the night. I was cold and careless after my forced bath, and, without thinking much about the nature of the house, I turned in.

It was built in ordinary posada style, the ground floor only open space, and a series of arches keeping up the ceiling. There was an immense open chimney in one corner, and within its circular dome were placed stone seats and a few brackets for holding water pitchers and delf. Whilst the women were shutting in the fowls and locking up the house, I managed to take a few pence out of my bag and tied the balance of my store in various articles of clothing. There was a " puchara " simmering on the small fire, and I agreed to take a share of it for twenty-five cents.

Just as the women had turned the " puchara " into a clay dish and stood it out on the floor, three men rapped at the door and asked to be admitted, saying that they were "aceituneros" (olive gatherers) from Antequerra, going towards Granada. Two were medium-sized men, and very fair for Spaniards, and the other was a tall, dark-skinned, sharp-faced fellow, with very restless flashing eyes. The two women and myself sat down to the " puchara," and as the men would not join us they found nothing better to do than to ask questions about me. They asked who I was, where I was going, was I alone, and finally, was I worth looking after? The two smaller men fell to talking under their breath, and I soon heard enough to make me believe they meant mischief. How I managed to go on eating and preserve an indifferent demeanour, I hardly know.

They spoke of the river, and of the ease with which one could be drowned in it, and my heart almost failed me. I am not a timid being. I do not fear men or death if either come to me in any guise which I may call fair; but the idea of being put out of the world by such wretches as these for the sake of the little I possessed was simply unbearable. In a moment I reviewed my whole life, and could call up nothing good I had done that would survive me. If I were killed this night there was little chance that my end would ever be known. I took out my note-book, wishing to write a few words, so that if any of my effects were ever found they might record my fate, but I could only muster courage to write: " At the ventas just over the olives, where the bridge is broken down; a rough crowd whom I do not like. I dread the sleeping part of the night; indeed, there will be very little sleep for me." And so it proved.

When the meal was over, the three men, who by this time spoke quite openly of their ruffianly pro-jects, asked to be shown to their sleeping place. One of the women told me to accompany them, but I made the excuse that I wished to sit up and mend my stockings, so the three were lighted to a loft by one of the women, and the other stayed with me. Whilst we were sitting in the semi-darkness another loud knock came to the door, and a man spoke from the outside. The woman recognised his voice and opened at once.

He was a big, old man, dressed as a farmer, and in a few seconds the two were talking and posing in a manner which led me to think them a pair of ancient lovers. The man and the two women went off into a small room at the opposite end of the posada, and I was left alone.

Near where I sat was a small doorway, and curiosity tempted me to look into the chamber. It was evidently meant for a store-room, but was now quite empty, except that a sack-bed lay in the centre of the floor.

This looked like a safe sleeping-place, and I waited for the women to return that I might make a bargain and sleep there.

I felt that it would be better to go to the room where the man and the women were, rather than endure this killing suspense. But I was unnerved—I confess it—and I waited and waited, because I had not strength to move !

At last the three came out of the room. The old man had a big "bolsillo" (sack purse) in his hand,

and when the women were seated he emptied the contents of it into their laps. It was about a thousand pieces, all in copper (a little over three pounds). The tally seemed satisfactory, and the money placed in the bag again, the old man wished the women "good-night," mounted his donkey, which had been tied to a pillar outside, and rode away.

It was nearly midnight, and a howling wind made the night more wretched. I thought this late departure strange, for the Spaniards dread night travelling, and are ever conscious of the traditional dangers of the road.

The man away, I asked permission to sleep in the little room. One of the women said, " Yes," on payment of a real, but the other would not allow it at any price. So I gave in, and elected to sleep on the floor in the chimney corner.

The women went off to their room, and I cooled down ; in fact, I grew quite cold, and the thought of that straw bed was too much for me. I gathered up my rug and knapsack, went in and lay down on it ; but in a few moments I heard a heavy door open and shut, then whispering—from a man's and then a woman's tongue ! Heavens ! what was going to happen ? I seized the bag which held my clothing, also my satchel and rug, and crawled to a corner of the room behind the door. And not a moment too soon, for it was pushed open, and something which rattled like a chain was thrown, and fell heavily on the bed where I had been lying. All was darkness. The two voices grew nearer; they came into the room; I heard sounds of disrobing; the sack bed was shaken up, and the dreaded visitor or visitors went to sleep. Then I crawled out of the room and sat down on a chair, and asked myself if I was awake or dreaming.

At last I stretched out under the great chimney and looked up at the stars and piling clouds which the wind was driving rapidly along. Slowly, very slowly came the first gleam of daylight, and when it penetrated the chimney and threw a gleam of light across the door beyond which lay the mysterious sleepers, I felt that I was safe. In spite of the horrors of that night, in part real, in part imaginary, I felt that all would soon be well with me.

When the light had increased, the door of the little room opened, and out came the old man and the younger of the two women. He carried the bag of money in his hand; this was what I had heard fall on the bed.

The incidents that wrought that unhappy night were now plain to me.

But whatever the moral character of the old man

may be, I am glad he came to the ventas that night, for I have little doubt that he was the indirect means of saving me from bad hands. His arrival and subsequent movements about the house prevented the three men from carrying out their designs.

The latter left before me, and I saw them no more.

When I had paid my little bill I took a good look at the ventas by the river, and thanked my lucky stars that I had survived the most unpleasant night I have known in sunny Spain.

Fear is quickening, for that day I walked nearly twenty-five miles, and at night found rest and security within the walls of Granada.

CHAPTER XVII.

GRANADA.

THERE is a house in Granada well known to every traveller in Spain. It is owned by Agrela Brothers,—and very real brothers they are to those who call on them. I called, and after a short interview I found it convenient to take up my quarters at a hotel in the " Plaza Pineda,"—a plaza with a heroine in its centre,—the now pure and spotless Maria Pineda, a revolutionist of fifty years ago, who was first put to death and then pardoned.

My motto has always been, " If you want to know a people make yourself one of them." Whilst I am on this journey, I want nothing from Paris or Piccadilly. In town or country the Spaniard and his fare shall be mine, and if I don't enjoy many easy luxuries, I shall certainly get a better chance of understanding native customs than at the monotonous board of the universal tourist.

At the house where I stayed were several military men of good rank, a couple of colonels, and others but a step or two lower in degree. There were also two families whose dress and accessories indicated that they considered themselves members of the upper class. A handsome and showily dressed man, who was an "impresario" running an opera in the town, sat near the two matrons, and seemed very anxious to make love to both at the same time! These with myself formed the resident boarders.

No Englishman could look on this group and expect to find less than decent manners at table, but, alas! these were absent. Soups were shovelled into the mouth or sucked up from the plate ; objectionable morsels were shifted from plate to plate, and where kindness was shown it took the form of piggishness, as little bits were fingered and clawed, bitten in pieces and poked in the mouths of those befriended. The children regularly amused themselves by throwing pellets of bread at the shakos of the military men, and by placing olives about the floor that people might slip and be accused of being drunk. The dessert served to entertain more than to satisfy the body's needs. It was cut and chopped up and used as missiles to annoy and soil every one in turn. This was not a mere child's game or exceptional breach. It formed a set portion of the table programme, and was looked on as quite decent and proper form. I was counted out of these "revels," and thought a very sad and particular dog because I could not see the fun of them and raise a laugh over such animal play.

Later I had a peep at one or two clubs—the "Circulo Artistico" and "Liceo"—where I heard some good music and saw some pretty pictures, and was permitted to draw a breath of Granada "life." It is chiefly composed of "coffee" and "talk," but much coffee is debilitating, and the other is a light and unsatisfactory article in Spain.

Guide-books of Granada are easily made, consequently they are abundant. All Spain has raved and shed its salt tears here. Cervantes has been selected to "speak a piece," and Chateaubriand lauds it in company with Washington Irving. Coming down to modern times, I read with delight the majestic outburst of a great military genius of the United States army, and the equally flashy prattle of a merchant of Denver city. Granada needs none of these to make its idols worthy of worship. But the Spanish guidebook maker loves "fat" and gush. I once heard a famous woman say that "the highest sense of civilisation was shown in seeking to be amused." Does a guide-book amuse? Is that its mission? But I am not here to write a guide-book, only to record a few impressions.

As a "thing of beauty" the Alhambra has lost much of its old charm. In company with most respectable old things, it loves the shade, and it gets enough of it. It is always in the shade, for Charles V.'s unfinished palace hugs two of the sides; and the church and monastery walls of Santa Maria tower above a third, and a little wilderness of tall trees—which fill the spaces between these buildings and rise around the front of the Alhambra —hide it from every direct ray of sunlight. It is so completely shut in and so low that it is with difficulty, when standing on the opposite hill of San Nicolas, which is but a few hundred yards away, that one distinguishes it between the larger buildings. Have you always thought the Alhambra a big building, a kind of Quirinal-Tribune or Versailles? It is not! It is a tiny palace. It is its story which stretches it out over such a vast area; but the area is not ground space, only time and tradition. And yet though so little, how long it takes to get through it! It is so full. There are no bare walls, no corridors, passages, or patios which do not count. The eye never rests in the Alhambra. There is a something

to be noticed everywhere. To-day that something
is only enough to show how beautiful it has been in
the past. The great charm consists in the symmetry
and harmony of the whole. The decoration is daring,
but the combinations of colour never offend the eye.
Nature has been wooed to bestow her sweetest pictures
on these walls and ceilings.

You look up at blue heavens peopled with
beckoning stars and fragments of moon-lit clouds,
all as far away and ethereal as those which the real
night reveals. You see the Muses and Graces of
the Orient garnering earth's flowers and fruits, or
hand-in-hand treading lightly to a measure which
sets your pulse a-ticking to summer heat, even though
it be a dull November day. Some guide-books say,
" The Alhambra is sensual but severe." I quote but to
complain of these hard words ! I saw the Alhambra
first with surprise (I was disappointed), then with
wonder, and lastly with much delight; and when I made
my farewell visit I found more to help me upwards
than to tempt me down. The Alhambra has buried
all its sorrows and its sins. It is no longer the pas-
sion-firing shrine it is said to have been in the past.
To-day it is *untenanted.* I underline the word with
some reason, for the visitor feels so forcibly that no
earthly or sensual influence steals over him here.
The warmth, the brightness, the life of the Alhambra

have gone for ever, and its most substantial trophies wear the garments which time puts on all things. The marble columns have become discoloured; mosses and lichens are struggling to possess themselves of the white marble floors of its patios. The fountains are no longer young: they do not play, and the tanks and fonts of once crystal waters are green, turgid, and foul. The shrubs and flowers have outgrown their allotted space and degenerated into unkempt weeds. The little beehive-shaped towers and domes, once ablaze with showy enamelled tiles, have yielded to the sombre tones which time lays on all things; and the lattice windows in these towers, which were once made fantastic by man, have also been· re-stained by the master artist. The divans, cubinals, and alcoves, once so full of sweet-scented loveliness, are now dank, cold, and clammy: no longer tiring-houses for the happy living, their pure white walls, all fretted and hung around with fantastic draperies in stone, look like the cerements of the grave.

One is continually reminded of the two Alhambras —past and present. There is no doubt about the past; who does not worship it in book, and who would not love it more on looking on the old reality? But drop all knowledge of it, forget its story and come to it—I don't say on a dull November day, but when the air is hot with an August sun, when all the trees are green, and the birds are carolling in them,—or better still, when they are all silent, save the nightingale and the cigarone,—and comparing your impressions with the rhapsodies of the guide-books, see how moderate they will be.

The Alhambra is a great novel, and its characters are just as real as the world likes to make them. The personality of the Moor is over it all. The life and history of a marvellous people are said to be written within its walls; but we dare not separate fiction from fact. We must stick fast to the prejudices of early beliefs, for the cold material things before us will not suffice to preserve the witchery of the old idol.

In the company of an intelligent old Spaniard I went to Albacin, the most perfect example of a Moorish town in Spain.

It covers the hill of San Nicolas, and is in full view of the Alhambra. There are hundreds of houses of entirely Moorish construction, and the interior walls are covered with fantastic figure relief work, which is delicate and lovely as the choicest lace embroidery.

The patios within these houses are in many instances veritable pictures of mediæval luxury, as it was known to the ordinary citizen.

The grape-vine, cypress, and myrtle grow beside

the white walls, and afford a strong relief to the gipsy-patterned tiles ornamenting the windows and doorways.   The hanging balconies are still green and sweet with jessamine and carnations ; and the beauties of the place wear red petticoats, white sandals, and cream and pink mantillas about their heads and shoulders, and cast side-long glances because they dare not speak, much as we may suppose the Moorish maidens to have done in these same courts five hundred years ago.

I mention the Albacin because it is not as well known and recorded as the more classical sights of Granada.   We saw the Gitanos in their caves which lie round the base of the hill.   They are so many—I need not write "questionable" characters, as it is well known whence the beautiful Granadina gipsy draws her praises.

The crowns of gold and the tombs and coffins of Ferdinand and Isabella are displayed in the " Capilla Real " of the old cathedral, and in the Calle Gracia stands the plain little house where the Empress Eugénie was born.   Hard by, at an old-fashioned and splendid house bristling with little brass cannon from basement to roof, we found the sword of Boabdil lying in a sheath of leather and gold, the leather work beautifully coloured with Oriental mosaic work.

We promenaded in Bib Brambla—now a plain open square surrounded by very high Parisian-like houses, but once the famed of all famous arenas for the baiting of bulls and the breaking of Moorish and Christian lances to defend the name and fame of the beauties of old. Here stands Columbus presenting his petition to Isabella. He has been doing this for three years, and shows no sign of fatigue.

Every one must enjoy visiting the sacristy and chapel of the Cartuja, with their artistic blendings of marble, wood, tortoiseshell, ivory, mother-of-pearl, gold, and silver. The massive cabinets placed around the sacristy were fashioned by friars of the monastery. Each was the work of a lifetime, and a lasting proof of devotion to their Church. A cross, painted high up on the wall, is so well executed, that the birds are constantly flying in and endeavouring to perch on the arms. I am glad the mob treated San Bruno badly, or this lovely monastery might never have existed.

We should not speak of the castles, but rather of the churches of Spain. The church is the national theatre of all lands, but more especially of Spain, where the performance is always going on. Here your programme includes the world's history, detailing incidents from the time of Moses to the last pilgrimage to Rome. The actors are finished artists and know their public well. You can get your delight, be it music or oratory, with splendid scenic effects, or if you will, as plain as an undress rehearsal. The manager is a genius who knows the value of the kaleidoscopic pictures he presents to the faithful.

I saw Granada churches by day and night—when they were made homely by the presence of the living, and weird and uncanny by the spirits of the dead. There is no building like a church for pleasing and scaring you, driving you away and whispering you to come back and rest on its motherly bosom.

When you have seen Granada piecemeal and have grown weary, as I confess I did, of trying to fathom the mystery which hangs about all its parts, you should climb the hill behind the Alhambra and Generaliffe, and, sitting in old Boabdil's Chair, contemplate the picture as it lies below. It is a hard seat of cold stone; but—if you believe there is interest in all that is beautiful—you will be warmed into life, even though the winds blow from the heights of Mully-Assan.

Who has not heard that the view from the Alhambra is the finest from any royal palace in the world? It is a wonderful scene. One looks out on a portion of everything—except the sea. Were

there only one little headland—a single blue wave
and line of sand—then the world would lie in
miniature at our feet. The mountains behind are
capped with deep snow ; bare hills slope down to
the right, and below them are gardens of cactus and
orange trees.   On one of these right-hand peaks
is a little châlet-like house, and running down
towards the fruit trees, is an old Arabic wall. From
Boabdil's Chair there is a leap of six or seven
hundred feet into a soft shady vale—all foliage and
rushing water. Beyond lies the hill of San Nicolas,
and the Albacin rising terrace above terrace, its
narrow " calles " showing between the lichen-covered
roofs and white walls. Half a dozen churches send
their towers above the rest, and beyond stretches the
long, broad valley of the Genil,—now all green and
gold, for it is autumn and the leaves have not yet
fallen. A tall chimney shows here and there in the
distant valley (sugar refineries). The scene is bounded
by great bare hills, relieved by several watch towers,
which keep one in memory of old times. Slightly
out of the centre of the picture stands the famed
city as motley and beautiful as Man and Time could
make it. The mingled waters of the Darro and
Genil send a silver streak through the green lawn
which stretches towards Santa Fé. A stream of
rich emerald light pours through a breach in the

southern hills, as if borne direct from the sea which lies beyond. The strong walls of the citadel prevent our seeing the southern slopes of the Sierra Nevada, now sparkling in the sunshine.

These are the easy features of this famed spot. I closed my eyes to see how much I could call up and inflict upon a surfeited world. I brooded and pondered till I almost wept, and, no mistake about it, I had got hold of some ideas which pleased me immensely. I stuck fast to the dream, and the panorama unfolded itself splendidly. I had well-nigh got at the most sacred secret of all the glory of this scene, when I heard a rattle of feet, then a girl's dress, and before I could open my eyes and sit upright, a rich contralto voice called, "Come on, Jack!" Now wasn't this enough to make a man swear? There had I been sitting like a blind idiot getting all my "ribbons" in order that I might drive the general public over the ground in true four-in-hand fashion, and yet though I occupy a king's chair I must be disturbed in this rude way! My dream is for ever gone! I cannot tell you a word of what I was going to say. I looked round for the intruders—a governess with six bonny little boys and girls, and "Jack" was the very worst of them. He had not the least respect for the creeping ivies and other modest greens which the Zegries may have planted.

and scrambled and bound himself up in their long tendrils till he became a pretty little prisoner. The straight path was not romantic enough for him, or in any way to his liking. He was hungry and he said so. He would stray away and get lost, or he would go home and fill himself with Spanish chestnuts. So Jack was obeyed, and the English children and my dream of Granada passed away.

I had another dreamy moment in old Granada, when an invisible presence seemed to keep me company. Perhaps in the by-and-by I shall be saying, "Don't you remember the morning when we sat together on the parapet wall of San Nicolas and looked at that wonderful piece of world that lay around, and above, and below us?

"Can't you see now, as plainly as you did then, the old Moorish quarter of the Albacin lying at our feet, and, flowing past it, the rattling, prattling Darro; and up the poplar-decked slope, now golden with lingering autumn leaves, the Alhambra towers showing through a maze of cypress and other greens; and away to the left, still higher up on the hillside, the plain-faced palace of the Generaliffe, and Boabdil's Chair of everlasting stone, and in the background fifty miles of craggy peaks, bold headlands, and wild ravines, all sparkling and glittering in the sunshine under a deep mantle of November snow?

"You remember how long we looked, marvelling more and more that these inanimate glories should last for ever, and we, the highest atoms in the world, should so soon pass away?

"And then the valley, the vega of the Genil, the great plain laid out as a vast carpet, twenty by thirty miles in dimensions; the church towers, and factory chimneys, and the most complex city in Spain sending up its murmurs to our ears as we sat and looked and dreamed; the clear blue sky, the wild hills, the rivers and the trees, the watch-towers on every peak, and the labour of twenty centuries crumbling round us?"

Granada made a fool of me. I was fired with an extravagant imagination all the time I was there.

I came near making an enemy in Granada. A newspaper man would have me go to the Alpujaras and I would not! He dared to tell me that if I did not go there I should know nothing of Spain. And now I want to know how many people do know Spain if this man spoke the truth.

Alpujara is famous. I remember the pretty ballad which goes—

" 'Twas thus Granada's fountain by spoke Alpujara's daughter."

But what if she did drop her earrings in the well?

Is it my place to fish them out, or go in search of the house where that old-time maiden lived? No! I went in search of Dulcinea's house in Toboso and didn't succeed, and that was enough. This man says Alpujara has the loveliest scenery in the world! But then to what world does he allude? Probably to his own! I expect he was born there or fell in love with some beauty of the place. Birth and first love make a paradise for us all. The loveliest places I can recall are those where I walked with ———. Love makes more and keeps more things beautiful and satisfying than all else in this world.

On leaving Granada, I took the shortest road to Malaga, and after three days saw what was more delightful to me than a hundred Alpujaras—the sea! I slept the first night at La Mala, and the next day I made a frightful journey of thirty miles through deep and still falling snow.

At Alhama on the Mount (there is another in the valley) I was succoured for the last time by the authorities, who granted me a resting-place on a posada floor.*

---

* The record of a journey across Spain would be incomplete without reference to the amusing tavern signs one sees at every turn. A common one in South and Central Spain is the inscription, "Vino de Valdepeñas." The literal statement is plain enough, as Valdepeñas wine is famous, but the words are frequently mutilated so that they can be construed, " Wine for

The country was very wild and uninteresting, but the prospect before me brightened the way.

From Alhama I took a mountain-track, which, as it was bearing south, I knew must lead me to the coast. The way was terribly wild ; I encountered not a soul or sight of a habitation until nearly midday, when I arrived at a gap in the Sierra Tajedra,

nothing" ("Vino de Valde" is painted on one side and "peñas" on the other). A wine shop north of Madrid stands facing a cemetery. A hand on the sign-board points to the Rest-house over the way, and bears the inscription, " 'Tis better to be here than there."

At El Palo, near Malaga, one can choose between "The New Five Minutes" and "The Old Five Minutes." "The House of Progress" is a common sign. Other taverns bear the discreet names of "The Reformation," "The Thought," "The Star," "The Lighthouse," "The Truth."

"Here It Is" and "Here is Everything" are frequently inscribed over grocers' shops and cafés. The shoeing-smith displays an iron horse fashioned out of shoes. The unqualified medical man shows a dainty foot and arm, with a streak of blood flowing from the wound made by his lance. In a *calle* not far from the Puerta-del-Sol in Madrid, a corset of gigantic proportions is placed over the door of a "corseteria"; on it is written, "Inside we make little ones."

The wine-skin maker hangs fully blown skins over his door, and sometimes adds an inscription in praise of their quality. In a street in Pamplona I saw painted on a huge skin swinging to and fro over the door, "I am so strong that I can carry eight arrobas the whole year long" (two hundredweight).

It is not the barber's pole, but his bowl, that one sees in Spain. He hangs out two shining discs of brightly burnished brass, recalling Mambrino s helmet, and, as these attract and reflect the

from whence I got my first glimpse of the Mediter-
ranean in the far distance.

Oh the joy of looking on the wide waters once
again! for it meant the end of my journey. These
many months I have been more alone than any one
could be made to understand. Yes, I have laughed
and capered, and rattled off Spanish songs, and
appeared quite merry ; but it was laughing against
fate. I have lived hard, worked hard, slept hard ;
and these three make the world a weary place ; and
I have been awake to feel a few of the most bitter
pains and pangs that mortal may know.

It was easy work to descend to the village of
Vinuela, where I passed the night at a posada in
company with several other " men of the road."

sun's rays like little suns, they are probably the most striking of
all the Spanish signs.

In many plazas and cloister gardens stands a cross with a
coarse bell rope and a board saying, " Here we administer
extreme unction."

Perhaps the most touching of all the inscriptions is that which
is often seen over a hole in the walls of certain nunneries. The
unfortunate Spanish girl has no claim on the man who degrades
her. When her child comes into the world, her only resource
lies in cloaking her misery by placing it in the convent cradle,
which fills the hole in the wall. This is made to revolve, allow-
ing any one to turn the portion containing the little bed towards
the outer world. The mother deposits her babe, rings the heavy
bell, and departs. Over the cradle are the words, " You are
neglected by your parents and received into the hands of God."

The next morning saw me at Velez-Malaga. It was at this little port that Cervantes landed after his captivity in Morocco; and here, I, the prisoner of my own free will in the wilds of Spain, regained my liberty as I walked the shore of La Torrox.

As Malaga was still over seventy miles distant, I set out along the beach, and before nightfall covered more than half the way. The fisher folk afforded me some pretty pictures, "and brightened all the strand," till, night coming on, I was forced to halt at a very clean cottage, where I was accommodated with a fish supper and a bed in the chaff-house.

The bright sunny morning which followed sent my spirits up to jubilee point, as I realised that I had come to the end of my journey across Spain, and could lay aside the character, as well as the knapsack, of a Tramp.

THE END.